Rest Not
in Peace

The chronicles of Hugh de Singleton, surgeon

Rest Not in Peace

The sixth chronicle of
Hugh de Singleton, surgeon

MEL STARR

LION FICTION

Published by Lion Fiction
an imprint of
Lion Hudson plc
Wilkinson House, Jordan Hill Road,
Oxford OX2 8DR, England
www.lionhudson.com/fiction

ISBN 978 1 78264 008 0
e-ISBN 978 1 78264 009 7

First edition 2013

Acknowledgments
Page 15, drawing of Bampton Castle: Used by kind
permission of Professor John Blair, Queens College, Oxford.
Redrawn by Jonathan Roberts, Lion Hudson.

A catalogue record for this book is available from the
British Library.

Printed and bound in the UK, August 2013, LH26

Another one for Susan

Acknowledgments

Several years ago when Dan Runyon, professor of English at Spring Arbor University, learned that I had written an as yet unpublished medieval mystery, he invited me to speak to his fiction-writing class about the trials of a rookie writer seeking a publisher. He sent sample chapters of Master Hugh's first chronicle, *The Unquiet Bones*, to his friend, Tony Collins. Thanks, Dan.

Thanks to Tony Collins and all those at Monarch who saw Master Hugh's potential. And thanks especially to my editor, Jan Greenough, who excels at asking questions such as, "Do you really want to say it that way?" and, "Wouldn't Master Hugh do it like this?"

Dr. John Blair, of Queen's College, Oxford, has written several papers about Bampton history. These have been invaluable in creating an accurate time and place for Master Hugh. Tony and Lis Page have also been a wonderful source of information about Bampton. I owe them much.

Ms. Malgorzata Deron, of Poznan, Poland, offered to update and maintain my website. She has done an excellent job. To see the result of her work, visit www.melstarr.net

Glossary

Angelus Bell: rung three times each day, dawn, noon, and dusk. Announced the time for the Angelus devotional.

Arbolettys: a cheese-and-herb egg custard.

Ascension Day: forty days after Easter; May 25 in 1368.

Bailiff: a lord's chief manorial representative. He oversaw all operations, collected rents and fines, and enforced labor service. Not a popular fellow.

Boar in confit: honey-glazed pork fillets, served cold.

Bodkin: a sharp, slender tool for punching holes in leather and heavy cloth.

Book of Hours: a devotional book, usually elaborately decorated and illustrated.

Boss: the decorative junction in a ceiling where the barrel vaulting joins.

Braes: medieval underpants.

Buttery: a storage room for beverages stored in butts, or barrels. A butler would be in charge of it.

Cabbage with marrow: cabbage cooked with bone marrow, breadcrumbs, and spices.

Candlemas: February 2. Marked the purification of Mary. Women traditionally paraded to church carrying lighted candles – hence the name. Tillage of fields resumed this day.

Capons farced: chicken stuffed with hard-boiled egg yolks, currants, chopped pork, breadcrumbs, and spices.

Chamberlain: the keeper of a lord's chamber, wardrobe, and personal items.

Chardewarden: pears cooked in wine sauce with breadcrumbs and spices.

Charlet of cod: fish beaten to a smooth paste, then cooked with wine, vinegar, ground almonds, sugar, and spices.

Chauces: tight-fitting trousers, often of different colors for each leg.

Chewet: a meat or fish pie, rather like a pasty.

Claret: originally a yellowish or pale-red wine from the Bordeaux region.

Commissioner of Laborers: Officials chosen to enforce the Ordinance of Laborers, which limited wages to pre-1348 levels.

Coney in cevy: rabbit stewed with onions, breadcrumbs, and spices in wine vinegar.

Cormarye: pork roasted after marinating in red wine and spices.

Cotehardie: the primary medieval outer garment. Women's were floor length; men's ranged from thigh to ankle.

Cresset: a bowl of oil with a floating wick used for lighting.

Crispels: pastry made with flour, sugar, and honey, and fried in lard or oil.

Cyueles: deep-fried fritters made of a paste of breadcrumbs, ground almonds, eggs, sugar, and salt.

Dexter: a war horse; larger than pack horses and palfreys. Also, the right-hand direction.

Dirge: a song or liturgy of grief and lamentation.

Eels in bruit: eels served in a sauce of white wine, breadcrumbs, onions, and spices.

Egg leech: a thick custard, often enriched with almonds, spices, and flour.

Farthing: one fourth of a penny; the smallest silver coin.

Fast day: Wednesday, Friday, and Saturday; not the fasting of modern usage, when no food is consumed, but days upon which no meat, eggs, or animal products are consumed.

Fewterer: the keeper of a lord's kennels and hounds.

Garderobe: the toilet.

Gathering: eight leaves of parchment, made by folding the prepared hide three times.

Gentleman: a nobleman; the term had nothing to do with character or behavior.

Grocer: a wholesaler of staples.

Groom: a household servant to a lord, ranking above a page and below a valet.

Haberdasher: a merchant who sold household items such as pins, buckles, buttons, hats, and purses.

Hallmote: the manorial court. Royal courts judged free tenants accused of murder or felony; otherwise manorial courts had jurisdiction over legal matters concerning villagers.

Hanoney: eggs scrambled with onions and fried.

King's Eyre: a royal circuit court, presided over by a traveling judge.

Kirtle: a medieval undershirt.

Lammas Day: August 1, when thanks was given for a successful wheat harvest. From Old English "loaf mass."

Leech: a physician.

Liripipe: a fashionably long tail attached to a man's cap and usually coiled atop the head.

Lychgate: a roofed gate over the entry to a churchyard under which the deceased would rest during the initial part of a medieval funeral.

Malmsey: the sweetest variety of Madeira wine, originally from Greece.

Mark: a coin worth thirteen shillings and four pence (i.e. 160 pence).

Marshalsea: the stables and their associated accoutrements.

Maslin: bread made with a mixture of grains, commonly wheat and rye or barley.

Matins: the first of the day's eight canonical hours (services). Also called Lauds.

Nones: the fifth daytime canonical office, sung at the ninth hour of the day (i.e. mid afternoon).

Page: a young male servant, often a youth learning the arts of chivalry before becoming a squire.

Palfrey: a riding horse with a comfortable gait.

Pantler: a valet in charge of the pantry.

Pantry: from the French word for bread, *pain*. Originally a small room for bread storage. By the fourteenth century other items were also stored there.

Passing Bell: ringing of the parish church bell to indicate the death of a villager.

Pears in compost: pears cooked in red wine with dates, sugar, and cinnamon.

Portpain: a linen cloth in which bread was carried from the bakehouse to the hall.

Pottage: anything cooked in one pot, from the meanest oatmeal to a savory stew.

Pottage of whelks: whelks boiled and served in a stock of almond milk, breadcrumbs, and spices.

Poulterer: a manor employee in charge of chickens, ducks, and geese.

Reeve: an important manor official, although he did not outrank the bailiff. Elected by tenants from among themselves, he had responsibility for fields, buildings, and enforcing labor service.

Remove: a dinner course.

Rice moyle: a rice pudding made with almond milk, sugar, and saffron.

Rogation Sunday: the Sunday before Ascension Day. Monday, Tuesday, and Wednesday were Rogation Days, also called "gang days." A time for beseeching God for a good growing season.

Runcie: a small, common horse of lower grade than a palfrey.

St Benedict's Day: June 11.

St Beornwald's Church: today the Church of St Mary, in the fourteenth century it was named for an obscure Saxon saint.

St Boniface's Day: June 5.

St John's Day: June 24.

St Stephen's Day: December 26.

Screens passage: a narrow corridor which screened the hall from the kitchen and from which the buttery and pantry were accessed.

See: the authority or jurisdiction of a bishop.

Set books: the standard textbooks used by medieval undergraduates.

Shilling: twelve pence. Twenty shillings made a pound, although there was no pound coin.

Sinister: the left-hand direction.

Sobye sauce: a sauce for fried fish made with white wine, raisins, breadcrumbs, and spices.

Solar: a small room in a castle, more easily heated than the great hall, where lords preferred to spend time, especially in winter. Usually on an upper floor.

Sole in cyve: fish boiled and served in a yellow onion sauce.

Statute of Laborers: following the first attack of plague in 1348–49, laborers realized that because so many workers had died, their labor was in demand, and so demanded higher wages. In 1351 Parliament set wages at the 1347 level. Like most attempts to legislate against the law of supply and demand, the statute was generally a failure.

Steward: the chief officer of a manor. Occasionally a steward would have authority over all manors belonging to his lord.

Stockfish: the cheapest salted fish, usually cod or haddock.

Stone: fourteen pounds.

Subtlety: an elaborate confection, made more for show than for consumption, often served between removes.

Toft: land surrounding a villager's house, often used for growing vegetables and keeping chickens.

Valets: the highest-ranking servants to a lord.

Verderer: the forester in charge of a lord's forest.

Villein: a non-free peasant. He could not leave his land or service to his lord, or sell animals without permission. But if he could escape his manor for a year and a day, he would be free.

Void: dessert – often sugared fruits and sweetened wine.

Week-work: the two or three days of labor per week (more during harvest) which a villein owed to his lord.

Whitsuntide: White Sunday; ten days after Ascension Day, seven weeks after Easter. In 1368, June 4.

Yardland: about thirty acres. Also called a virgate and, in northern England, an oxgang.

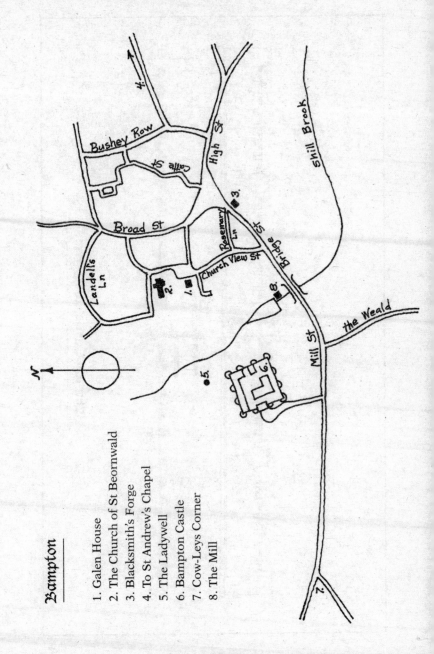

Bampton

1. Galen House
2. The Church of St Beornwald
3. Blacksmith's Forge
4. To St Andrew's Chapel
5. The Ladywell
6. Bampton Castle
7. Cow-Leys Corner
8. The Mill

15

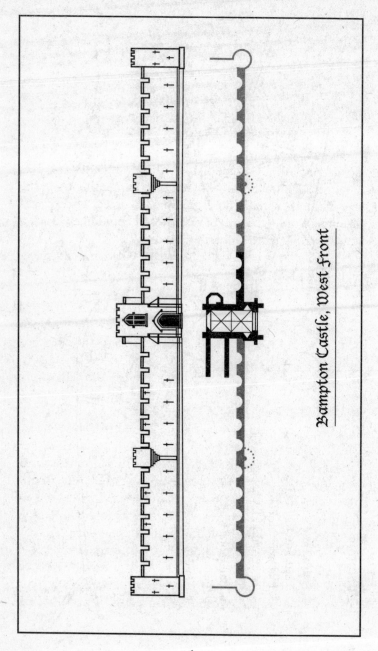

Bampton Castle, West Front

Chapter 1

Unwelcome guests may be a tribulation, and when they depart 'tis usually considered a blessed occasion. But not so if the visitor is a knight, and he departs to make his new home in St Beornwald's churchyard.

Sir Henry Burley was a small man, with a face that sloped back in all directions from a prominent nose, like a badger's. I should probably not be commenting upon the size of another man's nose. If ability to detect a scent was dependent upon the size of one's nose I could likely track a stag as well as Lord Gilbert's hounds.

Evidently in battle at Poitiers more than a decade past, Sir Henry had done some service for my employer, Lord Gilbert Talbot. What this service was I did not learn 'til later. Lord Gilbert said only that it would cost him little to repay the knight's valor. From this brief explanation I judged that Sir Henry had distinguished himself in battle, to Lord Gilbert's advantage. How this could be was a mystery to me, for Lord Gilbert is nearly as tall as me, and is squarely built, while Sir Henry is – was – small and slender and, I judge, weighed little more than eight stone.

But after nearly a month entertaining Sir Henry, his wife and daughter, two knights and two squires in Sir Henry's service, and several valets and grooms, Lord Gilbert was clearly ready for them to depart. Sir Henry was a demanding sort of man who seemed to delight in finding fault with Bampton Castle and its inhabitants; the garderobe was not perfumed to his liking, and Lord Gilbert's grooms and valets did not show him proper deference.

Three days before St John's Day, in the year of our Lord 1368, Sir Henry went to his bed hale and healthy after enjoying a long evening of music, conversation, and dancing in Bampton Castle's hall. The next morn his valet found him cold and dead. Death is but the path to God, but most men would prefer to travel that way in some distant future day.

Shortly after Sir Henry's valet made this disagreeable discovery I was breaking my fast when a loud and insistent thumping upon my door drew me from my morning reverie. Kate was feeding bits of a wheaten loaf to Bessie and continued her occupation, an early summons not being unusual in Galen House. I am often sought at such an hour, either because of my profession, surgeon, or due to my service as bailiff to Lord Gilbert Talbot's manor of Bampton. My summons this day was because of my training as surgeon, but soon called for a bailiff's work as well.

John, Lord Gilbert's chamberlain, stood before me when I opened the door. I knew immediately some great matter had brought him to Galen House. A groom or valet would have been sent for some routine business.

"Come quickly, Master Hugh. Sir Henry is dead."

Why the presence of a surgeon was required quickly, when the patient was dead, did not seem to have occurred to John, but I did as he bid. I had yet a part of a wheaten loaf in my hand. This I left upon our table before Kate, then explained my hasty departure, the reason for which my wife had not heard. Bessie has discovered language, and makes incessant use of the knowledge, often at great volume if she believes her words are not awarded sufficient importance. So Kate did not know who was at our door or what the reason until I told her.

Two days earlier a page had called at Galen House. Lord Gilbert's guest, he said, was unable to sleep. Lord Gilbert wished me to send herbs which might calm a troubled mind and bring rest. I sent a pouch of pounded lettuce seeds, with instruction to measure a thimbleful unto a cup of wine an hour before Sir Henry went to his bed.

Usually when I am called to some place where my skill as a surgeon is required I take with me a sack of instruments and herbs, so as to be prepared for whatever wound or injury I may find. I took no implements this day. Of what use would they be to a dead man?

I questioned John regarding the matter as we hurried down Church View Street to Mill Street, crossed Shill Brook, and approached the castle gatehouse. As we spoke I heard the passing bell ring from the tower of the Church of St Beornwald.

"Lord Gilbert wishes your opinion as to what has caused this death," John said. "The man was in good health yesterday. Complained of no illness. Lord Gilbert, I think, fears poison or some such thing which might cast blame on him and his household."

John did not say, but I suspect Lord Gilbert worried that the lettuce seed I provided to aid Sir Henry's sleep might have contributed to his death.

"Is there reason to suspect evil in this?" I asked.

"None... but that the man was robust one day and a corpse the next."

"Men may die of a sudden. 'Tis known to occur."

"Aye, when they are aged."

"But Sir Henry was not. I dined with him a week past, when Lord Gilbert invited me to his table. How old was the man?"

"Forty-six, his wife said."

Faces of those who greeted me in the Bampton Castle hall were somber, lips drawn tight and thin. Lord Gilbert and Lady Petronilla sat in earnest conversation with an attractive woman whom I recognized as Lady Margery, Sir Henry's wife. Lord Gilbert stood when he saw John usher me into the hall, spoke briefly to the widow, then approached. Over Lord Gilbert's shoulder I saw Lady Margery rise from her chair, her face twisted into a venomous glare. She began to follow Lord Gilbert, but Lady Petronilla laid a hand upon her arm and spoke, and the woman resumed her place. The hate in her eyes remained.

"I give you good day," I said to my employer.

"Much thanks, Hugh, but the day is ill. John has told you?"

"Aye. Your guest was found dead this morning."

"He was. And no sign of what caused the death… which is why I sent for you. A surgeon or physician might more readily see what indisposition has caused this."

"You have seen the corpse?"

"Aye."

"And you saw nothing out of sorts?"

"Not a thing. All was as a man should be when asleep, but for his eyes. They were open. The body is unmarked. Sir Henry was not a young man, but he was in good health yesterday."

"John Chamberlain said you feared poison?"

Lord Gilbert shrugged, then whispered, "'Twas but the thought of a moment. We are all baffled. I would not have Lady Margery hear of poison."

"John," Lord Gilbert continued, "take Master Hugh to Sir John's chamber." Then, to me he said, "'Tis an odious business, I know, to ask of you, but I wish to know if Sir Henry's death is God's work or man's."

"You suspect man's work?"

"Nay. I do not know what to think. So I have called for you. Is it possible that the sleeping draught you sent did this?"

"Nay. The seeds of lettuce are but a mild soporific. A man would need to swallow a bucket of the stuff to do himself harm."

Lord Gilbert turned back to Lady Margery and left me to John, who nodded and led me to the stairs which would take us to the guest chambers beyond Lord Gilbert's solar.

Past the solar the passageway grew dark, but at its end I saw two figures. I recognized one. Arthur, one of Lord Gilbert's grooms, stood at the closed door of a chamber, and another man, wearing Sir Henry's livery and badge, stood with him.

The two men stood aside as I approached, having been notified, no doubt, that I was to inspect the corpse and give reason for the death. I opened the heavy door and entered the chamber, but none followed. Death is not pleasant to look upon, and the three men who stood outside the door were content to allow me to do my work alone.

Sir Henry lay as he had been found, upon his back, sightless eyes staring at the vaulted ceiling and boss of his chamber. Would a man die in his sleep with his eyes open? Perhaps some pain seized him in the night and awakened him before death came.

A cresset was burning upon a stand, where it had been all night should Sir Henry have wished to rise and visit the garderobe. I lifted it and held it close to the dead man's face. Two windows gave light to the room, but they were narrow, and one faced north, the other west, so that the morning sun did not illuminate the chamber.

I first inspected Sir Henry's neck to see if any contusion was there. None was. I felt the man's scalp, to see if any lump or dried blood might betray a blow. All was as it should be. I pried open the lips – no easy task, for rigor mortis was begun – to see if Sir Henry might have choked to his death upon regurgitated food. His mouth was clear.

Because Sir Henry was already stiffening in death I assumed that he was dead for some hours before he was found. De Mondeville wrote that rigor mortis begins three or so hours after death, and becomes severe at twelve hours after death.

A blanket yet covered the corpse. I drew this aside, and with my dagger slit Sir Henry's kirtle so I might inspect the body for wounds or evidence of blows. There were none.

Beside the bed, next to where the cresset had been placed, was a cup. I held it to the window and saw in the dregs the few remains of the pounded seeds of lettuce which had been in the wine. Was some other potion added to the cup? I touched the dregs with my fingertips and brought them to my lips. I could detect no foreign flavor, although this is not telling, for there are several malignant herbs which leave little or no taste when consumed. Monk's Hood is one. And for this they are all the more dangerous.

The walls of Sir Henry's chamber were of stone, of course, and the door of heavy oak. If he felt himself afflicted in the night, and cried out for aid, he might not have been heard, especially if his call was weak due to an affliction which took his life.

I went to the door, where Arthur and Sir Henry's valet stood, and asked the valet if anyone had heard Sir Henry shout for help in the night.

"Don't know," he replied. "I spend the night in the servants' range. I wouldn't have heard 'im."

"Has no other, those whose chambers were close by, spoken of it?"

"Nay. None said anything."

"It was you who found him?"

"Aye."

"Has anything in his chamber been moved since then? Has Sir Henry's corpse been moved?"

"Nay... but for Lady Margery throwin' herself upon 'im when she was brought here an' saw Sir Henry dead. Lord Gilbert drew her away. Told her he had a man who could tell why Sir Henry was dead. That would be you?"

"Aye. I am Hugh de Singleton, surgeon, and bailiff at Bampton manor. You are...?"

"Walter Mayn, valet to Sir Henry... was valet to Sir Henry."

"Two days past I was asked to provide herbs which might help Sir Henry fall to sleep. Was there some matter which vexed him, so that he awoke of a night?"

Walter did not reply. He looked away, as if he heard some man approach at the end of the passageway. A valet is to be circumspect, and loyal, and hold his tongue when asked of the affairs of his lord. The man did not need to say more. His silence and glance told me that some business had troubled Sir Henry. Whether or not the issue had led to his death was another matter. Might a man die of worry? If so, this was no concern of Lord Gilbert Talbot's bailiff.

"Who slept in the next chamber?" I asked the fellow.

"Sir Geoffrey Godswein."

"And across the passageway?"

"Sir John Peverel."

"They are knights in Sir Henry's service?"

"Aye."

"And they did not speak of any disturbance in the night?"

"Not that I heard. There was lots of screamin' from Lady Margery and all was speakin' at once when Sir Henry was found."

I decided that I should seek these knights, and the Lady Margery, if she was fit to be questioned. I told Arthur and Walter to remain at Sir Henry's door and allow no man, nor woman, either, to enter the chamber 'til I had returned.

Lady Margery I had seen in the hall, so I returned there and found Lord Gilbert and Lady Petronilla comforting the widow. Lady Margery's eyes were red and her cheeks swollen. She had seen me an hour before, but through teary eyes.

"Master Hugh," Lord Gilbert said, rising, "what news?"

"Hugh?" the woman shrieked. "This is the leech who has poisoned my husband?"

Lord Gilbert answered for me. "Nay, Lady Margery. Master Hugh is as competent as any at his business. He has assured me that the potion he sent to aid Sir Henry's slumber could not cause death."

"Of course he would say so. Something did. And Sir Henry took none of the potion until the night he died."

The woman stood, her fists clenched, as if prepared to strike me. Lord Gilbert saw, and took her arm.

"'Tis of that night I would speak to you," I said. "Your chamber is not far from your husband's. Did you or your maids hear anything in the night? Some sound which might now, when you think back upon it, have told of Sir Henry's distress, even if in the night, when you heard it, you paid no heed?"

"Nay, I heard nothing. 'Twas the potion you gave which caused his death. It was to bring sleep, you said. So it did, the sleep of death. This man," she turned to my employer, "should be sent to the sheriff for trial before the King's Eyre for the murder he has done."

"Surely Master Hugh has done no murder," Lady Petronilla said. "If so be his potion brought death 'twas surely mischance, not felony."

Lady Margery stared skeptically at Lady Petronilla, but said no more.

Across the hall, as far from the grieving widow as could be yet remaining in the chamber, I saw two knights sitting upon a bench, their heads close together in earnest conversation.

"Sir John and Sir Geoffrey occupied chambers near Sir Henry, is this not so?"

"Aye," Lord Gilbert replied, and nodded in the direction of the solemn knights.

I walked in the direction of his gaze and the two knights stood when they saw me approach.

"I give you good day," I said courteously, although my words were but an affectation, for no such day could be good. "You are knights in service to Sir Henry?" I asked, although I knew the answer.

"Aye," the older of the two replied. "I am Sir John Peverel. This is Sir Geoffrey Godswein."

Sir John was a large man, taller than me and three stone heavier. His hands were the size of a dexter's hooves. Sir Geoffrey was smaller, a man of normal size.

I introduced myself and my duty, and asked if they had heard any cry in the night, or any other sound to indicate that Sir Henry might have been in distress. Both men shook their heads.

"Heard nothing amiss 'til Walter shouted for help," Sir Geoffrey said.

"When he did so you went immediately to Sir Henry's chamber?"

"Aye."

"Who entered first?"

"I did," Sir Geoffrey replied.

"What did you see? Tell all, even if it seems of no importance."

"Walter stood at the door, which was flung wide open, bawling out that Sir Henry was dead. I pushed past and saw 'twas so."

"Were the bed clothes in disarray, as if he'd thrashed about?"

Sir Geoffrey pursed his lips in thought, turned to Sir

John as if seeking confirmation, then spoke. "Nay. All was in order. Not like Sir Henry'd tossed about in pain before he died."

Sir John nodded agreement, then said, "His eyes were open. You being a surgeon would know better than me, but if a man died in his sleep, they'd be closed, seems like."

I agreed. "Unless some pain awoke him before he died."

"Then why'd he not cry out?" Sir Geoffrey asked.

I had no answer.

"When did you last see Sir Henry alive?"

"Last night," Sir John said.

"After the music and dancing," Sir Geoffrey added. "We retired same time as Sir Henry and Lady Margery."

"Did he seem well? Did any matter trouble him?"

The two knights seemed to hesitate, slightly, but I noted it, before they replied.

"Nay," Sir Geoffrey said. "Lord Gilbert had musicians and jongleurs to entertain here in the hall after supper. Sir Henry danced an' seemed pleased as any."

"When he went to his chamber did he stand straight, or was he perhaps bent as if some discomfort afflicted his belly?"

Again the knights exchanged glances, but this time Sir John spoke with no hesitation. "Sir Henry always stands straight, being shorter than most men. Wears thick-soled shoes, too. Was he bent last eve we'd have noticed, that being unlike him."

"Think back again to this morning, and when you first entered Sir Henry's chamber. Was anything amiss, or in disarray?"

"When a man is found dead," Sir John said, "other matters are trivial. I paid no heed to anything but the corpse." Sir Geoffrey nodded in agreement.

I thanked the knights, bid them "Good day," whether it was or not, and motioned to Lord Gilbert that I wished to speak privily to him.

"What have you learned?" he asked when we were out of Lady Margery's hearing.

"You saw the corpse?" I asked.

"Aye," he grimaced.

"Sir Henry's eyes were open in death."

"Aye, they were. What means that?"

"I do not know, but the fact troubles me."

"Why so? You think violence was done to him?"

"Nay. I examined the corpse. I found no injury. If a man dies in his sleep, his eyes will be shut. I'm sure of this. If Sir Henry awoke, and felt himself in pain, he would, I think, have called out. But no man, nor Lady Margery, heard him do so."

"The castle walls are thick," Lord Gilbert said.

"As are the doors. But between the bottom of the door to Sir Henry's chamber and the floor is a space as wide as a man's finger is thick. If Sir Henry cried for help I think he would have been heard through the gap, unless the affliction had greatly weakened him."

"Mayhap the malady took him of a sudden."

"Perhaps," I shrugged.

"You are not satisfied to be ignorant of a matter like this, are you?" Lord Gilbert said.

"Nay."

"'Tis why I employed you. But you must remember that only the Lord Christ knows all. There are matters we mortals may never know."

Lord Gilbert Talbot, baron of the realm, valiant knight, now theologian and philosopher.

"You wish me to abandon my inquiry?"

"The longer you continue, the more distress for Lady

Margery. If you think it unlikely you will ever discover the cause 'twould be best to say so sooner than later. Men often die for no good reason."

"There is always a reason, but other men are ignorant of understanding the cause."

"And you do not like being deceived, even by death, do you?"

"Nay. And if I cannot discover what caused Sir Henry's death, Lady Margery will tell all that 'twas my potion which did so."

"Another hour or two, then. Have ready an opinion by dinner."

I promised to do so. As I left the hall Sir Henry's daughter entered, as red-eyed and puffy-cheeked as her stepmother. Lady Anne, I had been told, was Sir Henry's daughter by his first wife, the Lady Goscelyna. The lass looked to be about nineteen or twenty years old, and was followed by two youths – squires, I remembered, to Sir Henry. The lads were somber, but showed no sign of terrible loss. Lady Anne is a beautiful maid, and surely accustomed to being followed by young men.

I returned to Sir Henry's chamber, nodded to Arthur and Walter, and entered the room. Perhaps, I thought, murder was done here in some manner I had not discovered, and when Sir Henry was dead all marks of a struggle had been made right. But if such had happened, why did Sir Henry not shout for assistance when he was attacked? Whether the man died of some illness, or was murdered, I could make no sense of his silence.

I sat upon a chair, ready to abandon the loathsome task I had been assigned. The Lord Christ gives to all men their appointed tasks, but occasionally I wish that He had assigned another profession to me. My eyes fell upon the fireplace. It was cold, and the ashes of the last blaze of winter were long since disposed of, but 'twas not the hearth which seized my attention.

A poker stood propped against the stones, and my mind went to a rumor which passed among students while I studied at Balliol College. A rumor concerning the death of King Edward II. Mortimer and Edward's faithless queen deposed him nearly a half-century past, and he was taken to Berkeley Castle where, some months later, he was found dead of a morning. Folk living near the castle were said to have heard terrible screams in the night, but, as with Sir Henry, no mark was found upon the King's corpse to tell of violent death.

A red-hot poker, rumor said, was thrust up the deposed King's rectum, doing murder and cauterizing the wound at the same time, so no blood flowed to disclose how the felony was done. And no visible wound was made to indict the murderers.

There had been no blaze in Sir Henry's fireplace, but I went to the hearth to examine the poker nevertheless. The iron bar was dusty with ashes from its last use, which had been as was intended, not to do murder.

I replaced the poker against the wall, but the thought of Edward II's death caused me to consider again Sir Henry's corpse. Surely if a man was murdered as the King was, his screams would have been heard throughout the castle, stone walls and oaken doors notwithstanding.

But what if he was silenced with a pillow over his face? Would that muffle his shrieks? Or might a pillow have been enough to suffocate the man and silence his protest at the same time?

I turned to the door of the chamber to seek Arthur and Walter and conduct an experiment with the pillow. 'Twas then I saw the tiny brown droplet upon the planks. I knelt to inspect the mark, thinking at first it might have been made by a drop of Sir Henry's wine. The color so matched the wood that 'tis a wonder I saw it at all. Some man, or men, did not.

The circular stain was smaller than the nail upon my little finger, and when I scraped a thumbnail across it I was able to lift some of the substance from the floor. Wine will not thicken so. A tiny drop of dried blood lay before me.

Could this be Sir Henry's blood? If so, whence did it come? I approached the corpse, turned it upon the bed, and spread the legs so I might inspect the rectum for some sign of violence. I saw none, although I admit I might have performed the examination more carefully.

When Sir Henry was again upon his back I made another search of the corpse for some wound from which the drop of blood might have come. As before, I found none. Was there some other orifice of a man's body whereby he might be stabbed and murdered, the wound invisible? I had already peered into Sir Henry's mouth and seen nothing amiss. I tilted the head back and inspected the nostrils to see if any trace of blood was there. None was.

Sir Henry was stiff in death, but I managed to turn his head so that I could inspect his left ear. 'Tis all dark within a man's ear, so at first I saw nothing, but it seemed to me that Sir Henry's ear was darker than might be expected. I drew my dagger and with the point teased from the ear canal a flake of dried matter identical to the drop of dried blood upon the floor. If a man died in the throes of apoplexy would the strain cause an eardrum to burst? I had never heard of such a thing, and Galen and de Mondeville wrote nothing of such a phenomenon.

I needed my instruments. I bid Arthur and Walter maintain their watch, told Lord Gilbert my examination was near complete, and hastened to Galen House. Bessie toddled to me, but I could spare her but a peck upon a cheek before I seized a sack which I keep always ready for a time when my skills are called for.

Often when I walk the bridge over Shill Brook I stop to observe the water pass beneath, but not this day. I hastened to the castle, and at Sir Henry's chamber I selected my smallest scalpel with which to prod the dark recess of Sir Henry's ear. A moment later I drew forth a clot of dried blood.

If an awl is driven through a man's ear, into his brain, will he die so suddenly that he does not cry out in pain before death comes? I did not know, and do not know yet, for there is no way to make experiment to learn if it may be so.

But I was then sure that Sir Henry was murdered. Some man thrust an awl or thin blade through his ear. If such a wound bleeds much – I had no experience of such a wound to know, and no writer has treated the subject – the felon had mopped up the blood so as to befuddle all who sought to find the cause of Sir Henry's death. They had overlooked one drop.

I must now report this sad discovery to Lord Gilbert, and he must send for Sir Roger de Elmerugg, Sheriff of Oxford. Murder upon Lord Gilbert's lands would generally be my bailiwick, but not when the deceased was a visiting knight. I was pleased that seeking a murderer would be another man's business. Sir Roger entertained other thoughts.

Chapter 2

I had no authority to summon the sheriff of Oxford to Bampton. Lord Gilbert must do that, and before he would do so I must explain the need. I found my employer in the hall, deep in conversation with Lady Petronilla and Lady Margery, sitting in chairs drawn aside while grooms erected tables for dinner.

Lord Gilbert saw me enter the hall. I did not wish to tell him of my discovery in the Lady Margery's presence, so stopped at the entry and with a nod of my head invited him to join me. He did so.

"What news, Hugh? Have you done with your examination?"

"I have, m'lord."

"And?"

"Sir Henry died at some other man's hand."

"What?" Lord Gilbert said, startled by this news, then peered over his shoulder to see if Lady Margery had observed or heard his response.

"Murder was done last night," I said.

"You are certain? How so?"

"Come with me and I will show you what I have found."

I motioned for Lord Gilbert to leave the hall before me, and as I turned to follow saw Lady Petronilla and Lady Margery look to me, their conversation halted, questions from their raised eyebrows. Few things will stop ladies' gossip, but I had managed to do so.

"Sir Henry," Lord Gilbert said as we strode the corridor toward the dead man's chamber, "had no wound upon him that I could see. How could this be murder? Have you found some poison?"

"Nay... no poison. I will show you. Come and see."

Lord Gilbert hesitated at the door to Sir Henry's chamber, where Arthur and Walter stood watch. I pushed past and motioned for him to follow. At Sir Henry's head I stopped and turned to Lord Gilbert.

"I had nearly given up learning the reason for this death," I admitted, "when my eyes fell upon yon poker." I pointed to the iron rod.

"Sir Henry was beaten to death with that?" Lord Gilbert asked incredulously.

"Nay."

"Stabbed, then? But where?"

"Nay. Not stabbed with the poker, but he was pierced."

"But there is no sign."

"There is if one seeks for it in the proper place. You have heard the tale of the death of King Edward's father?"

"Aye," Lord Gilbert grimaced. "Mayhap 'tis no tale, but true. But you said that poker was not employed to do murder."

"It was not. The soot of the last fire of winter is yet upon it. But when I saw it I wondered if another weapon might have been used to penetrate some other orifice."

"And you found it so?"

"Aye. So I believe. Look there." I pointed to the fragment of dried blood which I had teased from Sir Henry's ear, and which yet lay upon the pillow beside his head.

Lord Gilbert bent to examine the clot and perceived readily what it was he saw.

"Blood?" he said.

"Aye."

"From whence has it come?"

"Sir Henry's ear."

Lord Gilbert scowled. "Could not some spasm cause such a rupture?"

"I have never heard nor have I read of such a thing," I replied.

"But yet it could be so."

"Mayhap. But if Sir Henry died of a fit, I think he would have thrashed about in its throes, left his bed in disarray, and made some racket before death came upon him."

"Hmmm." Lord Gilbert stood from examining the blood, raised one questioning eyebrow, then spoke again.

"Some man within Bampton Castle walls did murder last night, then?"

"Or woman."

"What woman would wish Sir Henry dead?"

"What man?" I replied.

"Surely some man has done this."

"Why so? 'Twould take little strength to plunge a bodkin through a man's ear and into his brain."

"But would a woman have the stomach to do so?"

"That, m'lord, I cannot say. There are some men, I think, who could not bring themselves to do such a sleeping murder, no matter the provocation. As there be some men who could not, there may be some women who could."

"Oh," Lord Gilbert said thoughtfully. "Just so. Well, if you are certain of murder you must discover who has done it."

"Is that not the sheriff's duty?"

"He must be told, of course. I will send for him straight away."

"And we must bring Hubert Shillside to see what has happened here."

Shillside is Bampton's haberdasher, and has been the

town coroner since before I came to the place. I have had many dealings with him and his jury. More than I would wish. I do not dislike the man, but it seems that whenever I have discourse with the fellow some man has died.

"We will have our dinner first, then you must travel to Oxford and fetch Sir Roger."

"Me?"

"Aye. You must explain to Sir Roger what has happened, and why you suspect murder. John Chamberlain or some valet could not do so in convincing fashion."

June twenty-first was a fast day, so Lord Gilbert's table was not so lavish as otherwise would be. Lord Gilbert, Lady Petronilla, Lady Margery, Lady Anne, Sir John and Sir Geoffrey sat at the high table. In times past I had also had a place there, but not this day. There was room enough. Perhaps Lord Gilbert thought that Lady Margery might take it amiss, being yet convinced that my potion had slain her husband. Neither Lord Gilbert nor I had announced yet the cause of Sir Henry's death.

The first remove this day was sole in cyve, wheaten bread with honeyed butter, and mussels boiled in wine. I watched Lady Margery consume her portion of this first remove. I thought she might have little appetite, but not so. She attacked her dinner eagerly. Her cheeks were yet pink and swollen from the morning's tears, but her conversation with Lord Gilbert and Sir Geoffrey, who sat on either side of her this day, showed little sign of bereavement. Sir Geoffrey, I was surprised to see, stuffed himself crudely, and wiped honeyed butter from his lips with the back of his hand. Lady Margery did not seem to notice.

For the second remove the cook presented boiled salmon and a pottage of whelks. During this remove I turned my attention to Lady Anne. She seemed less enthusiastic for discourse, speaking to Lady Petronilla and

Sir John only when spoken to, and ate but a small portion of the boiled salmon.

Directly across from me, at the head of the other side table, sat the two squires. I watched them as valets brought the third remove, eels in bruit and a pike fried and anointed with sobye sauce. One squire ate heartily, and spoke frequently to his companion, but the other seldom made reply, consumed little of his meal, and from a corner of his eye seemed intent on those who sat at the high table.

For a subtlety there was gingerbread and a chardewarden. I gave up trying to learn anything from Sir Henry's household and enjoyed these sweets.

Sir Henry's and Lord Gilbert's grooms and valets, who sat at the far ends of the side tables, received only maslin loaves, eels, and stockfish, of course, but they seemed to enjoy the meal as much as we who dined on more refined fare.

"Your chaplain," I said to Lord Gilbert when the meal was done, "has he offered Extreme Unction?"

"Aye. When Sir Henry was discovered dead. Before I sent for you."

"What is to be done with the corpse? Will Lady Margery return her husband to Bedford?"

"Nay. She said 'tis too far. June days are warm. Sir Henry will begin to stink before he can be got home. She will have him buried here, in St Beornwald's churchyard."

"She does not wish him interred in the church?" I asked. I was somewhat surprised that a knight would await the Lord Christ's return under the sod with common folk.

"What she wishes and what she will pay for seem two different things."

"Lady Margery will not pay for Sir Henry to be buried within the church?"

"Will not, or cannot," Lord Gilbert said.

"Surely a knight's widow has coin enough to see him rest under the church floor."

Lord Gilbert shrugged. "Father Thomas has been sent for. Lady Margery will treat with him about costs. But when I asked this morn, before you were sent for, she named the churchyard as his burial place. 'Tis my belief," he added after a moment of silence, "that Sir Henry was in straitened circumstances."

"Ah… I understand. He's been under your roof, dining at your table, since Ascension Day."

"Day after."

"Had he said aught about taking himself home?"

"Nary a word, though I'd begun to hint of it. Gambled a bit, did Sir Henry. Lost often in France, while we awaited battle. He'd wager upon nearly anything; dice, two lads wrestling, which dog would win a fight. Lost ten shillings when he wagered Sir Ralph de Colley that next day there'd be no rain."

"There was rain?"

"Came down in buckets. Sir Henry had little luck when he put his coin at risk."

"That's why he came to Bampton, you think? Because of his poverty he wished to take advantage of your table?"

"Aye," Lord Gilbert answered. "And likely why he'll sleep under the churchyard rather than under the church floor, or in his own parish church."

It is no dishonor to be poor. The dishonor in poverty is often found in the manner in which a man becomes poor. Or remains so.

I wondered that Lord Gilbert would not offer funds to see Sir Henry laid under the floor of the Church of St Beornwald, but there are things even a bailiff finds it injudicious to ask of his employer.

It was by then past midday, too late to travel to Oxford,

seek the sheriff, and return before night, even as the longest day of the year drew near. And Bruce, the old dexter given to my use, has such a jouncing gait that such a journey all in one day would be a torment to my nether portion.

I told Lord Gilbert that I would take Arthur with me to Oxford, and return next day with the sheriff, was Sir Roger not otherwise engaged. Lady Margery could, with Father Thomas, make plans for her husband's funeral, and after Sir Roger had seen the corpse, and been shown the damaged ear, Sir Henry might be placed beneath the grass of St Beornwald's churchyard, there to await our Lord Christ's return.

Kate awaited me, hands on hips, lips drawn tight, when I returned to Galen House. She had expected me for my dinner, a chevet, which is a meal I enjoy. Well, as Kate knows, there are few meals I do not enjoy.

"I left it upon the coals so long, awaiting your return, that it is scorched and gone dry," she said through pursed lips.

The subject was troublesome. I thought to change it. "There has been murder done at the castle," I said.

"Oh." Kate put a hand to her mouth. "Sir Henry?"

"Aye. Found dead in his bed this morning. 'Twas not a natural death."

"What has happened?"

"Some man thrust a bodkin or awl or some such thing through his ear and into his brain whilst he slept."

Kate's eyes grew wide and she shuddered. "I am sorry that I was short with you. The pie is not so badly burnt."

"Lord Gilbert asked me to dine at the castle."

"You did so?"

"Aye. I wished to observe Sir Henry's family and retainers."

"Because one of them slew him?"

"It must be. Lord Gilbert wished him away and back to his own demesne, but would not have murdered him to be rid of him, nor asked another to do so."

"What did you learn, watching them eat?"

"Nothing. Sir Henry's wife believes my sleeping potion to blame, and ate heartily of her dinner. But only one of Sir Henry's squires had appetite for his dinner. Lord Gilbert has promised to tell Lady Margery how Sir Henry died, and I must travel to Oxford and return tomorrow with the sheriff. The murder of a knight is more his business than mine. It happened in my bailiwick, but his shire."

* * *

Sir Roger de Elmerugg possesses champion eyebrows. They cross his face like a hedge through a meadow. When I told him of death at Bampton Castle and its cause, his ruddy forehead furrowed above his brows.

"You do not know who has done this murder?" he said.

"Nay. Lord Gilbert wishes you to attend him and seek the felon."

"You are bailiff there. Does he not trust your competence?"

"Sir Henry," I shrugged, "is... was a knight. And," I added, "I am suspect."

"You? How so?"

I explained that Sir Henry had slept uneasily and had asked for a sleeping draught.

"You provided this?"

"Aye. 'Twas but the pounded seeds of lettuce, a physic I have often used to bring slumber."

"What if a man took your potion, yet could not sleep, so consumed more? What then?"

"The seeds of lettuce are a mild soporific. We may see how much remains in the pouch of what I gave him, but he could have consumed all and it would not have stopped his breath. Lettuce seeds may poison a man if taken to excess, but there were not enough in the pouch to sicken Sir Henry. And I told you of the blood I found in his ear."

"Aye. Well, Lord Gilbert asks, and I will come. You may sleep this night in a guest chamber, and your man may sleep with the castle sergeants. We will set out tomorrow after we have broken our fast."

I had slept in Oxford Castle before, but not under a clean blanket. I had been charged with stealing another man's fur coat, which I had not done, so until I was freed at Lord Gilbert's command I spent several days in the castle dungeon. The experience returned to my mind and so occupied my thoughts that I did not readily find sleep.

A sergeant pounded upon the chamber door shortly after dawn and announced that Sir Roger would have me and Arthur join him to break our fast. We found the sheriff in the hall, his mouth stuffed with wheaten bread and cheese. No maslin loaf for the sheriff of Oxford. Another sergeant was there also, and Arthur and I joined readily in consuming the loaves and cheese and ale.

Sir Roger, the two sergeants, Arthur, and I, our bellies pleasingly full, rode under the Oxford Castle gatehouse half an hour later, crossed the Isis on Bookbinder's Bridge, passed Osney Abbey, and set off for Bampton.

Whole families were in the fields as we passed. Men swung long-handled scythes to cut hay close to the ground. Women and children followed to turn the hay so it would dry evenly. In other meadows, where the hay had been cut some days past, men were gathering it into great stacks. Many of these laborers watched our party pass upon the road, and some noticed that Sir Roger and I were garbed as gentlemen and tugged at a forelock as we passed.

The hall was prepared for dinner when we arrived at Bampton Castle. Lord Gilbert had expected Sir Roger's arrival, so the meal this day featured many pleasing dishes: roasted partridges, cony in cevy, stewed pigeons, and boar in confit, amongst others.

Place was made at the high table for Sir Roger, and I, again, sat at the head of a side table. Sir Roger was seated beside Lady Margery, and throughout the meal she continued an uninterrupted conversation with the sheriff, turning from him occasionally to cast a baleful eye in my direction. I did not see the woman exchange even one word with Lord Gilbert, who sat also beside her.

To avoid Lady Margery's hostile gaze I watched other diners. None seemed to have lost his appetite in the past twenty-four hours. Even the youthful squire who had picked at his pike a day earlier consumed his portion of the meal this day. Perhaps he preferred boar over pike.

'Twas well we dined before I took Sir Roger to Sir Henry's corpse and not after, for in the warmth of June the corpse was beginning to bloat, and would in a few days stink, reducing even a stout sheriff's hunger.

"Lady Margery believes you at fault in this business," the sheriff said as we walked the corridor leading to Sir Henry's chamber. "Lord Gilbert has told her what you found, and that murder was done. She scoffed at that, he said, and claims you seek to turn suspicion from your own malfeasance."

"You will see soon enough," I replied, and led Sir Roger past Walter and Uctred, who had been pressed into the melancholy duty of guarding the corpse in Arthur's absence. For reasons I could not then explain, I wanted a Bampton Castle man at Sir Henry's door as well as one of Sir Henry's retainers.

Sir Henry lay as I had left him the day before, the dried clot of blood from his ear yet upon the pillow. I pointed to it.

"That is what I drew from Sir Henry's ear."

"I'm no surgeon," Sir Roger said. "Is there no other explanation for such a wound?"

"I know of none. Even if he was taken with a fit in the night, I do not believe blood would issue from his ear."

"What of the other ear? If a fit drew blood from one ear, seems likely it would be found in the other as well."

"I did not look there, not after finding the injury done to this ear."

"Look now."

I did. Rigor mortis was beginning to fade, so 'twas no trouble to turn Sir Henry's head upon the pillow. The light in this chamber, as I have written, was poor, but enough to show that no blood could be seen in the ear. Nevertheless I took the thin blade I had left in the chamber and probed as deeply as I could. I found no crusted blood there.

"Wouldn't need to pierce a man's head through both ears to slay him," Sir Roger said when I withdrew the scalpel and held it up for him to see the clean blade. "Can you be certain such a thrust took his life?"

"Not without opening his skull, which I cannot do without Lady Margery's permission."

"Oh... aye. Would not the pain of such a stab cause a man to shriek, even if but for a moment, before he died?"

"Who can say? Perhaps he was silenced with a pillow over his mouth. Or perhaps my potion had to do with the business."

"Your potion? I thought you said it could not harm a man."

"I did, and I spoke true. But my thought is this: perhaps Sir Henry was given a larger dose of the pounded lettuce seeds than I advised. It might be that a greater amount could put a man so deeply asleep that he would not awaken when his head was turned and he felt the first prick of the weapon."

"You think this possible?" the sheriff asked.

"It is outside my experience," I replied. "But yes, I believe it possible. I would like to see the pouch I gave to Sir Henry, to see how much remains of the lettuce seeds."

"You shall, and I will speak to Lady Margery. Can you open Sir Henry's head to learn if a thrust through his ear did this, without disfiguring his visage before burial?"

"I can."

Chapter 3

Lady Margery would not permit me to open Sir Henry's skull. This did not surprise me. The woman was convinced, or said she was, that my sleeping draught had taken her husband's life and had no wish to be proven wrong.

"Said you wished to mutilate her poor husband to turn suspicion for the death from yourself to some other man," Sir Roger said.

Lord Gilbert also attended this conversation. "I asked if she wished Sir Henry embalmed," he said. "'Who would do it?' she asked. When I told her Master Hugh had the skill, she refused. Of course, it may be she would not pay your fee."

"There is little reason to embalm a man who will await the last judgment in the churchyard," I said. "A putrid corpse there will not torment a parish as might be if the corruption was entombed within the church and the seal lacking."

"Lady Margery wishes to bury Sir Henry tomorrow," Lord Gilbert said. "Is there any reason she should not?"

Sir Roger and I exchanged glances and waited for the other to speak. He did not, so I finally told Lord Gilbert that the corpse could tell us nothing more and that Lady Margery's wishes should be granted.

Bampton has been without a carpenter since Peter Carpenter fled, but Edgar Haute, a groom in Lord Gilbert's service, has shown some skill with saw, chisel, and drawknife, and so has been pressed into service when castle or village requires a man to build with wood.

Lord Gilbert sent Uctred to find Edgar and tell him that the coffin he was assigned to fashion would be needed Friday morning.

"Had Sir Henry enemies, you think?" Sir Roger asked.

Lord Gilbert chuckled and looked to me with one eyebrow raised. "Must be," he said. "No friend would drive a bodkin through a man's ear."

"Oh, aye, just so," Sir Roger replied.

The sheriff looked to me. "How do we go about finding the man? Whoso did this is clever. I'm a soldier. If an evil fellow must be brought to justice at sword's point, I'm your man. But this..." Sir Roger waved a hand above the corpse. "This is work for a scholar."

He said this while gazing fixedly at me. I turned to Lord Gilbert, seeking his aid in turning the task back to Sir Roger, but received no support.

"Master Hugh's a scholar, is that not so, Hugh? And he's been bailiff here long enough to ferret out felons in a wink. He'll have the culprit in your hands within a fortnight."

I wished for Lord Gilbert's confidence. There is but one thing a scholar can be relied upon to do, and that is to disagree with other scholars. Discovering felons is not taught in the set books.

"What is to be done first?" Sir Roger asked, and thereby placed himself, the high sheriff of Oxford, under my command. I would have preferred it otherwise. Humility is a virtue, and one which I admire. I have never sought to rise above my station. St Augustine wrote that humility is the source of all virtue, and pride the root of all evil. Somewhere in Bampton there was that day a proud man, or woman, who had done murder. Likely there were in the castle that day many proud men, both gentle and commons, but only one, or perhaps two, had taken Sir Henry's life.

"I would like to find the pouch of lettuce seed I gave to Sir Henry," I replied, "to learn how much was put in his wine."

"If the seed did not stop his breath," Lord Gilbert said, "why seek it?"

"Because it seems to me that, if Sir Henry took a large portion of the seeds in his wine, one man might have done the felony, Sir Henry being in so deep a sleep that his head might have been turned upon his pillow and the murder done without him being awakened."

"Ah," Sir Roger said. "I see. If the dose was as you advised he might have awakened when a man sought his life. Then two men might have been required to do the deed."

"Aye. So let us first seek the pouch. Walter may know where it may be found."

He did. Lady Margery had asked for it after Sir Henry was found dead. It had been in Sir Henry's chamber, resting upon the table where was found the wine cup, until then.

"Hmmm. 'Twill not do for you to ask Lady Margery for the pouch," Lord Gilbert said. "I will do so. Wait here."

While he was away seeking the pouch I asked Walter of the potion and how it had been administered.

"Sir Henry sent Adam to the buttery for wine."

"Adam?"

"Another of Sir Henry's valets. I measured a thimbleful of the powder from the pouch an' poured it into the wine, like I was told. Used one of Lady Margery's thimbles. There it sits, upon the table."

"Did Sir Henry then drink it down, straight away?"

"Aye."

"And left the empty cup upon the table?"

"Aye."

I heard footsteps approach and a moment later Lord

Gilbert appeared in the doorway, the pouch dangling from his hand.

"Here 'tis," he said, and offered it to my inspection.

I had not measured a precise amount of the lettuce seed when I filled the pouch, just poured a handful in and sent it off to the castle. So I was required to cast my mind back two days to recall how much of the crushed seed I had placed in the pouch. I was certain that more than a thimbleful was gone. Lord Gilbert saw me frown as I peered into the pouch to examine its contents.

"You are troubled, Hugh."

"Much of what I placed in the pouch is missing."

"How much?" Sir Roger asked.

"Half, I should think."

"Enough to poison a man?" Lord Gilbert asked.

"Nay."

I turned again to Walter. "Did any other require an aid to sleep? Did some other man ask for some of the sleeping potion? Or woman?"

"Nay," he shook his head. "None that I've heard of."

Just then we heard footsteps approaching and the rustle of clothing in the corridor. Lady Margery and two of her ladies appeared, garbed in somber cotehardies of brown, and the Lady Margery veiled.

Sir Henry's wife stared through her veil for a moment, as if the obstruction to her vision caused her to misjudge who stood before her. She finally fixed her eyes upon Lord Gilbert and spoke.

"'Tis not meet for my husband to go unwashed to the grave. Has this miscreant leech finished with Sir Henry?"

Lord Gilbert looked to me for a reply. "Aye, I have done here," I said.

"I should hope so," Lady Margery hissed. "You have already done quite enough."

Then, before I or any man could react, Lady Margery lunged for me. Her fingernails scored my cheek.

Lord Gilbert hastened to my defense. He grasped Lady Margery's arms and pinned them to her side. "M'lady, Master Hugh did not poison Sir Henry. Your husband was murdered. Master Hugh has shown how 'twas done. Sir Roger and I are convinced that Master Hugh speaks true and has discovered here an evil felony."

I put a finger to my cheek and it came away bloody.

"Bah, what man wished to take my husband's life? A groom or valet? Sir John or Sir Geoffrey? A squire? Or mayhap one of your men? Absurd."

Lady Margery eyed the pouch in my hand. "'Twas that potion which murdered Sir Henry."

"My instruction," I replied, "was to give Sir Henry a thimbleful of the crushed seeds, but more than that is gone from the pouch... perhaps half of what I sent."

"You sent some herbs so hazardous that taking a larger dose would put an end to him?"

"Nay. He might have consumed the entire contents of the pouch and yet awakened next morn."

Through the veil I saw the woman's disbelief, so continued. "Mixing half of the contents of the pouch into his wine might have sent Sir Henry to a deep sleep, but would not have caused death."

The skeptical look did not leave Lady Margery's eyes, so I decided upon a measure which would prove my assertion. I asked Uctred to seek the buttery and bring a cup of wine.

Lord Gilbert peered at me from under a raised eyebrow.

"I will prove to m'lady that crushed seeds of lettuce, even taken in immoderate measure, will not send a man to his death."

"How will you do so?"

"I will consume what remains of the potion."

48

"Nay, Master Hugh. You must not do so. Perhaps some other substance has befouled the potion, unknown to you."

"I keep my remedies secure and clean of contaminants."

"But what if some man mixed some poisonous herb into the contents of the pouch?" Lord Gilbert said.

The thought gave me pause. I poured a generous amount of the pounded seeds into my palm and inspected the stuff closely. I am familiar with the appearance of pounded lettuce seeds, as the powder is one I use often to aid sleep when a man is injured or in pain. I saw in my palm nothing to indicate the crushed lettuce seeds had been adulterated.

The buttery was close by, down a stairway at the end of the corridor and adjacent to the hall through the screens passage. Uctred returned promptly with a cup of wine. Lord Gilbert, Sir Roger, Lady Margery, and the others crowded into the chamber watched silently as I emptied the pouch into the cup, then drank the coarse concoction in one prolonged gulp. I confess that, as I swallowed, I had a worrisome thought that perhaps Lord Gilbert was correct, and somehow my pots and vials and flasks had become confused upon the shelves and in the chest where I store them.

I placed the empty cup upon the table and wiped my lips with the back of my hand. The others remained silent and motionless, as if they expected me to swoon before their eyes. Only the Lady Margery seemed to watch with anticipation. The others seemed apprehensive.

"I put but a thimbleful of the powder into Sir Henry's wine," Walter said, breaking the silence. "'Twas not near what he has taken."

"Then how," Sir Roger asked, "did near half of the stuff disappear? This fellow said he gave Sir Henry but a thimbleful, as he was told to do, but Master Hugh says but half of the potion remains." The sheriff looked to Walter. "Where did you leave the pouch after you had prepared Sir Henry's draught?"

"There, on the table, where it now rests."

"Perhaps," Lord Gilbert said, "Sir Henry thought the draught too weak, and took more. Did you see him drink what you had prepared?"

"Aye, m'lord. Drank it straight down, 'e did."

"Was there any wine remaining in his cup?" I asked.

"Dunno. Don't think so. He tilted the cup so's to drink it all."

"How then did he consume more of the potion?" Lord Gilbert mused. "Did he eat it, mayhap?"

"I doubt so," I said. "The seeds of lettuce are bitter. And we do not know that he did take more of the potion. Perhaps someone else swallowed a part of it."

"But who?" Sir Roger asked. "Was there another," he looked to Lady Margery, "who was troubled in the night so they could not fall to sleep?"

Lady Margery shook her veiled head and replied, "What difference if half the potion did not stop his breath?"

"Aye," Lord Gilbert said. "What difference?"

"I will tell you tomorrow," I said. "As for now, 'tis near the twelfth hour, I wish to return to Galen House, and Lady Margery wishes to prepare her husband for burial."

"You will return on the morrow to seek a murderer?" Sir Roger asked.

"Aye. I will be well rested for the work."

Galen House and my bed loomed large in my thoughts as I passed under the castle portcullis and set out for Bridge Street and home. I had rarely dosed myself with even a thimbleful of crushed lettuce seeds, as sleep generally comes readily to me. I had no experience at consuming so great a portion of the herb. I did not pause at the bridge over Shill Brook, as I often do when no pressing business calls, for worry I might succumb to sleep while gazing into the flowing water and tumble into the stream.

I had forgotten my scratched cheek. When I arrived at my home and Kate saw me her eyes went wide and she asked what had befallen me. I told her of Lady Margery's anger, and for a moment thought she was about to strike out for the castle to avenge me.

"The woman must be forgiven," I said. "She is a new widow and does not see things as they are."

"But folk will see your cheek and think I have done this."

"Those who know us will know you would not do such a thing to your husband, and that I would not treat you so as to give you cause. Why should we care what others will think?"

Kate was not much pleased when she learned what I had done to prove to Lady Margery that Sir Henry's sleeping draught could not have caused his death.

"What am I to do," she asked, "if you fall to sleep upon the table while eating your supper?"

"Carry me up to our bed," I said in jest.

"You like my cookery too well. You are no longer the slender youth I wed."

"Am I grown fat?"

Kate frowned and assumed a thoughtful air. "Not yet," she said.

"But if you continue to feed me with mushroom tarts and coney pies and roasted capons I soon will be, eh?"

"'Tis a mark of honor for a wife that her husband is well fed."

"Then I will do what I may to bring you respect amongst other women. And if I fall to sleep here, over my loaf and ale, leave me. I may sleep as well with my head upon an elbow as upon a pillow, after so much lettuce seed as I've consumed. But I am alert enough yet, I think, to climb to our bed. When I am well asleep, turn my head upon the pillow."

"Turn your head?"

"Aye. I wish to know if a man could fall to such a deep sleep that he would not awaken if his head was moved."

I managed to remain awake through a simple supper, but became drowsy when the meal was done. I climbed the stairs to our bed chamber, lay down, and was deep asleep when the sun sank beyond the trees of Lord Gilbert's orchard and forest to the west of Bampton Castle.

Kate's rooster awakened her next morn, but not me. The sun was well up when I finally blinked awake. It occurred to my muddled mind that I was yet alive. My experiment had been a success. A surfeit of crushed lettuce seeds had not stopped my breath. I had been sure it would not, but yet... well, that is the point of an experiment – to learn what is unknown, even if the result seems sure.

I admit to being a bit unsteady as I descended the stairs. When Kate saw me enter our modest hall she said, "I could've shaved away your beard and you'd not have cared."

I was yet too stupid from sleep to understand her words. My spouse saw this, rolled her eyes, shook her head, and said, "I was to turn your head upon the pillow, remember?"

"Oh, aye. You did so?"

"Indeed. I turned your head one way, then the other, and prodded you in the ribs, too. I even poked where the arrow pierced you under your arm. I know the wound is yet tender, but you lay as dead. But that your chest rose and fell with each breath I might have thought you were."

I had little appetite this morn, which is surely a reflection of too much crushed lettuce seed the night before, as I am usually eager to break my fast. My tongue felt as though one of the poulterer's geese had molted in my mouth, however, so a cup of the baker's wife's ale was welcome.

My cup was near empty when Kate spoke again. "What did you learn when I turned your head last night?"

"I learned nothing when you turned it, but this morn I have learned that a man may be so deep in sleep that his head might be moved so as to drive a sharp object through his ear and into his brain, doing murder while the fellow is asleep."

Kate shuddered. "Is this what happened to Sir Henry?"

"So I believe. The Lady Margery thought my sleeping potion to blame for her husband's death. I drank a fistful of crushed lettuce seeds in a cup of wine to prove her wrong, but I have also proven that under the spell of such a draught a man might be murdered and be able to do nothing to prevent his death."

"Had Sir Henry enemies?"

"One, at least, although his wife and those in his service say not. What man who has achieved anything of import has not made enemies while doing so?"

"Either they are ignorant," Kate said, "or they do not wish to cast suspicion on one another."

"Aye," I agreed.

"Which do you believe it is?"

"I do not know Lady Margery or Sir Henry's daughter or his knights, squires, valets, and grooms well enough to say."

"But you have thoughts on the matter."

"Aye. Some man in Sir Henry's service has done this. And some others may have suspicions which they do not wish to voice."

"A friend of the murderer?"

"Or fearful for their own life, perhaps."

Kate was silent for a moment, then spoke again. "A man who would do murder once might do so again, if he thought he was about to be found out."

"Aye. A man can only hang once."

"Then I beg you take care. I need a husband and Bessie needs a father."

"You may trust me to do all necessary to keep body and soul entwined."

Kate had set a maslin loaf before me, but I had no appetite for it, nor did she. It lay untouched upon our table while we spoke.

"Why do men murder one another?" Kate asked.

"Many reasons, I suppose."

"Aye... but some reasons are rare and others common, I'd guess."

"And what," I asked her, "are the customary reasons for one man to slay another?"

"Surely you can imagine such causes."

"Aye, but I would know your thoughts." My Kate is quick of wit, and had provided good counsel in previous entanglements in which I had found myself.

Kate finally picked up the loaf and tore a fragment from it as she spoke. "Greed, of course. One man wants what another has."

"Sir Henry was in reduced circumstances."

"A knight with no funds?"

"So it seems."

"A man may possess things other than money," Kate said, "which another man may want."

"Such as?"

"A wife... or a daughter."

"Ah, just so. Sir Henry had both."

"I've not been to the castle since they arrived. Are they comely?"

Here was perilous ground, but I trod nimbly across it.

"Some men might think so. They are not repulsive."

"Hmmm. I suspect you of great tact," Kate smiled.

I am no fool. I changed the subject. "Why else, do you think, do men do murder?"

"Some grievance, perhaps. An ancient wrong, or a new one, for which a man might seek vengeance."

"'Twould have to be some offense Sir Henry did to one of those of his circle now lodged in the castle."

"Was he a hard man with his inferiors?"

"I know not. 'Tis a thing I must learn, and it should not be difficult. A man who holds a grudge against his lord can usually be persuaded to speak of it, especially if the lord is a corpse and can do him no injury for his words."

"What if," Kate replied while chewing a portion of the maslin loaf, "such a man fears speaking ill of his lord, lest doing so will turn suspicion upon him for his lord's death?"

"A possibility. You speak wisely. I must be discreet."

"Or devious," Kate said. "Cause a man to believe you suspect another, so he will lower his guard."

"His guard, or hers?"

"You think a woman struck down Sir Henry? It could only be his wife or daughter... unless one of Lady Margery's maids..."

"Aye, wife or daughter, and both have maids who wait upon them."

"Why would Lady Margery want her husband dead?"

"Who can know if she did?"

"Or the daughter," Kate added.

"If it is so that wife or daughter did this," I said, "there will be also a man in the business."

"A lover?"

"Aye. A wife who wishes to change husbands, or a

daughter who wishes to wed a man to whom her father objects."

Kate tore off another fragment from the maslin loaf and chewed it thoughtfully. "There must be other reasons men do murder."

"I believe there are but three," I said. "A man has what another man wants, and is slain for it. Or, a man has what another man wants, and murders the other to keep it. Or revenge... to requite some injury."

"Which of these brought Sir Henry's death, you think?"

"I cannot tell," I said. "But when I learn the reason I will have the felon, I think."

My cup of ale was not quite empty. I swallowed the dregs, kissed Kate and Bessie – who had been exploring her toes all the while her mother and I had tried to account for the evil men do to others – placed my cap upon my head, and set off from Galen House for the castle.

I was but a few steps from my door when I heard someone retching nearby. The sound came from behind my own house. I crept quietly alongside of Galen House 'til I could peer around the corner into the toft. Kate stood just outside the rear door, one hand upon her stomach, the other across her mouth. Her retching had ceased.

I remembered well the last time Kate was so afflicted and so walked with light heart to the castle. I was sure that Bessie would soon have a playmate.

Chapter 4

My joy was much reduced when I arrived at the castle, for there all was in mourning. Sir Henry's coffin, shrouded in black linen, lay upon a bier just inside the gatehouse, and as I watched, Lady Margery and Lady Anne appeared, garbed in their most somber cotehardies, ready to assume their places behind the coffin as chief mourners when the procession to the church began.

Father Thomas de Bowlegh arrived a few moments later. As I watched him pass under the portcullis I saw behind him, through the opening, that a small knot of Bampton citizens was gathering in the forecourt.

The priest spoke a few words to Lady Margery, then nodded to the four grooms who stood ready at the poles to bear the coffin to St Beornwald's Church. Father Thomas took his place at the head of the procession, ready to lead the way.

The grooms bent to their poles and followed Father Thomas through the gatehouse, Lady Margery and Lady Anne close behind. Lord Gilbert, Lady Petronilla, and Sir Roger walked behind the bereaved widow. Then came Sir John and Sir Geoffrey. I fell into the column with the squires William and Robert, as my rank ordained.

The bier was hardly out from under the gatehouse when Lady Margery set up a dreadful wail. Lady Anne joined in, but both were immediately overwhelmed by the small crowd which I had seen through the open gate and portcullis. Somehow Lady Margery had found funds to hire mourners for Sir Henry's funeral, and these now offered a howl of grief so as to earn their pay.

The procession crossed Shill Brook on Mill Street, and thence traveled on Bridge Street to Church View. Kate watched from the door, Bessie wide-eyed, clutching at her mother's cotehardie, as the procession passed Galen House. While I walked I tried to watch and see if any mourners before me seemed less enthusiastic in their grief than the others. This was difficult to do, observing the backs of heads. And behind me the Bampton citizens hired for the purpose set up a mind-numbing clamor which did not abate until the coffin was set down in the lychgate.

Father Thomas there began Sir Henry's funeral, but I paid little heed to the dirge. Any man who has survived the plague and its return has heard such many times. I watched to see if any of Sir Henry's mourners seemed complacent while others grieved, but either the felon was cunning, or I am unable to recognize guilt in a man's features.

Father Thomas completed the office, then turned and strode toward the church porch. The grooms who bore Sir Henry's corpse resumed their task, and we mourners followed, silent now, into St Beornwald's Church. Father Thomas can be eloquent when the mood strikes, and after the funeral mass, it did. His oration was as fine as any duke might deserve. I hope Lady Margery appreciated his effort.

When he was done Father Thomas led us to the churchyard and near to the south transept scraped a furrow into the turf with a toe. The grave-diggers plied their spades at this place, and there was soon a pit large enough for Sir Henry to await the Lord Christ's return.

The grooms lowered the black-veiled coffin into the grave and mourners who had brought with them sprigs of rosemary tossed the greenery atop the coffin. Father Thomas reminded all to remember to pray for Sir Henry, that his soul be released sooner from purgatory. It may be difficult for a wealthy man to enter heaven, but it is also sure that it is hard for a poor man to escape purgatory. If Sir Henry had not lived a life worthy of heaven I doubt that my prayers, or any man's, would send him there. But I keep such heretical views to myself. I am responsible for the care of a wife and a child. Perhaps soon two children. It would not do to provoke the bishops.

Sir Roger approached and drew me from the grave and those who surrounded it as earth was shoveled atop the coffin. We were near the churchyard wall when he turned and drew from his pouch a scrap of parchment the size of my palm. "This," he said softly, "was slipped under my door in the night, whilst I slept."

A few lines, hastily scrawled, filled one side of the fragment. The letters were so badly formed that at first I could not decide whether the words were Latin or English. A moment of scrutiny told me that before me was a message in English, written by some man unfamiliar with a pen.

"The squire has what you seek," was lettered in a crude hand upon the parchment.

"Who has written this," the sheriff asked, "and what is it that I seek?"

"You are here to seek a murderer, are you not?"

"Aye. Does this then say that one of Sir Henry's squires did murder, or does a squire know who is guilty?"

"Perhaps both. If one of the squires is the guilty man, the other may know of it. But why, I wonder, tell you in this manner? Why not speak of the knowledge directly to you?"

"Aye, why not? The man who wrote this wishes to be unknown."

"Some knight or valet or groom knows, or believes he knows, who has slain Sir Henry," I said, "but wants to conceal from you that he possesses such information."

"Which squire?"

"Perhaps the man does not know. Or perhaps the squires worked together to strike down Sir Henry."

"Then what is it we seek?" Sir Roger asked.

"Evidence. When we have returned to the castle I will tell Lord Gilbert that while others are at dinner in the hall we will inspect the chamber where Sir Henry's squires sleep."

"You believe what the squire has is a thing, rather than information?"

"Who can say? If some evidence is to be found in the squires' chamber, it may be more readily discovered than knowledge, which men may more easily obscure from the view of others."

"Lady Margery wishes to set out for Bedford on Monday," Lord Gilbert said when Sir Roger and I approached him. "What say you? Must she remain until this matter is resolved? We could require her men and maids to remain, and send her off with an escort of my own grooms. There will be men left behind at Bedford to serve her until those of her servants who are innocent of murder can be released."

"It may be possible for her to leave with her people... but for one," Sir Roger said. He produced the scrap of parchment and Lord Gilbert frowned over the crude message while he considered its import.

"One of Sir Henry's squires did the murder?" he asked.

"It is uncertain that this is what is meant," I replied. "Sir Roger and I wish to absent ourselves from dinner. While all are in the hall we will search the squires' chamber. Perhaps the murder weapon may be hid there."

"Ah. Very well. I will tell the cook to keep back some of the meal for you."

No doubt we were missed when Lord Gilbert's valets

began to serve dinner, but no one asked, he said later, of our whereabouts, being perhaps too polite to seem nosey.

The squires' chamber was on the ground floor of the castle guest range, its ceiling low, and with but one narrow window of glass which looked out to the marshalsea across an open yard. It was mid-day, or nearly so, but the small window provided little light for our search.

"What is it we seek?" Sir Roger asked as we entered the room. "A bodkin or other such device?"

"Aye. Something long and slender which could be plunged into a man's head through his ear. Assuming that we construe that note properly."

Two narrow beds occupied either side of the chamber. Between them was a small table, two chests, and on the far wall a fireplace. I pointed to one of the beds. "Search that mattress and bed clothes and I'll do the same here."

Silently we lifted and peered under the mattresses. I pulled back blankets but found nothing. I bent to peer under the bed but found only dust. Sir Roger completed his inspection of the other bed and likewise found nothing incriminating.

I stood and studied the chamber, then turned my attention to the chests. They had no locks, and the lids opened freely. In them were men's undergarments, kirtles and braes, extra cotehardies, caps, combs, and one chest held a pair of shoes with outlandishly curled toes, of finest leather, such as young men of fashion like to wear. In this same chest I found a vial of some liquid. I removed the stopper and passed the vessel under my nose. 'Twas no poison, but clove-pink, useful when a youth might wish to make his odor sweet before a maid. But no hidden weapon was found in either chest – but for the clove-pink.

Perhaps we looked for the wrong thing. The anonymous informer had written that we would find here what we sought, but how did the writer know what it was we sought?

I stood in the center of the small chamber, hands on hips, and studied the shadowed room. If I wished to hide an incriminating weapon, where would I do so?

The pillows and mattresses had seemed a likely place, but examination had found nothing but goose feathers and chopped straw. The sun, now slanting through the narrow window, illuminated the fireplace and at the top of the opening I saw a brief glimmer of some white object, pale against the soot of the mantel.

The white fragment hung, barely visible, from the inside of the mantel. A place where nothing white should be, nor would it remain so for long in such a place. I stepped to the hearth, reached into the cavity, and drew from behind the mantel a scrap of linen cloth about as wide as my foot and twice as long. It had evidently been stuffed hastily into a crack between the stones, and a corner had fallen free, which I had not seen until the afternoon sun began to penetrate the chamber and illuminate the hearth.

The linen cloth was white, but not completely so. Nearly half of it was speckled with a reddish-brown stain. The fabric had been used to absorb blood. Was this Sir Henry's blood? Was this what Sir Roger had been told to seek? Sir Roger thought so.

"Blood," he said, "or I'll swim the Isis on St Stephen's Day."

Both the sheriff and I had, in our work, seen much blood. There was no mistaking the stains upon the cloth.

"Sir Henry's blood, you think?" Sir Roger continued. "Some man wished to hide it, so it's not likely 'twas used to staunch a bloody nose."

"Aye. Forced into the crevice between stones, it might have gone undetected, but a corner fell free."

"So we've caught a murderer, eh? But which one? Two of Sir Henry's squires occupy this chamber."

"We must devise some way," I said, "of learning which is guilty. If we bluntly ask, each will blame the other – unless both conspired against Sir Henry – and we might never learn the truth of the matter."

"Hang 'em both. We'd be sure to have the guilty lad then."

I turned to study Sir Roger's face, but could not tell whether he was serious or spoke in jest.

"'Twould be best to be certain," I said. "And if this is Sir Henry's blood, the weapon which struck him down may be nearby as well. I don't think a felon would cast away his weapon, then keep the fabric with which he wiped away the gore."

"Keep both, or cast away both, eh?"

"Aye. Let's return to the search. Perhaps there is in this chamber some secret place where an awl or bodkin may be hid. Such a weapon is slender and requires little cover."

I placed the bloodstained linen fragment in my pouch while Sir Roger lifted the chests from the floor aside the table and inspected them. He then turned the table over, to see if any slim instrument of death was hidden underneath. None was.

This was a chamber fit for squires, not knights. Aside from the beds and table there was no other furniture in the room. I went to the hearth again and felt the crevices between stones inside the opening, seeking some tiny crack where a thin iron probe might be concealed. I found nothing but soot.

Only one other object remained in the chamber. A lampstand stood at the foot of one of the beds, where a cresset rested to light the chamber at night. Where upon a lampstand could a man hide a bodkin or an awl? The thought seemed absurd, but having no better thought, I moved the cresset to the table and upended the stand.

The shaft of the lampstand had been turned, and where the turner had fastened the work to his lathe there was a small hole. I know little of joinery, but enough to know that this cavity was to be expected. I gave it little attention, so nearly missed the stub of dark iron which had been driven into the lampstand through its base.

Sir Roger saw me studying the upturned stand and spoke. "What have you there?"

"A bit of iron rod where none should be," I said, and held the stand out for his inspection. The sheriff scowled down at the visible end of the iron shaft, then tried to pluck it out. He had no success. Some man had driven this slender bit of metal deep into the lampstand.

"The marshalsea will have pliers," I said. "Let's go there and see if we can draw this bit of iron from the stand. Perhaps if we can see all of it we will know better its use and how it came to be here."

"Lead on," Sir Roger said, and grasping the lampstand he followed me from the chamber.

We found Ranulf the farrier beginning his afternoon work, rested from his dinner. I showed him the lampstand and asked if he had a tool which could draw the thin iron rod from the spindle. He nodded, went to his bench, and produced an implement used for wrenching nails from horses' hooves.

So little of the iron pin extended from the base of the lampstand that Ranulf found it difficult to find purchase on the metal with his tool. The pliers slipped their grip several times before the farrier managed, with forearms bulging and knuckles white, to loosen and then extract the object.

Ranulf lifted the thin rod before Sir Roger and me, and I reached out and took it from his tool.

"What was that there for, d'you suppose?" Ranulf said. "Lampstand didn't need no bracin'."

The bodkin or awl or whatever it once was had been filed to a needle-point. No wooden sphere covered the blunt end, but somewhere in the castle or nearby I was sure such a ball might be hid or discarded. There was no need for so sharp a point on a rod unless it was made to plunge through some other thing, and a larger surface against a man's hand than just the blunt end of the rod would be needed for that work.

"Speak to no man," I said to the farrier, "of what has been found here."

"Aye... What is it, an' why was it there?"

"Don't know of a certainty. But when we learn of it we will tell you. Until then, keep silence."

The farrier tugged a forelock when Sir Roger and I turned to go, me with the iron pin in my hand and Sir Roger with the lampstand. The bodkin was a bit longer than my longest finger. This was likely long enough to penetrate a man's brain if thrust through his ear. Was this the thing we were to seek, which the crudely written message had advised us of? This seemed likely.

Dinner was finished when we entered the hall. Grooms and valets had already completed their meals and departed, and Lord Gilbert and Lady Petronilla were standing at their places at the high table. Lord Gilbert saw us enter the hall, saw the lampstand in Sir Roger's hand, and raised an eyebrow. The bodkin in my hand was too small to be seen across the hall.

The others who yet remained at the tables had stood when Lord Gilbert did so, and I watched the squires to see if one would flinch to see the sheriff holding forth the lampstand wherein he had hidden a murder weapon.

Conversation in the hall faded as first Lord Gilbert,

then the others watched us enter and approach the high table. The squires also fell silent, curious expressions upon their faces as they saw Sir Roger approach Lord Gilbert with a common lampstand which must have seemed similar to the one they had last seen in their chamber. Neither youth showed any sign of fear or apprehension. Their expressions were bland; no furrowed brows, darting eyes, or chewed lips. One of these squires, or both, I thought, should be a traveling player.

"What is this?" my employer asked when Sir Roger stood before him.

"Master Hugh has discovered…"

"A lampstand, m'lord," I interrupted Sir Roger. I did not know what more than that the sheriff might say, but thought the less others in the hall knew of the stand, where it was found, and what was discovered within it, the better.

"I can see that," Lord Gilbert sighed, "but why have you brought it to the hall in the middle of the day when no light is needed?"

"We will explain in the solar, m'lord," I said.

"Very well. Come."

Lord Gilbert left his place and strode toward the stairway which led to the solar and adjacent chambers. As I passed the high table I saw Lady Margery's eyes fall to my hand and the slender shaft of iron I held. Neither of the squires had shown any dismay at the appearance of the lampstand, but the Lady Margery seemed to stagger back a step when she saw what I carried, before she steadied herself with a hand against the linen covering of the high table. Her eyes lifted to mine, she fixed me with a brief, haughty glare, then turned to speak to Lady Petronilla.

"Whence came this lampstand?" Lord Gilbert asked when we had entered the solar and closed the door behind us.

"'Twas in the squires' chamber," the sheriff replied. "And 'tis no common lampstand."

Sir Roger upended the stand, pointed to the base, and said, "Look there."

Lord Gilbert did so, looked to Sir Roger, then to me, and said, "What am I to see? Is there something remarkable about the thing?"

"Do you see the hole in the center of the stand?" I said. "We drew this from it."

I held out the iron bodkin and Lord Gilbert took it from me. "Too fine to be a nail," he said, "and no head. Why was it in the stand?"

"'Twas hid there," Sir Roger said. "Show Lord Gilbert the message again that put us on the trail."

Reading is not a task which comes easily to Lord Gilbert, although he does possess a most excellent book of hours to aid his devotions. He once read well, but many folk of his age must hold a document at arm's length, or admit the frailty of age and seek spectacles in London. And the note was written in a poor hand. As my employer scowled at the parchment I repeated what words were there.

"Was this used to slay Sir Henry?" he said, peering at the tool with some distaste.

"It may be," I replied. "If so, 'twas wiped clean when the deed was done. There is no trace of blood upon it."

"Plenty of blood on the cloth that was stuffed up the chimney," Sir Roger said.

One of Lord Gilbert's eyebrows lifted. "A bloody cloth?"

"Aye. Hidden above the fireplace in the squires' chamber," I said. "A corner of it fell free, so 'twas visible."

I withdrew the cloth from my pouch and held it forth for Lord Gilbert's inspection. He studied it intently, but would not take it from me.

"So one, or both, of these squires is guilty of murder?"

"Likely," Sir Roger replied.

Lord Gilbert peered at me. "How will you discover which has done this felony?"

"Take 'em both to the dungeon at Oxford Castle, 'til they confess the deed," the sheriff advised.

"What say you, Hugh?"

I dislike contradicting my betters, but it seemed to me such a course would not be effective.

"The squires will protest their innocence," I said, "but after a few days in the dungeon, or perhaps a week, they will confess all."

"See," Sir Roger said. "Your bailiff agrees. I'll send my sergeants to arrest the fellows."

"They will confess," I continued, "that the other is guilty. It is unlikely that any man will admit himself a felon when to do so will send him to a noose. Each will deny the crime and try to entangle the other in it."

"Mayhap they are both guilty," Sir Roger said. "The King's Eyre may find it so."

"It may be, but our only clues are insubstantial."

"What?" Lord Gilbert said. "A bloody cloth, a murder weapon, and a note which told Sir Roger where these might be found. These are insubstantial?"

"Evidence enough," the sheriff growled.

"What if this iron pin was used for some other purpose and did not slay any man? And who left the message under your door? One of the squires?"

Sir Roger shrugged.

"If one squire had informed against the other, he would, I think, write of which was the felon and which was not, else he would know that his own life was at risk."

"Mayhap someone saw them approach Sir Henry's door in the night," Lord Gilbert offered.

"Why not say so? Why send this riddle to Sir Roger in

the night? What harm could come to a man who would tell of what he saw?" I said.

"Perhaps he feared that someone might ask what he was doing prowling about the castle so late at night," Lord Gilbert said.

"The garderobe is not far from Sir Henry's chamber."

"Ah," Sir Roger said, "just so. What then, are we to allow a guilty man to escape a just punishment?"

"Nay. But we must be careful that the punishment is meted out to the guilty and none other."

"Innocent men often suffer for the deeds of others," Sir Roger said. "Why so troubled about perhaps one more?"

"If the innocent are afflicted because of the deeds of evil men, or because of God's choice, then I am free from censure. But no blameless man, nor woman either, should suffer because you, or I or Lord Gilbert, are too slothful to do justice."

Sir Roger was not pleased, I think, with my words. He frowned at me silently for a time, then spoke. "Very well... we will seek justice. How? We have clues. Three of 'em. What more?"

"A clue is a mistake," I said. "Most of the time."

Lord Gilbert's eyebrow lifted again. "How so?" he asked.

"Felons seek to obscure their guilt," I said.

"Aye," Sir Roger agreed. "But those squires, one of 'em, anyway, made a mistake."

"And someone knew of it and sent the message under your door," Lord Gilbert said.

"I am not convinced of the mistake," I said.

"Oh, why so?" the sheriff asked.

"I watched the squires when we entered the hall. You had the lampstand in your hand. There would be no reason for you to have it but that it was evidence of the murder. Neither of the squires seemed troubled, as one, at least, should have, had he hid a murder weapon in the lampstand. He would know he had been found out. This clue is too simple. A man cunning enough to slay Sir Henry in the manner he chose would not be so stupid as to leave evidence of his guilt where it might be readily found."

"What then of the message?" Lord Gilbert asked.

"Someone, I think, wants to point suspicion at a squire, or both of them."

"To turn us from his guilt?" Lord Gilbert said.

"Aye. What other reason, if the squires are blameless?"

"Mayhap the squires are guilty but skilled at deception," the sheriff said.

"'Tis possible," I agreed. "But everything falls to place too readily for my liking."

"Bah," Sir Roger scowled. "Scholars! Want to complicate matters which are simple. We've found a felon, or two, and you protest 'twas too neatly done."

"Would two youths devise so devious a way to slay a man, then be so careless as to leave evidence of the felony where it might be readily found?"

"Wouldn't have been," the sheriff said, "but for we being told where to search."

"And that's another riddle," I said. "Would the squires, one or both, be so careful to plot a hidden murder, then be so indiscreet that some other learned of their crime?"

Lord Gilbert scratched at his bearded chin. "So you believe some murderer hopes we will send one or both of the squires to a scaffold in his place?"

"I do not believe it so," I replied. "But I believe it possible. Is there a lock upon the squires' chamber door?"

"Nay. You think some man entered while the squires were away and placed in their chamber the bodkin and bloody cloth?"

"It could be done."

Sir Roger puffed his cheeks, frowned, then spoke. "How could that be proved? If 'tis so, what mistake did the murderer make which will be a clue for us?"

"The bodkin and fragment of linen stained with blood came from somewhere," I said. "If we can discover their origins we may find who has slain Sir Henry. And no man pushed an iron point into the lampstand with the palm of his hand."

"Used a hammer, you think?" Sir Roger said.

"Or some such device. A rock would serve, or a small block of wood, such as would have been used to thrust the bodkin into Sir Henry's brain."

"Lady Margery wishes to return to her home," Lord Gilbert said. To Sir Roger he continued, "What shall we tell her? When she leaves she will take the guilty with her."

"Good riddance," the sheriff said. "But tell her that if she wishes for her husband's murderer to be discovered she must remain until the man is found out."

I saw Lord Gilbert's lips draw tight at the thought of Lady Margery remaining longer in Bampton Castle. Sir Henry was, at first, a welcome guest, but my employer had found his wife to be a greater burden even than Sir Henry had become. Little could please her. Her loaf was stale, or there was not enough wood delivered to her chamber to take away the morning chill, or the musicians and jongleurs Lord Gilbert provided for entertainment were unfit.

I produced the bloody scrap of linen from my pouch and displayed it before Lord Gilbert and the sheriff. Before it became so stained it had been purest white.

"To what use was this put, you think, before it was used to mop up a dead man's blood?"

Sir Roger took the cloth from me and examined it. "Could be some fellow's kirtle," he said.

"Or some woman's," Lord Gilbert replied.

If this was so, the murderer was likely some gentleman in Sir Henry's household, for grooms, or even valets employed by one so impoverished as Sir Henry was said to be, were unlikely to wear linen. Plain wool must do for such folk.

Next I held the bodkin before me. "To what purpose was this first put? Or was it made for the purpose of murder?"

Both men shrugged, being unfamiliar with tools. Men in their employ might know better the answer to that question.

"The farrier might have made such an object. Or Edmund," Lord Gilbert said.

Edmund the smith is not a friend. His past behavior has required that I speak to him firmly, even threaten the fellow upon occasion. This was not a task I enjoyed, as the smith, like others who follow his craft, is a beefy sort while I am shaped like a reed along Shill Brook.

"Your farrier has already seen the thing," Sir Roger said. "If he knew of it, seems to me he would have said, it being found in an odd place, where it was not needed to be."

Lord Gilbert nodded approval of this theory. So it was left to me to seek Edmund Smith and learn what I could from him. I placed awl and bloody cloth in my pouch, bid Sir Roger and Lord Gilbert "Good day," and set off for the castle gatehouse. As I left the solar I heard Lord Gilbert direct John Chamberlain to bring wine. The sheriff, whose duty this should be, would enjoy a cup of malmsey, or perhaps claret, while I sought enlightenment from a strapping man who dislikes me. His wife cares little for me, as well, but I have already written of that tale.

Chapter 5

Being in no hurry to seek a favor of the smith, I lingered at the bridge over Shill Brook to watch the bubbling stream make its way to the Thames. How long, I wondered, would it take a twig to float to London? I picked up a bit of broken branch the size of a finger and tossed it into the stream. Would I discover Sir Henry's murderer before it drifted past the Tower? I would not do so gazing into the brook. Pleasant things are oft unprofitable. Were it otherwise, all men would be prosperous.

For all his great strength Edmund must have feeble nostrils. The power of his odor is as great as his arms. The man does strenuous and filthy work, 'tis true, but seems not to mind the accumulation of grime and sweat which he seldom scours away.

So I was prepared for the fragrance of Edmund's forge when I entered the place; a mixture of coal smoke, hot iron, and unwashed humanity. Edmund looked up from his anvil as my shadow darkened his open door, saw who it was who entered, then returned to hammering at a slab of red-hot iron. I waited while the work cooled. Then the smith placed it back amongst the coals and turned to his bellows.

"Have you ever made such a tool as this?" I said, holding the slender, pointed rod before him and trying to breathe through my mouth. I wondered if the smith's stench would linger upon me so that Kate would demand I disrobe in the toft and bathe before entering Galen House.

Edmund squinted at the awl and mistook it for a nail. "Aye... make nails all the time. You never see one before?" he added sarcastically.

"'Tis no nail. Here, look closely. What is its use, you think?"

"Ah, a bodkin. Made one for Bogo Tailor. That was long ago, him bein' dead nearly five years."

"Of what use was it to the tailor?"

"Poked holes in leather an' canvas an' stuff as was too tough for 'is needle to pierce."

"Could this be the bodkin you made?"

Edmund snorted. "'Ow could I know that? They're all alike... an' it's been years past."

"You've not been asked to make anything similar since?"

"Nay," he said, and turned back to his bellows.

I had not entered Edmund's forge expecting to learn much, so was not disappointed. I left the forge and walked up Church View Street to Galen House, where I also expected to learn little. This assumption, however, proved wrong.

Kate was preparing our supper, Bessie at the hem of her cotehardie, when I opened our door. Kate was bent over the hearth, frying a dish of hanoney upon scattered coals. I had neglected my postponed dinner in a desire to be at the trail of a felon, and my stomach took the moment to remind me of its empty state.

"What news?" she said as she stood from her cramped labor.

"I have found a murder weapon, I think, and perhaps a bit of cloth used to wipe away Sir Henry's blood when the man was slain."

I drew the items from my pouch and held them forth. Kate shrank from the objects as from an adder.

"That bodkin was plunged into Sir Henry's ear?" she asked.

"So I believe. I found it hidden, driven into the base of a lampstand, in the chamber where two of Sir Henry's squires lodge."

"One of them has slain his lord, then?"

"So Sir Roger believes."

"You do not?"

"'Tis all too neat and simple. The sheriff found a scrap of parchment upon the floor of his chamber this morn. Someone slid it under his door in the night. It told him to seek for what he hoped to find in the squires' chamber."

"And that is the bloody cloth?" Kate asked, curling her lip in distaste.

"Aye. A scrap of linen, of the finer sort. Perhaps torn from a gentleman's kirtle."

Kate's curiosity overcame her distaste and she reached for the fabric. She took it daintily, seeking to avoid the dark stained portions, and examined it closely.

"Here is no kirtle," she said.

"What, then?"

"Men!" she smiled. "Fancy yourself a sleuth, but do not know the difference between undergarments and a table cloth."

"Table cloth? That?"

"Aye, or napery or perhaps a portpain."

"Why do you say so?"

"Look there," she said, and pointed to the edge of the cloth. "I think no kirtle would be hemmed so, and the weave is twill. Who would have a kirtle woven so?"

One hem looks much like another to me, but Kate is experienced with needle and thread.

"If I seek the pantler tomorrow and ask him to search the pantry, you believe he will find one of Lord Gilbert's napkins missing a fragment of this size?"

"Aye. And look, it has been cut neatly, with a sharp blade, not ripped or torn."

"Hmm, 'tis so."

This bit of linen fabric was not employed by chance, then, but sliced from some larger cloth with a purpose in mind. So it seemed to me.

As the long midsummer eve faded to night I heard townsfolk upon the street, making their way to a meadow north of the Church of St Beornwald where all the day men had gathered wood for the bonfire which signaled midsummer's eve. Kate and Bessie and I followed the throng, but before we left Galen House Kate plaited the flowers of St John's Wort into her hair, and into the wispy, silken locks of our daughter, to ward off evil for the coming year.

Those who possessed white garments, and few did in such a town, wore them in honor of St John's Day. The quarter moon gave such folk a ghostly appearance, but soon flames reflected yellow and red from clothing and faces. Unless a man was ill and confined to his bed he would be celebrating the summer this night.

Bampton Castle was empty as well. I watched as Lord Gilbert traded some witticism with Father Thomas and saw the old vicar chuckle. Even Sir Henry's household had joined the throng about the blaze. Most of these were conspicuous for their solemnity. But Walter seemed to enjoy himself, smiling and boisterous and dancing about the blaze, and Sir Geoffrey smiled over the shoulder of Lady Margery as the flames rose higher. Kate saw this as well, and looked to me with questions in her eyes.

Bessie soon grew bored with the fire. When it was first lit her eyes glowed with delight, but after a short time she laid her head upon my shoulder and fell to sleep. So sooner than most Kate and I left the blaze and returned to Galen

House and our bed. Three years past I would have frolicked through the night. Now I was content to seek my home with wife on my arm and babe upon my shoulder. I do not grieve for my lost youth.

A man with a clear conscience is said to sleep well, while the guilty will toss upon his pillow all the night. I hope whoever murdered Sir Henry slept less that night than I did, for Kate slumbered peacefully while I lay awake, and I saw dawn arrive through our chamber window before even Kate's rooster announced the new day. A note slipped under a door, a bodkin, and a bloodstained piece of linen occupied my mind to the exclusion of sleep.

Lord Gilbert's pantler is an aged valet, grown grey in service first to Lord Gilbert's father, Lord Richard, then to Lord Gilbert. I approached Humphrey next morning as he unlocked the pantry to prepare for dinner. The wizened fellow bid me "Good-day", and asked how he might serve me. I showed him the bloody linen and asked if any napery or table cloths in his care had recently gone missing or been found missing a fragment of the same shape and size.

"Nay," he replied. "Was any of Lord Gilbert's wares mutilated like that, I'd be sure to know. See to the linen every day. An' did I miss something like that, the maids in the laundry'd find it an' tell me straight away."

"How oft is the linen laundered?"

"Table cloths twice each week. Napkins every day. Portpains whenever needful."

"So if this bit of linen came from your pantry it would not have been carved from a napkin, else the damage would have been found the same day. When were the table cloths last laundered?"

"Half was done yesterday."

"And none were found marred?"

"Nay."

"How many portpains are kept in the pantry?"

"Fourteen."

"Is more than one needed for a meal?"

"Not generally. But when Lord Gilbert welcomes guests we'll use more. Since Sir Henry come we need three portpains for dinner an' three more for supper."

"And then these are washed?"

"Aye. Six laundered every day since Whitsuntide."

"Has any of Lord Gilbert's table linen gone missing?"

"The pantry's kept locked, an' only me an' John Chamberlain's got keys."

"But do you count the table linen often, just to be certain 'tis all accounted for?"

"Don't see the point. The closet's locked. 'Course, I do a tally every year, when steward comes for hallmote."

"So the linen has not been counted since January?"

"No need."

"I'd be obliged if you would count your stock now, whilst I wait."

Humphrey sighed his displeasure at the unwanted and, to him, unnecessary task, but swung open the heavy door and with a candle to light his way entered the pantry.

I had no desire to crowd behind the valet into the cramped, dark chamber, so waited at the door in the screens passage. I heard Humphrey rummage about in the pantry, then silence. The fellow muttered something to himself, and I heard the audit resume.

A few moments later the pantler joined me in the screens passage, blinking in the light. "Must be one more'n I thought got sent to laundry," he said.

"One more of what?"

"Portpains."

"You sent six to the laundry yesterday?"

"Thought so. Must've been seven."

"Because you found only seven where there should be eight?"

"Aye," Humphrey agreed.

"I will accompany you to the laundry. We will see how many are there," I said.

The pantler locked the pantry door, then hobbled after me past the kitchen to where the laundresses labored. Kettles of water, soap, and soiled clothing boiled upon a great hearth. The heat and steam were onerous on a warm summer morn, but the work would be pleasant enough when winter cast a chill over all other corners of Bampton Castle.

I stood at the laundry entry, where a cooling breeze kept the heat at bay, and watched as Humphrey approached a woman who seemed to be in charge of the place. I have served Lord Gilbert at Bampton for three years, yet I did not recognize the laundress. Perhaps her crimson cheeks and sweat-beaded brow rendered her unrecognizable to me.

The pantler spoke, and through the steam I saw the woman shake her head. Humphrey spoke again, and waved his arms about to punctuate his words. Again the laundress shook her head, more vigorously this time. I saw Humphrey then point to a shelf, visible through the steamy space as through a winter fog, and the two walked to it. Folded upon this shelf were stacks of white fabric; Lord Gilbert's table linen, I decided.

I watched as the laundress approached one of the pale piles and began to count through the stack. Even from my place across the room I could see that when she reached the number six all of the folded linen on that part of the shelf was accounted for.

The pantler's head swung to the other stacks of folded linen on the shelf and he gestured toward them. The laundress seemed to sigh, then turned to the remaining table linen and carefully sorted through the mounds. She completed the work, turned to Humphrey, and with palms upraised before her indicated to him a lack of success. The pantler spoke again, then turned and walked as quickly as he could from the shelf to my place at the door.

"Lost one," he declared when he faced me. "Incompetent woman! Lord Gilbert will hear of this. Portpains is made of finest linen. Cost near a shilling."

"And one of your portpains is missing?"

"Missing? Aye... some wench in the laundry has stolen it. Be sold to some burgher in Oxford soon, if not already."

"It could not have disappeared from the pantry?"

"Nay. 'Ow could it? Me an' John Chamberlain's got the only keys."

"Is the pantry ever left unlocked while you attend other duties? Before dinner, for example, or after?"

"Well, aye, but not for long. My work don't take me far from the screens passage when settin' things out for Lord Gilbert's dinner. You gonna see to this theft, you bein' bailiff?"

"Aye, I will. But I ask you not to speak of the loss."

"Best not to let the miscreant know we're on 'is trail, eh?"

"Aye. As you say."

The blood-soaked linen fragment was stolen from the pantry, of this I was now convinced. But was it taken while the pantler was about his work, or did some man gain access to his keys? Or to John Chamberlain's keys? The thought raised another question.

"You are no longer a young man. Lord Gilbert assigned a page to assist you last year, and learn your tasks, did he not?"

"Aye. Young Andrew."

"Is his work acceptable?"

"Aye... most times."

"Why is he not here to aid you in preparing for dinner?"

"Helps Cuthbert, also. Should be here anon."

Cuthbert is Lord Gilbert's butler, and no sooner had Humphrey said this than I heard the light footsteps of a youth approach the screens passage from the kitchen. Andrew is a beardless youth of fifteen years or so, orphan since plague returned to strike down his father seven years past.

The youth broke his stride when he saw me at the pantry door with his superior. I did not know much of the lad. I had even forgotten his name until Humphrey reminded me. But Andrew knew me, and when his lord's bailiff shows interest in a lad's life and work most youths are convinced no good will come of the matter.

"Andrew, come here, lad," Humphrey demanded unnecessarily, for it was clear the youth was bound for the pantry. In response to this command Andrew's countenance went from light to heavy more quickly than I can tell of it.

"Master Hugh seeks a thief, and we must help him find the felon."

I had told the pantler that the missing portpain must not be named, so interrupted him.

"Have you seen any man loitering about the pantry door before or after dinner, whilst the door was ajar, in the past few days?"

The lad seemed to tremble before my gaze. Why? Did my question or my office frighten him? Or did he quaver for the result of his answer?

"N–n–nay," he finally blurted.

"Have you seen any man enter the pantry but for Humphrey?"

"N–nay. No man."

Something in his tone caught my attention. "No man? Who, then? A woman?"

Andrew looked to Humphrey as if seeking guidance, but the pantler returned only a stern frown. The youth finally spoke. "The lady what's a guest of Lord Gilbert."

"Which lady... the lass, or Lady Margery?"

"The lass."

"Why did you not speak of this?" the pantler said through tight lips. Then to me he said, "Why would a knight's daughter steal a portpain?"

I saw a gleam of understanding flash in his rheumy eyes even as he asked the question. "You think the maid helped slay her father? Cut that bloody piece from what she took?"

"Mayhap." To the youth I said, "When did you see this?"

"Three, no, f–four days past," he stammered.

"Did you see her enter the pantry and leave it?"

"Nay. Didn't see 'er go in... only come out."

"What did she carry?" the pantler asked.

The page hesitated, considering, I think, whether he would find himself in more trouble by telling the truth or by deception.

"She was puttin' somethin' up the sleeve of 'er cotehardie," he finally said.

Stylish sleeves for a lady's cotehardie are voluminous, but it seemed to me unlikely that the Lady Anne would try to stuff a portpain into one. "What was it she hid there? Could you see?"

"Had some of m'lord's silver, spoons an' knives."

Gentlemen and ladies who dine at Lord Gilbert's table bring their own knives and spoons, as is the custom, but I knew that my employer kept a supply of silver utensils in the pantry for occasional use. I have found need of them upon the occasions I dine at the castle, but they are seldom brought forth, as they are rarely needed.

"Where," I asked the pantler, "is Lord Gilbert's tableware stored?"

Humphrey nodded toward the pantry door. "In a wooden box."

"Is the box locked?"

"Nay. Pantry's locked, so no need for a lock on the box... so I thought."

"How many knives and silver spoons are kept there? When did you last count them?"

The pantler now seemed as ill at ease as his assistant. "Don't count 'em regular, like."

"When did you last do so? How many knives and spoons are stored in the pantry?"

"Twelve of each," Humphrey said.

"Go count them now."

The pantler turned and entered his pantry. He disappeared behind the open door with his candle and I heard what I assumed to be the lid of a box fall upon a shelf. It takes little time to count a dozen knives and spoons, even less if some are missing. Humphrey appeared from behind the door, raised his palms, and said, "Eight knives an' ten spoons. That's all as is there."

"And when you last counted all were present?"

"Aye."

"When was that?"

"Afore Whitsuntide. Just before Rogation Sunday. Lord Gilbert was to have guests at 'is table that day an' wished to be sure all would have proper knives an' spoons, as some might not have their own, not bein' gentlefolk."

The pantler turned to his youthful assistant and, with as much anger as his aged voice could muster, demanded why he had not been told of the theft when it occurred.

"Who'd 'ave believed me if the lady said otherwise? An' when she saw that I'd seen what she'd done she gave me such a glare as I knew I'd be in trouble did I accuse her."

"But the spoons and knives are gone," the pantler said. "That would be evidence of your truthfulness."

"She'd 'a said I took 'em... that she saw me in the screens passage with 'em an' thought I was about me work."

"The lad speaks true," I said. "Lord Gilbert is a just man, but he'd sooner believe the daughter of a knight than his page."

"What you gonna do?" Humphrey asked of me. "You bein' Lord Gilbert's bailiff, it'd be your business to see to the return of 'is silver. And the portpain."

I had wished that knowledge of the missing portpain should remain between the pantler and myself, but now the page also knew of it. I turned to Andrew and faced him with my sternest expression.

"You will not speak of this with any other soul," I said. "Not the stolen silver nor the missing linen. You understand?"

The youth swallowed, his adam's apple bobbing like one of Kate's hens pecking at the ground, and nodded understanding.

"You will need to be about preparing for Lord Gilbert's dinner, so I will leave you to your work. Remember, not a word to any man of what has gone missing."

The two, aged and young, nodded, silent, evidently in awe of my fearsome visage. Here was much change in my life. Five years past I could not have summoned a scowl which would have frightened a nursling. Now, after serving some years as Lord Gilbert's bailiff, I was learning the potency of an occasional peevish frown.

I would be untruthful if I wrote that the experience was unpleasant, but I must guard against the subtle but inexorable onset of pride, for holy writ proclaims that the vain must soon fall. There are Oxford scholars I remember from my youth at Baliol College who are overdue for a tumble.

Chapter 6

I left the screens passage and sought my employer in the solar. I found him there, with Lady Petronilla, entertaining Lady Margery and Lady Anne. Lord Gilbert was out of his element, for when John Chamberlain announced me at the door to the solar I found the three women plying needle and thread at some embroidery whilst m'lord sat stiffly beside the cold hearth. When I asked if I might speak privily to him he leapt to his feet as if freed from captivity.

He may also have thought that my desire for confidential conversation indicated progress in discovering a murderer. I had to disappoint him. And rather than solving one problem for Lord Gilbert I laid another before him.

"The Lady Anne?" he said in disbelief when I told him of what Andrew the page had seen. "Why would the lass take my silver?"

"You said Sir Henry was destitute. Perhaps Lady Anne was tired of wearing the same worn gowns and desired new."

"Aye," Lord Gilbert agreed thoughtfully. "Well, she'll not have one by way of my silver. You must see that the spoons and knives are returned."

I had feared he would give the task to me, for 'twas sure to be unpleasant. But that is why gentlemen employ such as me: to do those disagreeable things they would prefer not to do themselves.

"But do not," he continued, "retrieve them in so impolitic a manner that Lady Margery will be embarrassed."

I nodded understanding and my employer concluded by saying, "You can be a tactful man, Hugh, when you put your mind to it. I have every confidence that you will see the silver returned with little fuss."

"Prying stolen spoons and knives from a thief of gentle birth without annoyance will be like taking bacon from a pig with no squealing."

"Hah," Lord Gilbert laughed and swatted me across the back. "I shall be pleased to learn how you do it."

And with that he returned to the solar, his wife and guests, one of them a thief, there to await dinner.

Confronting a beautiful lass with her felony would not be a pleasant task, especially so as she was of rank and I am not. So, as Lord Gilbert had presented the task to me, I decided to bestow it upon another. I sought Walter, Sir Henry's valet, and found him crossing to the hall from the servants' quarters, intent upon his dinner. He would not enjoy it much when he learned what he must do.

I greeted the fellow, but he was not interested in conversation. His eyes went from me to other castle servants who, like him, were hurrying toward the hall and a meal.

"I will not detain you long," I said, and went straight to the heart of the matter. "I have learned that Lady Anne took four of Lord Gilbert's silver knives and two spoons from the pantry four days past."

"What? Lady Anne? Surely you are mistaken. She..."

"She was seen. I have just this day learned of the theft. Lord Gilbert knows of it and demands that his silver be returned promptly."

"Who saw her do such a thing? The man lies."

"He does not. The silver has been counted and the missing pieces numbered. You are to speak to Lady Anne this day, at dinner, and tell her that her theft is discovered and the spoons and knives are to be returned immediately.

Tell her that an hour after dinner the screens passage will be vacant. No man will be there. She is to leave the stolen goods upon the floor beside the pantry door, where Lord Gilbert's pantler may find them and return them to their place."

"But what if she denies the theft?" Walter said. "I cannot believe it of her."

"Tell her that much unpleasantness will follow before this day is done if she does not do as I require. Remind her that the sheriff of Oxford is resident in the castle."

The valet made no reply for a moment, I think trying to invent some reason whereby my accusation might be impeached, or, failing that, to find some way to avoid the task I had laid upon him.

"Aye," he said finally, and I nodded toward the hall, releasing him to his dinner and his duty. He would appreciate neither this day.

I followed the valet, sought Humphrey, and told him that one hour after dinner ended neither he nor Andrew must be near the screens passage, nor the hall nor the kitchen, either. I did not tell him why I asked this of him, for fear Lady Anne would resist and the precaution would be for naught.

I took my meal in the hall again that day. It was a fast day, so Lord Gilbert's table featured baked herring, viand de leach, brydons, blancmange, sturgeon, salmon in syrup, and a void of sugared apples, wafers, and hypocras.

I once again sat at the head of a side table, from which place I could observe Lady Anne at the high table and Walter, far down the opposite side table. Walter appeared to have little appetite, and it is true that he did not enjoy the delicacies which we of higher estate consumed, but I believe his abstinence due more to the task I had assigned him than to the quality of the stockfish and maslin loaf before him.

The Lady Anne ate well and conversed freely with Lady Petronilla, beside whom she sat this day. I noted that several times Lady Anne's eyes met those of squire William, although when this occurred they both looked quickly back to their meal. And was it my imagination, or did a winsome pink blush spread across Lady Anne's cheeks after one of these exchanges?

It seemed sure that Walter had not yet presented my demand to Lady Anne. He had no opportunity to do so before dinner, and when the grooms and lesser folk had finished their meal he left the hall with the others.

But as we who remained finished the void I saw him peer from the screens passage and knew he waited to deliver to Lady Anne the requirement that Lord Gilbert's silver be returned. There was nothing now for me to do. I departed the hall and left Walter to the onerous task I had assigned him.

One hour passed slowly. When the time was nearly gone, and I was about to seek the screens passage, I saw Walter walking toward the marshalsea and hastened after him. He feared I would challenge him about Lady Anne, I think, and so when I came within earshot he said, "I repeated your words to Lady Anne. Does the silver not appear as you wish, 'twill be no fault of mine."

The valet was defensive, but in his place I might have been as well.

"There is another matter I wish to speak to you of," I said.

Walter's face, already somber, fell even more as he imagined other disagreeable labors I might assign him.

"Sir Henry," I began, "lay awake nights. I was asked to provide a potion which would help him sleep. When I asked you what caused his wakefulness you did not reply. It is now time for you to do so. You cannot be charged with betraying your lord. He is in his grave."

The valet did not answer at once, but looked about, and beyond my shoulder, as if to see if some man might appear who could extricate him from an uncomfortable place. No man did, so he finally spoke.

"S'pose can do no harm to Sir Henry now. He was penniless. Had debts 'e couldn't pay, an' gentlefolk an' bankers he'd borrowed from who wanted their coin."

"Could he not sell lands from his manor?"

"Tried. But others knew of 'is embarrassment an' thought to gain from him cheap. Wouldn't sell to such folk. Said 'e'd not give his house or lands away to any man."

Sir Henry was not the only gentleman to suffer financial reverses these past years. Since plague took so many lives, grain has declined in price, and with it the value of the land upon which to grow it. A knight who needs money will raise little from his lands.

"His debts were greater than his worth?"

"Probably. Didn't speak of such things when the common folk was about. Heard 'im arguin' about it with Lady Margery once. Shoutin' at each other, they was... not like I was tryin' to hear."

"What was Lady Margery's complaint?"

Walter's mouth twisted into a crooked grin. "What does most ladies want of their husbands? Silks an' furs for new gowns, an' shoes an' such, an' more servants to care for it all."

"Sir Henry could not afford these?"

"Nay. Said he'd told her before there was not a shilling to spare for new clothes, an' why would she not accept that."

"What was her reply?"

"Said if she'd known he was so poor she'd not 'ave wed. Wealthier men had sought her hand, an' still would was she free of him."

"Lady Margery spoke of being free of Sir Henry?"

Walter's eyes were downcast, and he moved a pebble with his toe, then said, "Aye… she did."

Holy Church permits no divorce. The only way an unhappy wife may be free of her husband is through his death, or annulment of the marriage. But annulment requires the good graces of a bishop, generally gained by a liberal contribution to the bishop's purse. Walter knew this well. I had another question.

"Did Lady Margery have any new husband in mind, you think, if she was free of Sir Henry? Was that another reason for Sir Henry's wakefulness?"

The valet was again silent for the space of a dozen heartbeats before he said, "Not for me to say."

"But you have, all but the man's name. Was it not so you would not have hesitated. Who is it who has caught the lady's eye?"

"Don't know," he protested. "Just talk."

"You've heard gossip, but are unsure 'tis true?"

"Aye."

"What does gossip say? What name is tied to Lady Margery?"

"More'n one."

"She'll bring little estate to any new husband. But more than one man is rumored to have an interest in Lady Margery if she were free of Sir Henry?"

"So I've heard. An' even a small estate is of value to 'im as has none."

"What names, then?"

"Haven't heard that."

"No names? From whence do these rumors come?"

"I speak to Lady Margery's servants. Hear talk from them… but never names."

"What do these women say? Was Sir Henry a cuckold?"

"May be. Isobel Guesclin, what's Lady Margery's companion, said as much."

Worries about money and a faithless wife might cause any man to stare at the ceiling of a night. I remembered then the reddened cheeks of the Lady Anne, and asked Walter what he knew of the lass.

"Children may sometimes cause a man to lose sleep. Lady Anne is a thief. Has she done other mischief which might have brought distress to her father?"

Walter's face twisted into a sardonic grin. "What lass don't cause 'er father worry? 'Specially be she as pert as Lady Anne."

"How did she bring worry to Sir Henry?"

"Wanted to wed, I heard."

"Who?"

"William, the squire."

This explained the stolen glances and pink cheeks I'd seen at table. "Sir Henry objected?"

"Aye. Wished her to wed another."

"Who?"

"Dunno. A wealthy knight of Sussex, is all I know. Needed money, did Sir Henry, an' thought to use 'is daughter to get 'is hands on some. So I heard."

Where Sir Henry would gather funds to provide a suitable dowry for his daughter was another question, but one Walter could not be expected to answer.

The valet, who had been at first reluctant to speak of his employer's family, had become loquacious, as if he found it a release to unburden himself.

"If any other reason for Sir Henry's sleepless nights occurs to you, I would hear of it," I said.

Walter touched a forelock and I bid him "Good day," confident that an hour had now passed since dinner had ended, and that I knew better how matters stood in the family and household of Sir Henry Burley, deceased.

The hall had long since been cleared of tables, and stood empty and silent. My footsteps echoed from the walls as I crossed the great room to the screens passage and looked toward the pantry door. The space is dark, even on a bright day, for the only light which penetrates there comes from windows in the hall. But when I looked toward the pantry I saw a white parcel upon the flags. A piece of linen cloth was wrapped about two spoons and four knives. Lord Gilbert's property was returned.

I set out to seek Humphrey, and found him a moment later, where he sat before the oven gossiping with John Baker, a groom nearly as ancient as the pantler.

I held the returned silver out to Humphrey and told him to replace the items in the locked pantry forthwith. "And perhaps count Lord Gilbert's spoons and knives more regularly in the future," I said.

Humphrey rose, took the silver from me, and hobbled off toward the pantry. I bid John "Good day," and set off for the solar where I might find Lord Gilbert to tell him that his property was recovered. 'Twas then I glanced to the white linen cloth which had been wrapped about the silver. It seemed to me much like the bloodstained fabric which I had plucked from under the fireplace mantel of the squires' chamber.

My route to the solar took me back through the screens passage and the hall. I stopped in the empty hall, withdrew the bloody linen from my pouch, and spread it upon the ewerer's table. I then took the cloth which had been wrapped about the silver and unfolded it next to the stained fabric. When I placed the two side by side I saw readily that they were parts of the same piece. They had not been sliced square, across the warp and in line with the woof, but on a slight angle, as if whoso wielded the blade which had divided the portpain had slashed through the fabric hurriedly. The angle of the cut on the two cloths matched perfectly.

Here was a perplexing discovery. Would a lass murder her father? What else was I to think? Lady Anne had taken Lord Gilbert's silver and was a thief. Would such a person find it troubling to add murder to a felony already committed? And if the lass would steal silver she would not balk at making off with a portpain. Perhaps she took linen and silver at the same time and Andrew overlooked the cloth when his eyes fell upon the knives and spoons.

'Twas sure that Lady Anne was the thief who made off with the silver. Walter spoke only to her to relay my demand that the silver be returned. Or did he mention the command to another?

No, that was unlikely. If some other thief had Lord Gilbert's silver in his possession and thought I suspected only Lady Anne, he would not return the stolen goods, but rather would allow me to continue in my error and accuse the lass.

But would the maid be so foolish as to return the silver wrapped in the same portpain she had used to wipe away her father's blood, a bloody fragment of which I was intended to find, so as to place blame for the felony upon a squire? Which squire? Not William Willoughby. 'Twas him she wished to wed. So said Walter. Robert de Cobham, then, was to fall victim to the plot, but how was I to know that when the only evidence I had against any man was the bloody linen and the bodkin embedded in the lampstand? I might pursue William as readily as Robert. Would Lady Anne, and her accomplice, had she one, risk that? Especially if aid came from William?

My confusion was complete. Either Lady Anne was uncommonly stupid or she thought I was. How else explain her use of Lord Gilbert's portpain in the commission of two felonies? Another answer suggested itself: she did not know of the bloody fragment, and so thought nothing of returning the purloined silver in cloth which could entangle her in her father's murder.

The door to the solar was open, and when I entered the chamber I found Lord Gilbert and Lady Petronilla laughing over some witticism of Sir Roger's. My appearance reminded them of more somber events and they fell silent. "Your silver is returned," I said to Lord Gilbert.

"Ah… well done, Hugh. Well done. With no fuss and feathers?"

"Nay, perhaps not."

"Perhaps?" Lord Gilbert raised one questioning eyebrow, as he does when puzzled.

"Aye. Perhaps there will be no fuss come of the theft, but the business may bear on another, more disquieting event."

"What is this about theft and silver?" Sir Roger asked.

I explained the matter to him, and repeated that the theft seemed a part of a greater felony.

"Sir Henry's death?" Sir Roger asked. A reasonable assumption, since the death was the most disquieting thing to happen under Lord Gilbert's roof in many years.

Lord Gilbert's eyebrow rose higher, an astonishing feat. "How so?" he asked. "What could silver spoons have to do with Sir Henry's murder?"

There is a table in the solar where Lord Gilbert occasionally works at accounts, being unlike most nobles, who prefer to allow their stewards and bailiffs to keep the manorial ledgers. Of course, most of Lord Gilbert's class cannot cipher well and so must leave the tallying of sums to folk like me and Lord Gilbert's steward, Geoffrey Thirwall. This is perhaps why stewards and bailiffs have a reputation for embezzling their employers' funds. It is easy to do, and unless the manor should become insolvent, their theft is unlikely to be detected.

I took the two pieces of linen, one pure white, the other stained with blood, and laid them side by side upon the table. Lord Gilbert and Sir Roger stood as I did so and approached to peer over my shoulder.

"What is here?" Lord Gilbert asked. "We've seen the bloody cloth, but what of the other?"

"See how they match?" I said. "This fragment, unless I am much mistaken, was used to mop away what blood came from Sir Henry's ear when 'twas pierced. And the unspotted remainder was used to wrap Lord Gilbert's stolen silver when it was returned not an hour past."

"Ah, then whoso took the silver also did murder," Sir Roger said triumphantly. "Catch a thief and we'll have the man who has slain Sir Henry, eh?"

"Perhaps, but I think not."

"Oh?" Sir Roger seemed dismayed at my response. No doubt he wished the matter resolved so he might return to Oxford.

"Would Lady Anne murder her father?" Lord Gilbert muttered.

"Lady Anne?" the sheriff said. "What has she to do with this business?"

"'Twas she," Lord Gilbert said, "who made off with my silver."

Lady Petronilla had also risen from her chair and crossed the chamber to see the two pieces of linen. She spoke next.

"Lady Anne seems most eager to leave Bampton and return home. The matter has arisen often when we are together, and she continually urges Lady Margery to be away."

"No wonder," Sir Roger growled, "if she did murder and took silver spoons as well. I'll take a sergeant an' arrest her this minute. Where will she be? Where is her chamber?"

"Not yet," I said. "We might learn more of this if we allow Lady Anne to roam free. She may do or say something which, without this knowledge, we might overlook. With these scraps of linen we may have answers to questions not yet asked. If, in a few days, we discover nothing more, you may then arrest the lass. If she is guilty only of theft, then the murderer may reveal himself, perhaps to save her, especially if it is William Willoughby."

"William? The squire?" Lord Gilbert said. "You do then suspect him of murder?"

"Sir Henry's valet said that William and Lady Anne wished to marry, but Sir Henry would not permit it, being eager to see his daughter wed to some wealthy knight."

"To help fill his empty purse, no doubt," Lord Gilbert said. "Though where he'd find coin for a dowry I cannot think."

"Are we then but to wait and watch for some man to do or say that which will incriminate him?" Sir Roger asked. The sheriff is a man of action. Patience is not his strong virtue.

"Lady Margery knows I have discovered the bodkin," I said. "She saw it in my hand yesterday. Whether or not she knows it might have been used to slay her husband we do not know. But I believe she does. When she saw it in my hand she took fright.

"No one yet knows we have found this bloody linen, unless the man who hid it has searched to see if it is gone from the fireplace. It might be good to spread the word now that these objects have been found and watch to see who seems uneasy at the rumor."

"Will we say where they were found?" Sir Roger asked.

"Nay. Should we do so, folk will wonder why one or both of the squires are not arrested."

"Wonder about that myself. The squires and Lady Anne seem mixed together in Sir Henry's death. Put the lot of 'em in Oxford Castle dungeon and soon one will tell who is guilty, so to free themselves."

"They will implicate each other, and we will be no nearer to discovering a murderer than we are now," I replied, "or William will play the man and take blame to save Lady Anne, whether he is guilty or not. We must be patient and alert."

"Not too patient," Lord Gilbert said. "Lady Margery wishes to return to Bedford and I wish the matter resolved to be rid of her."

Murder and stolen goods vexed my mind as I left the castle. I stopped at the bridge over Shill Brook to gaze into the stream, but this wool-gathering did nothing to clear my thoughts or suggest a solution to my problems.

Kate greeted me with an embrace and a supper of arbolettys and a maslin loaf. Bessie watched her mother clasp me close and lifted her arms to me to do the same. The babe was beginning to cut teeth, and so slobbered upon my shoulder as I held her close. This did not trouble me. There are fathers who would give much to have a babe drool upon their cotehardie rather than occupy a small corner of St Beornwald's churchyard.

I told Kate of the day's events while we ate our supper, and concluded by saying that, unlikely as it seemed, Lady Anne may have had something to do with her father's death.

"Perhaps she stuffed the portpain up a sleeve, before taking the spoons and knives," I said. "When the page saw her with the silver his attention was drawn to the utensils and he did not notice the bulging sleeve."

"You think she then gave the cloth to the squire... what is his name?"

"William. It may be. The sheriff believes it so, but 'tis all too simple, and who else would have known of their conspiracy?"

"Why would some other need to know of their connivance?"

"The message, slid under the sheriff's door."

"Oh, aye. Neither Lady Anne nor the squire would have done it were they guilty... or if they did, they would have named the other squire."

"And I do not know of a certainty that the bloodstains on the linen cloth came to be there at Sir Henry's death, or if the bodkin in the base of the lampstand was a murder weapon. 'Tis all conjecture, because we were directed to search the squires' chamber."

"How then will you find the truth of the matter?"

"It would be well if the Lord Christ would come to me in a dream and tell me how the felony was done and who did it, but that is unlikely."

"How, then?"

"There is not yet enough information for anything but supposition. I must learn more of Sir Henry and his life, as well as his death. Then my speculation will be less flimsy, and I may discard unworthy theories until but one remains."

"And then you will know who murdered Sir Henry?"

"Aye. When the impossible and the unlikely are all discarded, the felon will appear."

"Well," Kate said while munching thoughtfully upon the remains of her maslin loaf, "I think you can discard already thoughts of Lady Anne in collusion with her squire."

"Why so? Not that I believe you to be mistaken. I have my own doubts, but I would hear yours."

"The lass would not be so foolish as to return stolen silver in a cloth which could be identified with another used at the slaying of her father."

"I agree. But perhaps she is weak-minded."

"Have you seen sign of this?"

"Nay."

"She does not behave oddly at table, or scratch herself when and where she itches, or speak foolishness out of turn?"

"Nay," I replied.

"Then you must assume Lady Anne wise enough that she would not offer evidence of her guilt so carelessly."

"I agree, but I have no other direction for suspicion."

"Women can be as wrathful as men," Kate said.

"I suppose, although their temper does not usually result in the use of daggers and swords, or bodkins, either, I think. I am confused. Do you now say that Lady Anne might have slain her father in a fit of anger?"

"Nay. A resentful woman will seek to destroy her enemy with her wiles rather than blades. Being the weaker sex, she must use her wits for lack of brawn."

"So if Lady Anne is not stupid, you say she may be shrewd... enough so to devise ways to throw me and Sir Roger off her trail? But what I have learned points to her. How can that be shrewd?"

"There is another woman involved," Kate said. "Do Lady Margery and Lady Anne seem friendly?"

"Ah, I see your point. They cast no daggers with their eyes when at Lord Gilbert's table, but Lady Anne is Sir Henry's heir by his first wife, Lady Goscelyna. If Lady Anne went to the scaffold for her father's murder Lady Margery would not have to share the estate, such as it is."

"Such as it is? What do you mean?"

"Sir Henry went to his grave in debt. His valet is unsure if his possessions are of greater worth than his debts."

"So he was not likely slain for an inheritance."

"Nay. Lady Margery and Lady Anne would know there would be little profit to balance against the risk of discovery. A wife who slays her husband is considered guilty of treason against him, and likewise a daughter, I believe."

Kate shuddered. "They would be hanged, drawn and quartered?"

"That is a punishment reserved for men... but hanged, surely."

"But the valet said that Lady Margery was displeased with Sir Henry?"

"He did."

"And now she is free to wed some other. Perhaps you will not solve this murder until she takes another husband."

"And that fellow will be the felon?"

"Or the reason for Lady Margery's felony."

Chapter 7

Kate and I awoke next morn to the ringing of the Angelus Bell. Before I wed I was accustomed to seeking the church early on Sunday for Matins, but now that Kate and I have a babe we do not enter St Beornwald's Church until time for mass. May the Lord Christ forgive my sloth.

After mass, and a dinner of porre of peas, I left Kate and Bessie and sought the castle. I wished to speak more with Walter Mayn, and found him just leaving the hall after his dinner.

I greeted him pleasantly, but the valet seemed reluctant to speak to me. Perhaps he feared that I had another unpleasant duty to assign to him. He was not far wrong.

"Have you spoken since yesterday to Lady Margery's maids?" I asked.

"Nay."

"Make a point of doing so today."

"To what purpose?"

"Tell them that you believe the sheriff is about to seize Sir Henry's murderer."

"If they ask why I think so, what am I to say? Is it indeed so?"

"There are those more likely guilty than others, but if any ask of you how you know this, tell them only that Master Hugh has told you he has found grounds to accuse the felon. If you tell what I ask to Lady Margery's maids, gossip will soon send the rumor to every corner of the castle."

"That is all you wish of me?"

"Aye. For now. Set folk's tongues to wagging and we will see where it leads."

I suspected that Walter's gossip would envelop the castle before nightfall, and so it did, but other complications also encompassed Bampton Castle that day.

King Edward requires that all men practice with the longbow of a Sunday afternoon, and as bailiff to Lord Gilbert it is my duty to see that the charge is carried out. I had assigned Arthur to setting up the butts in the meadow before the castle, and after I told Walter what I required of him I wandered back through the gatehouse to watch the practice and oversee the competition.

Lord Gilbert provides four silver pennies each week as prizes for those who show the greatest skill with the bow, and when he is in residence at Bampton Castle delights in personally awarding the coins to those who prevail over their fellows.

Three of the coins went to Bampton men, tenants of Lord Gilbert, but one coin went to Sir Geoffrey Godswein, Sir Henry's knight. This was an oddity, as only the commons train to the longbow. Knights begin martial training with a sword when first they become pages, and then squires. How, I wondered, did a knight find such skill?

I was not alone in my curiosity, for as Sir Geoffrey let fly his arrows I saw others in the crowd of spectators whisper behind their hands. 'Twas nearly an admission of being baseborn that a knight would do this. I saw Lady Margery react with distaste when Sir Geoffrey seized a bow and took a place at the mark, and she scowled when he accepted Lord Gilbert's penny and bowed to his host.

Walter had stood with others in Sir Henry's service to watch the competition, and when the contest was done I sought him.

"None of Sir Henry's yeomen or grooms or valets went to the mark today," I said to him as we passed the gatehouse.

"Sir Henry was not one to set his men to archery as is Lord Gilbert."

"Too poor to afford even a few pennies as prizes?" I ventured.

"Aye," the valet smiled, "too poor to hand out even farthings."

"What of Sir Geoffrey? How did a knight come by such skill?"

"Wasn't always a knight, nor high-born, either."

"How was it that he was elevated?"

"Was a yeoman in Sir Henry's band at Poitiers. Just a lad, but keen to go to war. Went over with 'is father, who took sick an' died before the battle."

"Did he do some service for Sir Henry?"

Walter shrugged. "Guess so. He don't speak much of it, nor did Sir Henry."

"Do others of Sir Henry's retainers know of Sir Geoffrey's past? Does Lady Margery know?"

"S'pose so. Sir Geoffrey's rank is known to most as has been in Sir Henry's service, an' Lady Margery ain't always been a lady."

"Oh? Her father is not a gentleman?"

"Nay. Wealthy, though. A cordwainer of Coventry."

"If Sir Geoffrey did not speak of his origins," I said, "why take a bow and enter Lord Gilbert's competition and so make plain his family?"

"Pride, I'd say. Sir Geoffrey don't like to be bested at anything. Sees a man doing a thing that he can do better, he'd not resist showin' off."

"Even if to do so would lift eyebrows?"

"Even so," Walter shrugged again. "Mayhap that's why 'e

did somethin' what made 'im worthy of bein' knighted. Don't always think things through before he acts."

The valet may speak true, I thought. How many men would do heroic things if they first considered the risk of the deed which brought them glory? Perhaps this is why young men make the best warriors. They have less experience of the consequences of bold acts. Did the man who murdered Sir Henry think carefully of the possible result of such a rash act?

I bid Walter "Good day," and set off for the solar, where I hoped to find Lord Gilbert and Sir Roger.

I did so. The two men and Lady Petronilla, having just arrived from awarding the archery prizes, were quenching their thirst with cups of wine. Both men had fought at Poitiers, I knew, when the French king had been seized and held for ransom. I thought one or both might have a tale to tell of Sir Henry or Sir Geoffrey. I asked, and the sheriff and my employer peered at each other thoughtfully for some time. Some silent exchange passed between them, then Sir Roger finally spoke.

"We were much inferior in numbers to the French, so Prince Edward placed us upon a hill. The slope was a vineyard, and the archers he placed hidden amongst the vines. We men at arms were at the crest of the hill, dismounted, ready to repulse the French from whatever direction they might come."

"'Twas a perilous time," Lord Gilbert added. "Had the French king any wit he would have come at us from the flanks. His numbers were such he could have divided his army and enveloped us."

"But he rather chose to send his knights through the vines," Sir Roger said, "up a narrow path which wound through the vineyard. I could scarce believe a king would be so foolish."

"Our archers, hidden in the vines, waited 'til the French knights were nearly upon them," Lord Gilbert continued. "At such close range their arrows could not miss, and flew with such force that a knight's armor was of no more use to him than parchment.

"Some English knights became resentful that the battle might be won by archers before knights could seek glory or captives for ransom. An arrow does not take prisoners, but slays the man it strikes."

I began to envision what might have happened. "Sir Henry was one of these?" I asked.

"Aye," Sir Roger said, with a rueful grin, "as were Lord Gilbert and I."

"Sir Henry had but a small retinue, but when he leaped over the dry moat we had dug at the crest of the hill his squires followed, all eager for glory before it escaped them."

"Sir Henry was the first knight to attack?"

"Aye. When he set out for the grapevines we all followed, our blood being up and all unwilling to lose a chance for honor and to seize hostages."

Lord Gilbert hesitated, then continued. "Not all of the French knights were dead or even badly wounded. No sooner had I got amongst the vines than I came upon a knight who had hid himself in the grapevines so as to avoid the arrows which had destroyed so many of his fellows. We fell upon each other with swords, but neither could deliver a telling blow for the vines which entangled us.

"While I was thus engaged another French knight, all in black armor and with a white plume upon his helm, came up behind me and delivered a blow which dropped me to my knees."

"I was too far away to see," Sir Roger said, "lost amongst the vines and dealing with my own foe, else I would have come to Lord Gilbert's aid. But Sir Henry was fighting nearby, and saw him fall. Sir Henry left the knight he was battling and with a yeoman came to Lord Gilbert's relief."

"The knight that came upon me was a powerful man," Lord Gilbert said. "He laid such a blow across my helm, I saw all the stars and planets. Sir Henry had the courage of two men, but the size of a lad. He was overmatched against two. 'Twas then that Sir Geoffrey – not yet Sir, only a yeoman then – notched an arrow and from no more than four paces away put shafts through the French armor and dispatched both. 'Twas unfortunate. Dead men pay no ransom."

"Aye," Sir Roger agreed. "And Sir Henry needed funds even then."

"When I regained my wits the battle was nearly done," Lord Gilbert said. "King Jean was taken, along with many French knights who survived the slaughter. Prince Edward saw me being assisted back to our lines, as I was yet unsteady upon my feet. He asked my state, and Sir Henry, whose arm I leaned upon, told him all. The prince asked for Geoffrey Godswein and when the fellow was presented to him, he knighted him then and there."

"Along with a Welsh archer who had done him good service that day," the sheriff added.

"So you see, I owed much to Sir Henry, who came to my aid, and to Sir Geoffrey, whose arrows may have saved us both."

"You were pleased to award him a penny for his skills this day," I said.

"Aye," Lord Gilbert agreed. "He has had coins from me before."

"Did he ask for it?" I asked.

"Nay. Said a knighthood was pay enough for what he'd done, but Sir Henry presented him with a few shillings – all he could afford, I think – and I gave the fellow two marks."

"Sir Henry gave Sir Geoffrey a few shillings," I thought aloud. "Did Sir Geoffrey think that enough for his service, or was he resentful that he received no more?"

"Ah," Lord Gilbert said. "I see your point. The fellow seemed pleased with what he was given, then and now. And part of his reward was to enter Sir Henry's service. He's been under Bampton Castle roof for nearly a month, and if he's wrathful about what he was awarded twelve years past, he hides it well."

"We seek a man who wished Sir Henry dead," the sheriff said. "I think Sir Henry was worth more to Sir Geoffrey alive than dead. Whom now will he serve? Will Lady Margery keep him in her retinue?"

"Walter, the valet, has told me that Sir Henry and Lady Margery quarreled."

"Ha... what marriage does not have occasional dispute?" Lord Gilbert laughed. "The man who does not sometimes displease his wife has probably not enough spine to say 'boo' to a goose. And the woman who will not inform her husband when she is annoyed has not yet, I think, been born."

"If two people can live together without occasional cross words," Sir Roger said, "it shows a lack of spirit admirable only in sheep. Did the valet say what they argued about?"

"Money. Lady Margery said she'd not have wed Sir Henry had she known his circumstances. Said there were others she might have wed, and could do so yet, if she were free of him."

"Not whilst Sir Henry lived," Lord Gilbert said thoughtfully.

"Walter has overheard Lady Margery's maids. They speak of her interest in some knights, he knows not who. They spoke of more than one."

"Sir Henry was a cuckold?"

"Lady Margery's maids did not say. Perhaps they do not know of a certainty."

"A lady's maidservants know all there is to know of her business," Lord Gilbert said. "It might be well to speak to one."

"Lady Margery might not permit it," I said.

"She would if Lady Petronilla asked. I've heard my wife speak of one of Lady Margery's maids as having great skill with needle and thread. What if Lady Petronilla should ask for the woman to be sent to her chamber tomorrow, to mend some garment?"

"Lady Margery would smell a rat. Lady Petronilla has servants as skilled as any who wait upon Lady Margery, surely."

"Hmmm... aye, probably so. You do not wish to speak privily to one of Lady Margery's maids, then?"

"Aye, I do. 'Tis a worthy thought. But how might it be arranged?"

"I'll arrest one of 'em," Sir Roger said.

"On what charge?" Lord Gilbert asked.

"Your silver was stolen, was it not? We know of it, and Walter, and the Lady Anne, Humphrey and Andrew also, but who else? I'll send a sergeant to Lady Margery and have 'im seize one of her servants. What are their names? Which do you think most pliant?"

"Lady Petronilla would know who serves Lady Margery." Lord Gilbert turned to his wife, who had, to this time, had no part of our conversation, but had listened intently. I believe there were events of the Battle of Poitiers she knew not of 'til that day.

"The youngest of Lady Margery's maids is Isobel Guesclin. She might speak more readily than some, though I would be sorry to see her frightened in such a way. She is a shy, sweet young lass."

"I'll have my sergeant say only that she was seen near the screens passage the day the silver went missing, and Master Hugh wishes to ask if she saw any man lurking about the place."

"She may deny being near the pantry," Lord Gilbert said.

"My sergeant will say that's as may be, but he is to obey me an' take her to Master Hugh an' she can tell all to him."

I could think of no reason to dismiss this subterfuge, other than the fright the maid Isobel might feel. And that would be brief.

"Tell your sergeant to bring the woman to the chamber off the hall. I will await her there."

"Do be kind, Master Hugh," Lady Petronilla said.

"You may trust my discretion."

The chamber I spoke of was my own when I first came to Bampton to serve Lord Gilbert as his bailiff and surgeon to the town. A table, bench, and chair remained in the room. I moved the table and chair aside and placed the bench in the middle of the room, where slanting beams from the evening sun would illuminate whoever sat upon it.

Sir Roger's sergeant, the pale lass beside him, appeared but a moment after I had completed rearranging the chamber. Evidently neither the maid nor Lady Margery made serious objection to the young woman being drawn away to be questioned.

I dismissed the sergeant and bid Isobel enter. I nodded to the bench and told the maid to sit. Sunlight, as I planned, came through the slim window and into her eyes.

In the past, when I found need to ask questions of men who did not wish to answer, I found it advantageous to stand while my subject was seated and required to look up to me. I thought the same procedure would be effective with a maid.

The lass blinked in the golden sunlight and before I could speak, said, "M'lady sent me to the buttery for wine. But I saw no other but the butler in the screens passage."

Here was news which would make my task easier. The maid had evidently been near the pantry about the time Lord Gilbert's silver went missing.

"The sergeant told you of the missing silver?"

"Aye. Said spoons an' knives was taken."

"And you may have been seen in that end of the hall, near pantry and screens passage, when the theft occurred."

I saw a tear leave the maid's eye. I disliked myself for what I was about. But if the deed helped discover a murderer, my conscience would be soothed.

"Never been near the screens passage alone but that once... to fetch a cup of wine. Only go there with m'lady. Never by myself. Lord Gilbert's butler was there. I saw no other about, but perhaps he did. Was it he who said I was there?"

"Never mind. If you saw no other near the pantry, then perhaps 'tis you who made off with the silver?"

"Nay, I never did so."

"Someone did. Did Lord Gilbert's butler see you depart the screens passage with the wine?"

"Must have. Filled an ewer for me, an' I took it to Lady Margery."

"I shall ask him. If he saw you leave with the ewer you will be blameless. There is another matter I wish to speak to you about, as you are here."

I saw relief wash across the woman's face as I spoke. But the worried expression returned with my next question.

"There is gossip about the castle that Lady Margery does not grieve overmuch for Sir Henry's death. What say you?"

The lass did not soon reply, but cast her eyes about the chamber as if seeking some escape. I waited.

"M'lady wept when she heard of Sir Henry found dead."

"As might be, but tears may sometimes be false. When she is alone in her chamber, with only you and other of her servants, what does she say? What does she do?"

"Why do you ask this of me?"

"Because I am Lord Gilbert's bailiff, and 'tis my task to discover who murdered Sir Henry whilst he slept under Lord Gilbert's roof."

"M'lady believes your potion ended his life."

"She no longer does, and perhaps never did. She and Sir Henry quarreled, I am told."

Isobel was again silent, unwilling to report things which a good servant must keep concealed. Again I waited, 'til the silence in the chamber became uncomfortable. For Isobel, not for me. After some time, when I did not speak, she did.

"Most wedded folk quarrel upon a time."

"What were these quarrels about?"

Another period of silence followed. "Money, mostly," Isobel finally said.

"I've heard that Lady Margery wished herself free of Sir Henry."

Isobel's eyes grew wide and she sat upright upon the bench, as if I'd thrust a pin between her shoulders.

"She'd not slay him," the maid said.

"I did not say I suspect her of doing so," I replied.

"But... you said..."

"When a woman wishes to be free of her husband it often means she desires another. Who would Lady Margery have preferred to Sir Henry? What does the gossip say?"

Isobel was again silent, and this time my patience was not rewarded, for although I waited quietly for the maid to find her tongue she remained mute.

"Regarding Lord Gilbert's silver," I changed the subject. "Whoso did such a thing might hang." I was silent for a moment, then continued. "Sir Roger may wish to speak to you further on the matter of the silver, you being the only person near the pantry, other than Lord Gilbert's butler, at the time the silver may have gone missing."

Isobel became pale again as the implication of my words sank in. But the woman was no fool. She quickly grasped the reason for my changing the subject back to stolen spoons and knives and desired to leave the topic forthwith.

"M'lady has said often what a fine figure of a man is Sir Geoffrey."

"Do you and Lady Margery's other servants agree?"

Isobel blushed. "Aye," she agreed.

"Do Sir Geoffrey and Lady Margery seek each other in dalliance?"

The maid blushed again. "Not since Sir Henry was found dead."

"But before, they were oft together?"

"Not often."

"Sir Henry was in debt; did you know that?"

"Aye. M'lady spoke of it, an' we who serve her haven't had silk or even linen or wool for new gowns this past year and more."

"Sir Geoffrey might have left Sir Henry's service and attached himself to a more prosperous knight. Did lady Margery ever speak of him doing so?"

"Aye, both him and Sir John."

"How long past did she speak of these things? Does she talk of it often?"

"Aye. Says what kind of knight has no retainers to serve him? Soon he'll have no squires, nor pages, either."

"Do Lady Margery and Lady Anne quarrel?"

Silence once again followed the question, which was answer enough. Isobel, I think, was considering how much she might say. Enough to satisfy my curiosity, perhaps, but no more.

"Not often. Sir Henry wed Lady Margery soon after Lady Goscelyna perished. Lady Anne thought it unseemly haste."

"Not often, you say. What does that mean? Once each week? Once a fortnight? Every day?"

"Well, not quarrels, really. Disagreements, more likely."

"So, then, how often did they disagree?"

Silence again, and when Isobel did finally speak she replied so softly I barely heard. "Near every day," she said.

"What are these disagreements about?"

"Everything; gowns, how Lady Anne conducts herself, what man may be chosen as Lady Anne's husband. If Lady Anne wished to light a fire in her chamber Lady Margery would tell her 'twas warm enough."

Two of these subjects seemed ripe for controversy with little explanation necessary, but how a fire or Lady Anne's conduct could cause dissention required some further comment. I asked.

"Lady Anne is comely, as you, being a man, well know," Isobel replied. "She's sometimes not so modest as might be expected of a lass of her station."

"Leads men on, does she?"

"Doesn't mean to, I don't think. It's just her way. But Lady Margery thinks so. And between you and me, Lady Margery's not the beauty she once was. She resents Lady Anne, I think."

"I have heard that Lady Anne is fond of one of Sir Henry's squires. Is that another matter of contention between Lady Anne and Lady Margery?"

"Aye... but more like between Lady Anne and her father. Lady Margery only cared if Lady Anne was to wed a wealthy knight who could bring wealth to Sir Henry. She'd be pleased if Lady Anne did wed, and be gone. Of course, did she wed but a squire she'd have no place to go. Probably expect to stay under her father's roof... except she's got no father now, and so maybe no roof, either."

"No roof? Why do you say so?"

"Lady Margery weeps. I hear her in the night. Sir Henry's lands must be sold to satisfy his debts. What's left, if anything, is to be divided between Lady Margery and Lady Anne. Won't be much."

"She weeps for her poverty more than for the loss of her husband?"

"Aye," Isobel said softly. "What knight will wed a penniless widow? A comely face is no match for houses and lands, and Lady Margery will not have the last an' is losing the first."

"Has Lady Margery known of Sir Henry's empty purse for long?"

"Nay, don't think so. They were wed three years past. She'd inherited a house and business in Coventry from her first husband, but his will said was she to take another husband the house was to go to his younger brother."

"Lady Margery's father was a cordwainer, I have heard. What business did her husband pursue?"

"A grocer," Isobel replied.

"She had no children of her first husband?"

"One. A lad. They was wed for little more than a year when plague returned an' the babe perished, along with her husband."

Chapter 8

It was well that I was nearly finished with the interview, for in the distance I heard agitated voices. Isobel looked up to me as if she expected me to explain the shouting, but the clamor was too far away to be understood.

Any such uproar within Bampton Castle walls is likely to be my business, as a bailiff's duty is to keep the peace upon his lord's manor. I dismissed Isobel and hastened through the echoing hall to the heavy door which opened from hall to castle yard. When I pushed it open I heard more clearly the tumult coming from near the marshalsea.

The din increased as I approached, and not simply because I drew near to the scene of the disorder. When I rounded the corner of the marshalsea I saw a crowd of castle folk gathered about some event which caused their animated attention. From the opposite side of the castle yard I saw Lord Gilbert and Sir Roger appear at the top of the stairs which led from the yard to the solar and Lord Gilbert's private chambers. I saw my employer scowl and hasten down the steps. Soon his voice was added to the uproar.

Lord Gilbert and I approached the shouting crowd from opposite sides. I had at the time no sense of what had caused this noisy mob, but Lord Gilbert had looked down upon the throng from an elevated position at the head of the stairs and so knew the source of the tumult. Two men fought, their daggers unsheathed, the blades glinting in the afternoon sun.

Lord Gilbert and Sir Roger pushed through the mob from one side, and I did the same from the other. We met in the midst of the conflict. With a roar Lord Gilbert commanded the combatants to cease their brawl. When they saw who it was who moved between them they did so, breathing heavily from their exertions.

It was William Willoughby and Sir John who had so disturbed the peace of the castle. I saw blood issuing from the squire's nose, and Sir John's fine grey cotehardie was slashed and a crimson stain was seeping between the fingers of his left hand which he had pressed against the edges of the cut.

Sir Roger seized the squire's dagger and Lord Gilbert snatched Sir John's. "What means this unseemly contest?" he bawled.

"The knave struck me," Squire William said. As if to prove his assertion drops of blood fell from his nose to the dirt of the castle yard.

Lord Gilbert turned to Sir John and said, "Why did you do so?"

The knight opened his mouth to speak, but no sound came forth. He swayed upon his feet, collapsed to his knees, his eyes rolled back, and he fell face first into the dust, arms outstretched before him. He had evidently received a perilous cut.

I stepped to the fallen knight, turned him to his back, and inspected his wound. It bled freely. The thrust seemed deep, but I could not know this for certain without a closer inspection. A shadow fell across Sir John as Lord Gilbert knelt opposite me.

"Is he dead?" he asked.

"Nay. He breathes, but mayhap 'tis mortal. He must be carried to a table where I can see how severely he is hurt."

From the corner of my eye I saw Arthur. I motioned to him to approach and when he did I told him to take Sir John's shoulders whilst I grasped his feet. Together we lifted the insensible knight from the mud and carried him to the hall. This was not an easy task, for Sir John was not a small man. He was a near twin in size to Lord Gilbert, and surely weighed fourteen stone or more.

Uctred was nearby as well, and I shouted for him to hasten ahead and set up a table under a window. He did so, closely followed by two other grooms who had, moments before, been stunned into inaction but now saw a way to make themselves useful.

"Put that man in the dungeon," Lord Gilbert said to John Chamberlain, who had also appeared. He pointed toward Squire William. "We will deal with him later."

Sir Roger and Lord Gilbert followed Arthur and me and our burden through the great oaken door and into the hall. Once past the door I heard the clatter of trestles and boards as Uctred and his companions hastily erected a table. Someone would later need to scrub bloodstains from the planks, and from the flags, also, for Sir John bled freely, crimson drops falling even upon my shoes.

No sooner had the knight been laid upon the table than he blinked and tried to lift his head. He had regained his wits.

I told him to be still, drew my dagger, and slashed at his cotehardie and kirtle until I had cleared the clothing away from the wound. What I saw gave me some hope for the man's life. The cut was as long as my hand. Such a laceration is generally the result of a slashing stroke rather than a thrust. The wound bled much, but was not, I thought, so deep as I had feared. A smaller puncture could be the result of a stabbing blow, which might seem at first of less consequence. But if such a wound penetrated to some vital organ the knight would surely die. William's blade had cut deeply enough that I saw two ribs through the blood and flesh, but the bone had prevented the stroke from doing harm to any vital organ.

I had no instruments at the castle with which to deal with this injury. I grasped the fragment of kirtle I had cut away from the wound and pressed it firmly against the cut to stop, so much as was possible, the flow of blood. This seemed effective. I told Arthur to hold the linen in place whilst I ran to Galen House for instruments with which I might close the wound. I also requested of Lord Gilbert that wine and a basin of hot water be brought to the hall, to cleanse the wound. I then hastened from the hall.

I was longer in returning to the castle than I would have been three or four years past. This sluggishness is Kate's doing. I have enjoyed too many coney pies and egg leeches since we wed. When I lived alone and made my dinner of bread, cheese, ale, and an occasional roasted capon I was more fleet of foot.

I hesitated at my home only long enough to blurt out the news to Kate and throw instruments into a sack. By the time I crashed through the doors into Bampton Castle Hall I was breathless and unfit for any surgery. Lord Gilbert saw my state and offered a cup of wine from the ewer the butler had provided.

I drank from the proffered cup whilst I regained my breath, and inspected the knight's wound. Someone had provided a new cloth. The rag which I had left with Arthur lay red-stained beneath the trestles, and he was pressing a new, larger piece of fabric against the cut.

Sir John lay quietly during this inspection, but when he saw me produce a needle and spool of silken thread from my sack he spoke.

"Am I a dead man?"

"Mayhap. There is no way to know 'til a day or two passes. If you are yet alive come Tuesday, or Wednesday, I think then you will live. But Lord Gilbert's chaplain should remain close by to shrive you."

In my absence another table had been erected, and upon it I saw one of Lord Gilbert's napkins, missing a fragment which now stopped Sir John's blood from gushing from his wound. I ripped a length from the napkin, soaked it in wine, and wiped the wound as Arthur lifted the blood-soaked cloth. What good this might do I cannot tell, but it has always seemed to me that if a wound might heal better after being stitched and then bathed in wine, then to wash a cut with wine before any surgery or work with needle and thread might also help a wound to heal.

Squire William had already made the first cut, so 'twas too late to test the theory fully, but I poured more wine into the empty cup, then poured this directly into Sir John's cut. He gasped, and clenched his hands into fists, but was otherwise still.

I cut a length of silken thread as long as my arm and began to stitch Sir John's wound closed. The day was near done, and light from the window above my head was growing dim. The day had been sunny and warm. So as I bent over my patient, the better to see what I was about, drops of sweat beaded upon my lip and forehead and I was required to wipe the perspiration away with what remained of Lord Gilbert's napkin, else I would have dripped sweat upon the knight's wound.

The cut was in a place where others would be unlikely to see it, but I was careful to do fine work so that should the man live, his scar would be thin and faint. Perhaps, I thought, should he marry, his bride will appreciate my competence.

Twenty stitches closed the wound. A few tiny drops of blood yet oozed from the cut. These I wiped away with an unstained corner of the cloth Arthur had used to staunch the flow, then I soaked another scrap of napery in wine and once more washed the wound.

I could do no more. Whether the knight lived or died was now in God's hands, not mine.

I stood away from Sir John, washed blood from my hands in the basin, wiped sweat from my brow again, and placed my hands behind my back to stretch my complaining muscles.

"Will he live?" Lord Gilbert asked. He, Sir Roger, Arthur, Uctred, and several others had watched as I sewed Sir John back together, but so intent was I on the task that I had taken no notice of spectators.

"God knows. If the cut is not deep, he will survive, I think. But if the blade went under his ribs, which I think it did not do, he will likely die soon."

"What caused this row, I wonder," Sir Roger said.

"Sir John is not in fit condition to be asked," I said. "If he is alive tomorrow we may inquire of him then. Meanwhile, you might send a sergeant to bring Squire William from the dungeon to the solar and we may examine him to hear his account of the business."

"After supper," Lord Gilbert said. I glanced toward the screens passage and saw there the scowling face of Thomas Attewell, Lord Gilbert's cook at Bampton Castle, peering into the hall. He had prepared a meal and if 'twas not eaten soon it would grow cold.

Uctred and another groom were assigned to bring a pallet to the hall and transport Sir John to his chamber. I told the knight I would visit him in the morning and saw him nod in understanding.

I had no interest in dining this evening at Lord Gilbert's table. So when he asked me to remain I declined, told him I would return shortly to seek information from William, and made my way to Galen House and a simple supper in the peace and quiet of my own family.

"You believe this fight is connected to Sir Henry's death?" Kate asked as we consumed a maslin loaf. "Or is it but a coincidence?"

"Bailiffs do not believe in coincidence."

"Ah... then one or both of the fellows knows of Sir Henry's murderer, and the other..."

"The other knows, or believes that he knows," I completed her thought.

"And the squire is now in the castle dungeon?"

"Aye. Nothing like a dungeon to concentrate a man's mind upon his sins."

"And give him time to devise a tale which will turn guilt to the other fellow and ascribe innocence to himself."

"Aye, that also. Which is why I am to return to the castle this hour and with Lord Gilbert and Sir Roger question the squire about the brawl. If he does not have the night to invent his excuses we may more readily get the truth from him."

The sun rested just above the treetops of Lord Gilbert's forest to the west of the castle when I re-entered the gatehouse. I went directly to the solar, for supper was over and done and grooms were disassembling tables and benches. This was Sunday eve, so there would be no entertainment, no musicians or jongleurs. Lord Gilbert does not think such frivolity meet for the Sabbath.

Sir Roger was in attendance with Lord Gilbert and Lady Petronilla, enjoying wine and conversation, when I arrived at the chamber. Lady Petronilla excused herself and Lord Gilbert called for a sergeant to bring Squire William to us.

The youth's eyes were turning black from the blow he'd taken, and his nose was swollen and askew, clearly broken, if no longer dripping gore. William eyed us cautiously from the slits his eyes had become. Lord Gilbert and Sir Roger sat facing the lad, arms crossed, intent but waiting. Waiting for me.

"You might have killed Sir John," I began.

"He will live?" the squire asked.

"Aye, most likely."

I thought I saw regret flash across William's battered face. Not regret that Sir John might perish, but that he might not.

"Why did you thrust a dagger into him?"

"Because he first attacked me."

"You speak of your nose?"

"Aye. And when he struck me down he drew his dagger and would have plunged it into me was I not too quick for him."

"He knocked you down," Sir Roger asked, "then made to stab you whilst you were on the ground?"

"Aye... but I saw him coming and rolled away."

"Then you drew your own dagger?" I asked.

"Aye. I'd got free of him, but he came for me again, so I took a swipe at him with my dagger as I twisted away. Made him back away, an' I was able to get to my feet."

"That's when we came upon you and stopped the fray?" Lord Gilbert asked.

"What did you do to cause Sir John to smite you so?" I asked.

"Didn't do anything," William replied.

I saw one of Lord Gilbert's eyebrows rise, as is common when some matter strikes him as curious. "If you did nothing, then you must have said something," Lord Gilbert said. "A man will not aim such a blow at another for no reason."

I realized that Lord Gilbert had chanced upon the cause of the fray when William made no reply. For him to

123

do so would mean that we who interrogated him might learn a thing he wished us not to know.

"The fight was near to the marshalsea," I said. "Were you and Sir John going to attend your horses?"

"Aye. They'd not been exercised since day before Sir Henry died. We thought to go for a gallop."

Men who dislike each other would not agree to a companionable ride through the countryside. Something went seriously awry between Sir John and William between the time they made plans to ride and their approach to the stables.

"Is Sir John an irascible fellow?" I asked.

The squire shrugged. "Never seemed so," he said.

"Then you must have said something objectionable. What was it?"

William was again silent. Sir Roger responded.

"Say what Master Hugh requires, else you will return to the dungeon 'til your tongue is loosened."

"I don't remember my exact words," he said.

"Nonsense," I replied. "When a man says a thing which causes another to strike him to his knees, he is not likely to forget what he said which brought him two blackened eyes and a broken nose."

"Broken? My nose is broken?"

"Aye," Lord Gilbert said. "All askew. Now answer Master Hugh."

William tenderly touched his nose, discovered the truth of Lord Gilbert's assertion, then spoke.

"Can it be set right?" the squire asked.

"Aye," I said. "I will deal with it when you have answered our questions. If you will not, then you may go through life with a nose seeking scents to the sinister side, and through which you may never breathe properly."

William was, I knew, smitten with Lady Anne, and

reports said the lass wished to wed the youth. Would she do so had he a disfigured face and a nose which would draw laughter behind upraised hands? I believe William considered these same thoughts.

"'Twas meant as a jest," the squire finally said.

"What was? Your words to Sir John?" I asked.

"Aye."

"What did you say that he took amiss?"

"We spoke of horses... I said 'twould not be long before Sir Geoffrey would be riding Sir Henry's mare."

"You did not see that Sir John would see this as an insult to Sir Geoffrey and Lady Margery?" I said.

"Nay," the squire said ruefully. "All know that Sir Geoffrey and the Lady Margery..."

William's voice trailed off. I prodded him to continue. "'Sir Geoffrey and Lady Margery' what? It would be well if I could restore your nose as soon as possible. A broken nose left crooked for too long can sometimes not be made right."

William gingerly touched his swollen nose, grimaced, then continued.

"That Sir Geoffrey and Lady Margery would wed if she was free of Sir Henry."

"All knew this? Did Sir Henry know?"

"Think so. If he didn't, he was the only one, man or woman, on his estate who didn't."

"What else do folk know? Did Sir Geoffrey and Lady Margery connive in Sir Henry's death?" Sir Roger asked.

"Oh, nay. Surely not," William replied.

"Then how did they expect Lady Margery to be free of Sir Henry?" Lord Gilbert asked.

"Lady Margery was to seek an annulment."

"On what grounds?" Lord Gilbert scoffed. "That they had no issue? She had no funds. How would she gain the coin a bishop would require of her?"

"Don't know what ground she was to claim. Did all work according to plan, she wouldn't have needed grounds."

"Oh?" I said.

"The Bishop of Lichfield is old and ill and will not live much longer. Lady Margery's cousin is thought to have the see when the old bishop dies."

"Ah," Lord Gilbert said. "The new bishop would grant the plea of kinfolk."

"So men said."

"And this is why Sir Henry was distressed and lay awake nights?" I asked.

"Mayhap," the youth agreed. "That and his debts."

"The old bishop is dead," Sir Roger said. "Word came to Oxford early last week."

"Then Lady Margery will soon know if her cousin will receive the see," I said.

"She may know already. Rumor in Oxford is that a scholar at Merton College will be elevated to the post," Sir Roger said.

"Is Lady Margery's cousin an Oxford scholar?" I asked William.

"Nay. He's Dean of Hereford Cathedral, and not of noble birth."

Here was interesting information. If Lady Margery hoped to be free of Sir Henry when her kinsman became Bishop of Lichfield, that hope was dashed. Did she know of this already? And did the news cause her or Sir Geoffrey to seek another way to dissolve her marriage?

"Will you set my nose right now?" William asked.

I looked to Lord Gilbert and saw him nod. "We have what we asked of this fellow," he said. "Put his nose in place."

"To do so will cause him much pain," I said. "'Tis late, near dark, and I have no sedative herbs with me to reduce the hurt. I brought only instruments to deal with Sir John's wound. I will return in the morning and set his nose right then."

"But you said it must be done betimes or I may suffer the blemish all of my days," the squire protested.

"Tomorrow will be soon enough," I replied. "And you do not want me to tug your nose straight until you have swallowed a dose of crushed hemp seeds. You may trust my judgment on this."

"What is to be done with the lad 'til then?" Sir Roger asked. "Back to the dungeon?"

Lord Gilbert looked to me with that curious, raised eyebrow, and waited for me to speak.

"I think William will not try to flee the castle in the night," I said. "And if Sir John lives he'll face no charge of murder in the King's Eyre."

"Very well," Lord Gilbert said. "You may return to your chamber for the night. Where you spend the morrow will depend upon where Sir John's soul may be then."

William bowed, backed away from his betters, and felt behind him for the door from the solar to the corridor. I could guess how uneasy a night he would spend. In his chamber he would likely find Robert de Cobham already abed. Word of William's brawl had surely passed the ears of all in the castle, so that even those who were not present at the fight knew of it, so likely Robert would demand to be told all. The recounting, and his painful nose, would drive sleep far from William. And worry that he might be returned to the castle dungeon would also make him wakeful. So be it. My own bed called. I would concern myself with the squire and his troubles tomorrow.

Shill Brook flowed dark and quiet under the bridge. As was my custom when I had no pressing business, I stopped upon the bridge to gaze into the water, although, truth to tell, the evening had become so dark that I could see little of the stream. But I knew it was there. As was a murderer in the castle. There was not enough light yet for me to see the felon, but, like the brook below my feet, I knew he was there.

My thought traveled back to the evils which had come to Bampton Castle in past days. Whence did these evils come? Not from God. But if the devil created evils, who created the devil but God, who is all goodness? Could not God, all-powerful, change the sin in me and other men to good? How does wickedness exist in God's world, against His will?

As I pondered this I remembered St Augustine's assertion that all God has made is good, even the perverted things, like human nature. If they were not good, they could not be perverted. A thing which is already evil cannot be defiled, for it is so already. If men were the supreme good, like God, they would be incorruptible, as is He. But if they were not good at all, there would be nothing in them worthy of corruption. Being only evil, men would be incorruptible.

Men, and women also, must fall between the two. Events at the castle in past days displayed man's perversion. But those evil deeds are an argument that men were originally made good, as Holy Scriptures teach. We are not perfect. Only God is. But neither are we irreversibly evil. There we are, caught in the middle, and unable to save ourselves. We are moral beings, made good in the image of God, but we are corruptible, as God is not, as we abuse the gift of free will. And thence we are inevitably corrupted.

Was it not for the Lord Christ's death upon the cross we would all suffer the penalty of our depraved free will. I turned from the dark stream and set out for Galen House with a lighter spirit. Not because I had been considering how evil influences men, but because the Lord Christ has freed all who accept His sacrifice from the penalty of their depravity. Even me. Somewhere this night within Bampton Castle walls was a man, or perhaps a woman, who had freely chosen sin and would pay the penalty for the choice, in this world, was I wise enough to discover them; and even if I failed, they would suffer for it in the next.

Kate awaited me at Galen House. She was full of questions about events at the castle, as anyone would be. I had been in haste when I returned to collect my instruments, so had left Kate with only the rudiments of what had happened, and at supper had not yet questioned the squire. Kate is not a woman who is satisfied with partial knowledge. I sat with her on our bench and in the light of a cresset explained what I knew of the fight between Sir John and William.

"It seems to me," Kate said when I finished the tale, "that there are few folk sorry of Sir Henry's death."

"Aye, but few had cause to do murder, even if they feel no loss that he is gone."

"The night before Sir Henry was buried someone placed a message under the sheriff's door, telling him that the squires had what he sought. Is this not so?" Kate said.

"Aye. And written in a poor hand, as one unaccustomed to a pen."

"Then you found a bloody cloth and a bodkin in the squires' chamber."

"Just so."

"And one of the squires had cause to dislike Sir Henry, as he sought the Lady Anne's hand but was rebuffed."

"Mayhap was rebuffed. Whether or not he asked to pay her court I do not know... but Sir Henry knew of his interest and was opposed."

"Sir Henry was so poor his daughter stole silver spoons and knives from Lord Gilbert's pantry. I wonder did she resent her poverty enough to join William in wishing her father dead?"

"Who can know? Did Squire William wish Sir Henry dead? Both would deny it, so there is no point in asking either of them. And having a suit rejected has rarely drawn a man to homicide."

Kate was silent a moment, thinking. I was silent as well, content to watch the glimmering flame of the cresset light her cheeks and hair.

"And the portpain," she said. "Missing from the pantry at about the same time, you said, as the silver was taken. Then a fragment is discovered in William's chamber."

"Also Robert de Cobham's chamber," I reminded her.

"Sir Henry cannot sleep because of his debts and because he knows his wife seeks another husband. Now you say that Lady Margery may have had a design to escape her marriage, but no longer, as her cousin is not made bishop."

"I wonder," I said, "how badly Lady Margery wanted to escape her marriage?"

"And how much Sir Geoffrey might have been willing to assist her to free herself?" Kate added.

"Aye, that also."

We sat in silence then, lost in private thoughts. Kate's head began to sway, and soon rested upon my shoulder. I was loath to interrupt the moment, but the night grew cool, and the cresset burned low. I lifted Kate from the bench and carried her to the stairs and our chamber. This life includes many sorrows, but some simple things may soothe the hurts and make trivial the pains which come, soon or late, to all.

Chapter 9

Next morn, after a maslin loaf and ale, I set off for the castle with a few instruments and a vial of crushed hemp seeds. William would require a strong dose if the pain of my work upon his nose was not to overcome him.

The gate to Bampton Castle was open and the portcullis raised when I arrived. Wilfred the porter greeted me with a tug of his forelock, and I went straight to the hall and the stairs to Lord Gilbert's solar.

I found my employer and Sir Roger there, having just arrived from the castle chapel and morning mass.

"You are about early today, Hugh," Lord Gilbert greeted me.

"I promised to set the squire's nose straight, and I wish to see Sir John."

"Sir John lived the night," Sir Roger said, "and took some ale and part of a loaf to break his fast."

This was welcome news, both for Sir John and for Squire William. The lad would not face the King's Eyre if Sir John lived. Of course, he might face other sorrows if Sir John recovered health and strength and sought vengeance upon the lad. If he did so I hoped the reprisal would take place elsewhere and be no concern of mine.

"I've seen nothing of William this morning," Lord Gilbert said. "He did not break his fast nor attend mass."

"Hah," Sir Roger laughed. "With such a nose and eyes as he had last night, 'tis no wonder. He'll wish to take his meals in his chamber for a fortnight. He was not a handsome lad to begin with. If Master Hugh cannot repair his nose you might toss him in the Isis and skim ugly for a week."

"If you hear a yelp from the lower level," I said, "take no notice. It will mean I have put the lad's nose straight."

"Mayhap he will think before he offers another such jest," Lord Gilbert said.

"Aye," I agreed. "But I am puzzled why Sir John took his wit so badly. If William had spoken so where Sir Geoffrey heard, and was then struck, I could understand."

Lord Gilbert's eyebrow rose. "Aye, 'tis a puzzle. You believe it important?"

"Everything which happens in your castle may be important. Our problem is that some things may not be of consequence and we do not know which are which... so we must treat all events as significant to Sir Henry's death, even though some may not be, as we do not know the difference."

"Oh," Sir Roger frowned. "Just so."

I departed the solar with the sheriff's brow furrowed in thought and Lord Gilbert's eyebrow yet raised. They might puzzle out the mystery over a cup of wine whilst I ministered to William.

I found the squire groaning in his bed. His nose was more swollen and his eyes blacker than the day before. It seemed likely that William had slept little.

Robert de Cobham sat upon his bed, watching his companion, when I entered their chamber. Robert's visage, clouded with worry, lightened when I entered, as if he thought his friend's anguish would be soon ended. Not so. Pain may come in but a moment, as in the arrival of a strong man's fist upon the point of another man's nose, but will generally take much longer to pass away.

William turned from his pillow and lifted his head when my shadow fell across him. His warped nose had long since stopped bleeding, but was evidently so painful that neither he nor any other had tried to cleanse the dried gore caked upon his upper lip.

"You've come to fix my nose?" William said, his voice sounding as if he spoke from the base of a garderobe drain.

"Aye." I turned to Robert and told him to seek the buttery and return with a large cup of ale, then described to William what I must do.

Robert returned with the ale as I concluded my explanation. It was impossible for William's eyes to grow wide, but when I told him of what I must do and the brief pain he would feel, his face reflected the fright in his soul.

I poured all of the vial of crushed hemp seeds into the ale, instructed William to drink it all, and watched to see that he did. It is my experience that such a physic is most effective an hour or so after being consumed, so I told the squire to wait upon his bed while I was about other business, and that I would return to set his nose straight when the potion had done its work.

I did not tell William that I intended to visit Sir John while I waited for the hemp seeds to make the lad lethargic. I wanted no further explanations from him until I had heard the knight's account of their brawl.

Sir John lay sleeping upon his bed. So silent was he that at first I feared he had died in the hour since I had spoken to Lord Gilbert. No man or woman attended him, which I thought strange. But I was pleased that Sir Geoffrey was not present. I wished to ask of Sir John questions he might prefer not to answer was his friend with him.

Sir John slept soundly, which was good, as I am convinced that healing of such a wound is hastened when the one so injured is rested. I shook the fellow by the shoulder to wake him, and he finally snorted from slumber and lifted his head from the pillow to see who had disturbed him.

"Ah," he mumbled. "'Tis you. I have lived the night. I heard you speak to Lord Gilbert after you dealt with my wound."

"Sir Roger said you took bread and ale this morning. Did the meal make you nauseous?"

"Nay... well, not much. Didn't lose it."

"I will draw back your blanket and see the wound."

I did so, and Sir John raised himself upon his elbows to see also. "You've not bound it, nor put a salve on it," he said in an accusatory tone. I explained that I follow the practice of Henri de Mondeville, who learned in dealing with wounds suffered in battle that those left dry and open to the air usually healed best.

"There's no pus," the knight said, and I heard fear in his voice.

"Aye," I replied. "This is best. Physicians have long taught that thin, watery pus is perilous, and thick, yellow pus issuing from a wound is good. But again, I hold with de Mondeville that no pus at all is best."

Sir John remained propped upon his elbow as I told him this. He seemed unconvinced, but I explained to him that his very posture was evidence of the likely success of de Mondeville's view. If his cut had festered it would be unlikely that he could raise himself as he did without pain.

My words seemed to remind the man that he was uncomfortable, and he slumped back to the bed.

"Why did you strike young William?"

Sir John was silent. He was unwilling to speak and although I waited for a reply, none came.

"You broke his nose and blackened his eyes," I finally said. I thought I saw a smile flicker across the knight's face. "Does that news bring you pleasure?" I asked.

"He might have slain me," Sir John finally said.

"After you struck him down and drew your dagger," I reminded him. "What did he do to anger you so?"

The man once again lapsed into silence, and turned his head from me as if to signal that he wished the conversation at an end. I did not.

"The lad spoke in jest when he said that Sir Geoffrey might soon be riding Sir Henry's mare. Why did you take his wit so amiss?"

I saw Sir John stiffen under the blanket, but he made no reply. My words had touched some tender place, but I did not know why.

I learned nothing more from Sir John. He remained resolute in his silence, his face turned from me. He did not respond even when I told him that I would return before supper to see how he fared, and that we would speak about this again.

The failed attempt at conversation had taken nearly an hour, so when I returned to the squires' chamber William was as ready as he was likely to be for the straightening of his skewed nose.

The work required no instruments. There was nothing to slice or stitch, to open or close. My only tools were two small, tightly rolled linen patches which I drew from my pouch and laid upon the table.

William sat upon his bed, but I thought this an unsafe posture. Should he swoon from the pain when I set his nose aright he might fall to the floor. I told him to recline against his pillow, which he seemed grateful to do, as the hemp seeds had stupefied him to a wonderful degree.

There was no gentle way to do what must be done. Quickly was best. To set William's nose straight with slow, steady measures would bring him more grief than to do the work in one rapid, if painful, wrench.

The squire lay back upon his bed and watched through the swollen slits of his blackened eyes as my hand approached and gently probed his battered nose. This touch evidently caused him little pain. He did not twitch or catch his breath while I examined the organ.

This inspection was done as much to calm William as to tell me what must be done. I wished the lad to be lulled into a false sense that the treatment he was about to receive would be but more of the same. Such he could endure.

The squire lay relaxed under my hand when, with a quick motion, I grasped his nose, pulled it straight, and a heartbeat later, seeing it now protruding as should be from between his eyes, released the offended appendage.

William responded with an awful howl, and tears welled from his eyes. He threw his hands up as if to provide some relief for his pain, but I grasped them so he could not undo the work I had just completed.

Robert saw his friend thrashing about and jumped to aid me in holding William quiet upon the bed. The yelping soon subsided. William's body twitched a few times and was then still. I believe he understood, through his torment, that the worst was past.

When I was sure that the squire would do no harm to his restored nose I released his arms and stood above him.

"Is there more?" he moaned. "Or are you done with me?"

"Nearly finished. What remains will cause you little distress."

The small linen patches I had placed upon the table had unrolled. I took one, rolled it tightly again, told William to remain motionless, and as gently as I could I thrust the linen up one nostril as far as it would go. The squire gasped once, but was perhaps relieved that this measure was not so painful as placing his nose in its proper place had been.

I prepared the second linen plug and as I was about to shove it into the other nostril saw a small drop of blood drip from the offended orifice. The linen would end the flow, slight as it was, so I did not hesitate but pushed the linen into the empty nostril.

"You must leave these plugs in your nose for a fortnight," I said, "and even a few days longer if you can bear it. This will ensure that your nose will remain in place until the swelling has subsided and it has begun to knit. If I were you, I'd avoid any words or actions which might provoke a strong man to strike a blow... until well after Lammas Day, at least."

I might have left the youth some crushed lettuce seeds to help him sleep, as his pain would likely keep slumber distant for a few days, but my supply was low and could not be replenished until the new-grown lettuce was gone to seed. Before I left the chamber I had another question for William.

"I have spoken to Sir John," I said. "I asked him why your jest provoked him to strike you."

"What did he say?" William asked.

"Nothing. He would not speak of the matter. Can you guess why he would not?"

Robert, who had returned to his seat after assisting me to restrain William, spoke. "Don't need to guess."

I said nothing, but looked from Walter to Robert, awaiting the enlightenment I felt sure would come. It did. Silence is occasionally better than a question.

"Sir John thinks much of m'lady," Robert said.

"The Lady Margery?" I said.

"Who else?" he replied.

"Not Lady Anne? I thought 'twas Sir Geoffrey who had caught Lady Margery's eye."

"He has, and likewise. But just because a lady seems to

choose one doesn't mean another mightn't have an interest."

I looked to William. "Did you know of this? That Sir John was enamored of Lady Margery?"

William shook his head, "No," and instantly regretted the action. His nose flexed slightly upon its unsteady base and he grimaced in pain.

"Who else knows of Sir John's infatuation with Lady Margery? Does Lady Margery know?"

"Don't know. He didn't speak of it."

"Then how did you learn of this?"

"He'd had much wine once, and I saw him leering at m'lady. Asked him what he was about, and did he not know that if Sir Henry saw him he'd likely be sent from the household."

"What did he say?"

"Said he cared little for what Sir Henry might think, and for me to hold my tongue. I did so. Sir John is a powerful man and I did not wish to offend him."

The lad had William's nose before him as evidence of what an angry Sir John Peverel might do to an unwitting squire.

"Why do you speak of this now?" I said. "Do you not fear what Sir John may do if he learns that you have spoken to me of this?"

"Nay. Now Sir Henry's dead what matter if all the world knows of Sir John's hidden desire?"

I admonished William again to take care for his nose, surely unnecessary but probably expected, and departed the chamber more confused than when I had entered. I had expected that the more I could learn of Sir Henry's family, retainers, and servants, the closer I would come to finding a murderer. But the opposite seemed true. The more I learned, the more perplexed I became. I sought the solar and Lord Gilbert, but he was absent.

"Gone to the marshalsea with Sir Roger," Lady Petronilla said. "A pleasant day for a ride in the forest, he said."

I found Lord Gilbert and the sheriff preparing to mount their beasts before the marshalsea. My employer turned from the stirrup and, one eyebrow raised, asked of my patients.

"Sir John will live, I think, and I have set William's nose straight. He will appear no worse for wear in a month, so long as he does not provoke Sir John again."

"Why did his words do so yesterday?"

"'Tis that I would speak to you about."

Lord Gilbert looked to Sir Roger and I saw the sheriff nod.

"Tell a page to saddle Bruce. You will ride with us this morning and tell us what you know. We'll wait here for you."

Bruce is an ancient dexter, given to my use as part of my service as bailiff of Lord Gilbert's manor at Bampton. The beast carried Lord Gilbert into battle at Poitiers eleven years past, and is now doubtless pleased to spend most of his days in the meadow west of the castle, or munching oats in the marshalsea. I rarely need use of the beast, and being untrained to the saddle am not a skilled rider. But Oxford is a long walk from Bampton and Bruce has carried me there and back often. Perhaps he thought that our destination this day also.

When Sir Roger and Lord Gilbert saw Bruce led from the stables they mounted their horses and I clambered upon Bruce's broad back. Lord Gilbert led the way under the portcullis. Wilfred tugged a forelock as we passed. Iron-shod hooves clattered across the drawbridge and we were soon upon Mill Street, where Lord Gilbert turned his mount toward the forest and Cowley's Corner.

"You've set William's nose straight, then?" Lord Gilbert said as we rode easily toward the wood.

"Aye. A painful lesson, but such are not soon forgot."

"Just so," Sir Roger laughed.

"You wished to tell us of Sir John's wrath," my employer said, "and why William's words goaded him to strike the lad."

"'Twas Robert told me that the Lady Margery has more than one admirer."

Lord Gilbert's eyebrow lifted under his cap, as I knew it would, and he cocked his head toward me, awaiting explanation.

"Sir John also holds the lady in much esteem."

Lord Gilbert sighed and glanced to the sky. "Had I known of the disorder in Sir Henry's household I would never have extended an invitation for him to visit. Well... too late for second thoughts now. So two knights wished the Lady Margery free of her husband?"

"But Sir John had kept his desire for the lady to himself, but for a drunken leer when Robert saw," I said.

"Did he not know," Sir Roger said, "that Sir Geoffrey wished also to supplant the lady's husband?"

"He did," I said. "All the household seemed to know, including, I believe, Sir Henry."

"Are not Sir John and Sir Geoffrey friends?"

"So they seem," I said.

"'Twould not be the first time friends have fallen out over a lady," Lord Gilbert observed.

Sir Roger went to the heart of the matter. "Now you have another who might have wished Sir Henry dead."

We rode through the forest in silence for a time, each considering in his own way the events of the past few days. Lord Gilbert soon tired of this, being a gentleman and thus easily bored. He spurred his beast to a gallop and Sir

Roger and I did likewise to keep up. We thundered past Cowley's Corner and toward Alvescot, frightening squirrels and jackdaws, for better than a mile before Lord Gilbert drew upon his reins and brought his steed to a walk. I was much relieved. Teetering upon Bruce while the horse is in full gallop is akin to riding upon a cart with square wheels.

Lord Gilbert had slowed his mount because of a path through the wood leading from the road which he wished to follow. The way was narrow, just a track cut through the forest for use of the verderer, so we went in single file. Conversation was then shouted rather than spoken, especially if Lord Gilbert wished to address me, as he led the way and Bruce and I were in the rear.

"Sir John will live, you say?" he yelled.

"Aye," I replied.

"Then I believe William has suffered enough for his indiscretion, and Sir John has paid the price of his temper and the blow to William's nose. What say you, Sir Roger? Are these sleeping dogs best left to lie as they now are?"

"Perhaps," the sheriff agreed, "if the dogs you speak of are willing."

Our shouted conversation echoed through the forest as the sheriff and I found agreement with Lord Gilbert that William and Sir John be strongly urged to end their quarrel with no further blows, with perhaps a thinly veiled threat as to Lord Gilbert's response were his wishes disregarded, at least while the two men resided within Bampton Castle.

I wondered who would deliver this proscription to Sir John and William. I learned soon enough. "Hugh... will you see your patients again this day?"

"Aye, m'lord."

"Tell them what is decided. Do not spare them harsh words. I want no repetition of their brawl while they remain under my roof. After you have discovered

Sir Henry's murderer, and they have departed with Lady Margery, I care not if they wish to continue slicing and battering each other."

We emerged from the wood north of Bampton, where the path found the road to Witney. Lord Gilbert turned his mount toward the spire of St Beornwald's Church, which could be seen in the distance, rising above the clustered houses of the town.

We returned to the castle in silence, enjoying the sun and contemplating dinner. As we approached the castle drawbridge I glanced down into the green, scummy water and saw floating there an object which I could not identify. Twigs and sticks and other such debris often may be found in a moat, but the thing I saw was worked by some man, shaped and rounded. I paid it no more attention and followed Lord Gilbert and Sir Roger under the portcullis to the marshalsea.

A few moments later we entered the hall, where all was readied for dinner, and a valet produced an ewer of water and towels for our ablutions. The morning ride and my labors had left me with an appetite, and so I did wondrous injury to the removes as they were placed before me.

While I ate I watched my companions but saw no behaviors which might indicate a guilty conscience. Sir John and William, who might have reflected in their countenances such a sentiment, were not present.

My thoughts also turned to the object I had seen floating in the moat. I decided that when the meal was done I would leave the castle and fish the thing out of the water. I was curious about what it might be, and how it had come to be there, as it did not seem to be anything common to a moat.

As there is no current in the moat, and this day the breeze was slight, the object I sought was in the same place

I had seen it when riding Bruce toward the drawbridge. A rounded piece of wood, about the size of my fist, floated amongst lily pads two or three yards from the bank. I had no desire to wade into the green, turbid water to retrieve the thing, and in any case it was far enough from the shore that it likely floated in water neck deep.

I returned to the marshalsea and interrupted a page at his work. I instructed the lad to get a rake and a length of rope and report to me with these items at the moat.

What caused my curiosity about the floating object I cannot say, except that such a thing was unusual in a moat, even though such bodies of water are likely to attract much which castle folk discard, though nobles frown on such practice. Someone had worked to remove the corners from a block of wood, and evidently then discarded the object of their labor. I wondered for what use the thing had been made, and why it now bobbed in the moat.

Rakes and ropes are common enough about a castle marshalsea, so it was not long before the page appeared, rake over one shoulder and rope coiled over the other.

"Do you see yon piece of wood floating there in the moat?"

"Aye," the lad replied.

"Tie the rope to the rake, then cast it out and draw the thing to the bank."

The page set about this work, and at the third cast of the rake succeeded in bringing the object close enough to shore that, with me holding him by one hand, he was able to lean over the moat and lift the thing from the water. He handed the rounded block to me gingerly, coated as it was with some of the foul stuff found floating in a moat. Some castles of the older sort are surrounded by moats containing filth from the garderobes, which drain into them. The garderobes of Bampton Castle are not so constructed, for which I was much relieved as I examined the circular wooden object I held before me.

It was actually not round, more a rounded oblong, and had once, I think, been square, or nearly so. Someone had carved edges away with a blade so that what once had been a cube was now pear-like in shape and of near the same size. Where the stem of a pear would be I saw a hole, about half the size of my little fingernail in diameter. Was this indentation accidental to the object's purpose, or was it significant to the intended use?

Along one side of the object I saw a line of smaller holes, four in number, as if some man had driven a row of tacks into the thing, then removed them.

I carried yet in my pouch the bodkin used, so I believed, to slay Sir Henry whilst he slept. I drew it from my pouch and attempted to fit the blunt end into the hole in the carved ball. It fit quite well, and I was able to push the thin iron rod deep into the wood. Was this coincidence, or did I now hold in my hand the completed weapon with which one man slew another?

If this was the weapon used to murder Sir Henry, it seemed possible to me that each part, the bodkin and the wooden brace, had first some other use, and was modified to do evil. If I could discover their original service I might find who had turned them to murder.

I had already tried to uncover the origin of the bodkin, with no success. Perhaps I would have better luck with the wooden knob.

Lord Gilbert and Sir Roger had likely retired to the solar after dinner, and I might there have sought their opinion of the object I had taken from the fetid water of the moat. I decided not to disturb them when I had only more questions, but no answers. Perhaps I should have done so. I might have learned its original purpose sooner.

The day had turned gloomy and as I stood before the drawbridge a light mist began to fall. The page had coiled his damp rope and awaited further instruction. I sent him back to his work at the marshalsea and turned to Mill Street and my home. I had become weary of my quest for a murderer, and I knew from experience that an hour or two with my Kate and Bessie would improve my ill humor.

The sun which had warmed the morning ride with Lord Gilbert and Sir Roger was now hidden behind low clouds. The mist which drove me from the castle moat soon became a gentle rain. I did not hesitate at Shill Brook to gaze into the water, but hastened to Galen House. The bell atop the tower of St Beornwald's Church rang for nones as I approached my door.

Rain had brought a chill to the afternoon, so I was pleased to be able to draw a bench beside the fire and steam myself dry while Kate stirred the pease pottage which would be our supper. No pork flavored the bland meal, for 'twas a fast day. I drew the pear-shaped lump of wood from my pouch, told my spouse where I had found it, and gave her my opinion of its purpose.

Kate took the thing delicately in her fingertips, as if it was yet bloody from use, and examined it in silence.

"The bodkin was fixed to this hole?" she asked, pointing to the cavity drilled into the end of the knob.

"Aye, so I believe. If not to this piece of wood, then to another very much like it."

"Why not throw the bodkin and wood into the moat together?" Kate asked.

"I have asked myself the same question. When the murderer thrust the iron into Sir Henry's ear the bodkin would have been forced against the wood and deep into the knob, but when the felon attempted to draw the point from Sir Henry's skull it was likely loosened from the wooden base. The bodkin was not fixed to the wood, so when the point entered Sir Henry's ear it was caught there and remained when the murderer tried to pull it free."

"If so, how did the felon free it from Sir Henry's ear?" Kate asked.

"'Twas not held so fast as it would have been had it been driven through another place in the skull. There is an opening in the bone within the ear, and a man's skull is weaker there."

"Oh," Kate said with a wrinkled lip. "A woman's also, I presume?"

"Aye. For all of our differences, for which much thanks to God, we are much alike."

Kate looked to the floor, where Bessie played with a wooden spoon, and spoke again. "Our differences will become plain soon. Bessie will have a sister or brother come Candlemas."

"I have guessed as much," I admitted.

Kate seemed disappointed. Her brow furrowed. "How so?" she asked.

"You take little or nothing to break your fast," I said. "And last Friday I heard you retching in the toft when I departed for the castle."

"Oh... I thought to surprise you with the news. You are pleased?"

"Indeed so."

"I had forgot," Kate continued, "that you are a bailiff and 'tis your business to bring hidden things to light."

"'Tis a gloomy business, and one I sometimes wish to abandon."

Kate was startled into silence for a time. "What would we do, if you did so?" she finally said.

"Return to Oxford. I have some reputation there as a competent surgeon. If enough folk do themselves harm I might keep the wolf from our door. And we would have the rent from your dowry house."

"I have grown fond of Galen House," Kate said, "and Bampton, also. Could you not find enough custom here?"

"I think not. If I surrender my post as Lord Gilbert's bailiff but remain in Bampton I fear we will soon be paupers."

"Perhaps your melancholy will pass."

"If I discover who did murder in Bampton Castle my spirits will improve, I think, but each day which passes seems to take me farther from a resolution, not nearer."

"I find," Kate said, "that on such a dreary day my mood is often as low as the clouds. Perhaps the sun will appear tomorrow and improve your humor."

"I wish it may be so."

We sat in silence for a time, then Kate returned to the subject of the knob and bodkin.

"You think the felon wished you or Sir Roger to find evidence of a squire's guilt, so kept the bodkin to serve the purpose, but cast away the wooden part of the tool?"

"Aye. But why not leave both parts where they might be found? It may be that the knob points more to the murderer than the bodkin does, and that is why the felon cast it away. If I can discover where it came from I may be on the trail of the murderer."

In truth my disposition began to recover at that moment, for Bessie had tired of counting her toes and toddled to my knee, begging to be held. I approved her request and spent the next hour jabbering with my daughter, escaping all thoughts of murder, and enjoying the warmth of the fire. Did I really wish to give up my post and my place in Bampton because of the vexation I felt at not yet discovering who had slain Sir Henry? By the time Kate ladled our supper into bowls and set them upon our table

I was ready to return to the search for a murderer. Perhaps it is a duty of children, although they know it not, to cheer their parents with the simplicity of a childlike joy and trust.

I brought a bucket of water from the well, and after Kate washed our bowls, nursed Bessie, and took her to bed, we sat together on the bench enjoying what warmth remained upon the hearth. The rain had ceased, but drops lingered upon the glass of our windows, and the cloudy evening grew dark early.

"When I think that I have sorted out the trail of evidence leading to Sir Henry's murder," I complained, "some new event or clue comes to muddle the business."

"And I know you well," Kate said. "You wish things to be orderly, tied up in neat bundles."

"Aye, but life is oft a muddle. I get my bundles knotted and tidy and someone comes by and cuts the cord and all is in disarray again."

"Perhaps such folk are the Lord Christ's tool to keep us from thinking too highly of our accomplishments. We need to see our plans and the things we have achieved laid waste so as to keep us humble."

"If so, the Lord Christ has achieved His purpose. I am no nearer discovering Sir Henry's murderer than when I was first summoned to the castle last Wednesday. Each day I fail to find the felon serves to increase my humility and thereby improve my standing before the Lord Christ."

Kate's brow furrowed. "Does failure then bring us closer to God than success? Does the Lord Christ not wish you to prevail over a felon?"

I thought upon her words for some time before I replied. "The Lord Christ wishes men to attain success, I think, so long as their desires accord with His will. But if a man reaches his goal and is convinced his own competence is responsible for the achievement, he will not likely seek the Lord Christ in humility, nor share with Him other men's praise."

"So failure is better for the soul than success?" Kate asked.

"Depends upon the soul," I replied. "If a man blunders at all he does, will he not soon lose heart? How then can he achieve any success, for himself or anyone else?"

"So then 'tis best for a man to sometimes succeed, and sometimes fail?"

"Aye. For life in this world success is necessary, but for assurance of life with the Lord Christ in heaven, some failure, and the abasement it brings, is perhaps needful. There are few prideful men in heaven, I think."

"Is the Lord Christ teaching you humility and preparing your soul for heaven because you have not yet discovered a felon?"

"Mayhap it is too soon to say. But I must learn to be content, after I have done my best, whether I succeed in some matter or fail. I must do my work, without allowing it to disturb the peace of my soul. The Lord Christ commands that we serve others, but I must not forget Him whilst I do so."

"You have come near to that?" Kate asked.

"Aye, but you and Bessie have reminded me of my duty."

"Duty to the Lord Christ or duty to men?"

"Is there a difference? I am thinking that a responsibility to one is a responsibility to both."

"It is your duty to God, then, to find who has slain Sir Henry... and a duty to Sir Henry, also, though he is not here to appreciate your effort?"

"Aye, as you say. And a duty to the Lady Margery and Lady Anne as well."

"Unless one was a party to the murder," Kate said.

"Even then, for if the sin goes undiscovered the guilty may never seek forgiveness of the Lord Christ, and imperil their soul because of my malfeasance."

"You will save the felon by discovering who 'tis and sending him to the gallows?"

"Aye. Strange as it may seem, the felon who goes undiscovered may be in greater peril than the one who is found out, if not in this world, then surely in the next. The man whose sin is revealed, and who faces the noose, has time and a strong goad to acknowledge his felony before the Lord Christ and seek His pardon, but he whose offense remains hidden may never appeal to the Lord Christ for His grace."

The embers upon the hearth had burned down to a faint glow, as eventually did our discourse. Kate and I sat silently upon the bench as darkness came upon the town, and only reluctantly did I break the spell and suggest we seek our bed.

Chapter 10

Tuesday dawned as bleak as Monday eve, so cloudy and grey that even Kate's rooster seemed uncertain of the time and produced but a half-hearted call to proclaim the new day. He need not have troubled himself. I awoke when Bessie announced that she wished to break her fast, and although Kate must deal with the demand, my thoughts kept me from renewing slumber even though there was but a hint of dawn in the eastern sky.

I lay warm under the blanket and considered the events of the past six days while Kate placed Bessie back in her bed and departed our bedchamber. I listened to Kate begin the day, and tried to order my thoughts so as to find some pattern in events which would point to a murderer. I was not successful, and Bessie began to stir again in her cot, so I climbed from my bed, dressed myself, and carried Bessie to the stairs.

The morning Angelus Bell had rung some time past, but I was in no hurry to begin the day. I lingered over my morning loaf and ale, considering and then discarding one measure for discovering a felon after another. I could not decide how I would proceed this day, when a thumping upon Galen House door took the matter from my hands.

'Twas John Chamberlain who again found me with my mouth full of maslin loaf. I saw in his eyes that some great matter troubled him and soon discovered my conjecture true.

"'Tis Sir John," he said. "His page took him a loaf and ale this morning to break his fast and found him dead. All bloody he is, too. His wound opened in the night. Lord Gilbert would have you come. Nothing to be done for the man, but you should see what has happened."

I suspected immediately that murder had been done again in Bampton Castle, for the wound across Sir John's ribs which I had stitched closed Sunday afternoon was not likely to reopen, nor was it deep enough to cause a man to bleed to death if it did so. I kept my thoughts to myself, downed the last of my ale, gathered a pouch of instruments should I find that some were needed, and followed John into the mud of Church View Street. Rain had begun to fall again.

Somber faces greeted me in the castle hall. Sir John may have had a temper – what knight does not? – but from the leaden expressions I saw upon the faces of members of Sir Henry's household, I believe the knight was esteemed.

I followed the chamberlain through the hall to the passage which led to Sir John's chamber. Lord Gilbert and Sir Roger greeted me at the chamber door and I saw immediately that at least a part of what John had said at Galen House door was true.

Sir John lay upon a mattress, soaked in blood from neck to knees. He had slept only in braes, and the linen was also sodden with gore.

"The wound you closed burst open in the night," Lord Gilbert said. There was an accusation in his voice.

I did not immediately reply, but walked to the dead man and bent to examine the wound. The light was poor, but I could see no other wound than the one I had closed, and it was true that the cut I had stitched was now open, a half-dozen or more stitches ruptured.

I looked about the chamber and saw drops of blood upon the flags and even a few scattered low on the wall beside the bed.

"You think he was in pain in the night," Lord Gilbert asked, "and thrashed about, undoing your work?"

"Nay," I replied. "He was stabbed."

"What? Who would do so? William? Surely it was but the thread you used which broke. Perhaps he twisted wrongly in his sleep."

"Six or more stitches have been cut through, not broken."

I searched in my pouch and brought from it the spool of silken thread I had used two days past to close Sir John's laceration. From the spool I cut a length as long as my arm, gave it to Lord Gilbert, and invited him to break it. He wrapped it about his hands and yanked against the silk. The thread did not yield, but Lord Gilbert did. His mouth tightened in pain as the silk cut into his hands and he quickly relaxed his grip.

"Not easily broken," he said with a grimace.

"You could pull against one end, and Sir Roger against the other, and the silk would likely not break. No man could toss upon his bed and break the silk, as you see. It was cut. Some man put a dagger into Sir John in the same place he was slashed, hoping all would believe he had died of the first wound, not of a second."

Lord Gilbert looked from his tender hands to the floor and wall. "Why is blood so scattered about?"

"Fought for his life," Sir Roger said. "Whoso did this thought that in his wounded condition 'twould be child's play to drive a blade into him."

"Sir Roger speaks true," I said. "When I saw him yesterday he was mending well. William's slash had weakened him but little."

"Then whoso did this murder will be splashed with Sir John's blood, eh?" Lord Gilbert said.

"Likely, though the felon will probably discard his apparel rather than send it to be laundered," I said.

There would be no keeping this death or its cause hidden. Lady Margery, Lady Anne, Sir Geoffrey, Robert de Cobham, Walter, and several other valets and grooms to both Sir Henry and Lord Gilbert crowded the passageway outside the chamber door. Squire William was absent, which, given his falling out with Sir John two days past, caused Sir Roger to assume guilt.

"I told you," he said to me, "that we should have seized that squire when we found the bodkin and bloody cloth in his chamber. We will do so now."

Squire Robert heard the sheriff, as did all who clogged the passageway outside the chamber. "William did not do this murder," Robert said.

"Oh?" Sir Roger replied. "Why do you say so?"

"William's nose vexes him much. He could not sleep. I heard him tossing and groaning upon his bed and could find no rest myself, so I arose and lighted a cresset and sat with William all the night."

"All the night? 'Til dawn?"

"Aye."

"What did you speak of?"

"What young men commonly talk about... glory in battle and fair maids and such."

"Where is William now?" Sir Roger demanded.

"In our chamber, resting, his eyes all black and his nose purple. I heard the fuss and came to see what it was about."

"Come," Sir Roger said to Lord Gilbert and me, "we'll take this fellow back to his chamber and seek a bloody cotehardie. I'll wager both came here to slay Sir John. One held him down and the other delivered the thrust."

'Twas a gamble the sheriff would have lost. I told Sir Geoffrey to allow no man to enter Sir John's chamber, and moments later we found William, as Robert said we would, restless upon his bed, his face all bloated and

154

discolored from the combined effects of Sir John's blow and my remedy. The sheriff and I ransacked the squires' chests, peered under their mattresses, and I examined their fingernails. We found no trace of blood. If one or both plunged a blade into Sir John they had been uncommonly thorough in covering the deed. Sir Roger demanded their daggers, and these also were free of any sign of blood. If they had been wiped clean there was no stained cloth hidden in the fireplace this day to expose a felony.

Sir Roger does not like to be proven wrong. Neither do I, which is why I have learned to avoid appearing assured of my knowledge when I am not. 'Tis better to seem wise later than foolish soonest. Sir Roger would not have appreciated the sentiment, so I held my tongue.

"Who else would have wanted Sir John dead?" Lord Gilbert asked as we returned to the dead man's chamber. I did not reply. Best to follow my own advice and remain silent.

I saw Sir Geoffrey blocking the entrance to Sir John's chamber when we returned to the passageway outside the room. The crowd was as we had left it, each pronouncing an opinion about the death. Above the other voices I heard Lady Margery's irritating soprano assuring Walter that my clumsy surgery was responsible for Sir John's demise, that no murder was done, and I said 'twas so to avoid blame for my malfeasance. She had begun to claim once again that I was also responsible for her husband's death, but heard our footsteps approach, turned, and fell silent.

"Send them all away," I said softly to Lord Gilbert. "I wish to examine Sir John and the chamber in peace and quiet, with no man peering over my shoulder to see what I am about or what I have found."

"It will be done," he said, and in a firm voice commanded all to depart. "When we gather for dinner

Master Hugh will tell us what he has found. Now we will leave him to his business."

The groom Arthur had joined the folk outside Sir John's chamber. I asked him to remain and guard the door so I might be assured of solitude whilst I studied the corpse. What I might learn from a dead man I did not know, but of one thing I was certain: if I did not examine the corpse and chamber they would tell me nothing.

The single window in the chamber faced east, which on another day might have provided good light for my work. But the morning was as dismal as a day in November, so whatever I might learn would be the result of close examination.

The blanket which had covered Sir John whilst he slept was in a rumpled pile about his ankles. If he had indeed fought his assailant he had done so without getting feet and legs free of entanglement in the blanket. This would surely be an impediment to a man struggling for his life.

The cresset in the room was not lit. The man who attacked Sir John had done so with only the light from the window to guide his stroke. The night had been heavy with clouds, but above them the moon was but four days from being full. Would this provide a man with enough light to send his dagger accurately where he would have it go? I cast my mind back to Bessie's awakening demand to be fed. Although the eastern sky had but a pale grey cast, there was enough light in our chamber that I could see Kate rise and lift Bessie from her cot. Enough light to do murder? I thought so.

I had already examined the open wound, but went to it again to see if I had overlooked some important thing. I had not, or if I did, I overlooked it again, for the only thing the gash told me was that some man had undone my work with his dagger.

The new wound had bled terribly. The thrust of the dagger had gone deep into some essential organ; the liver, perhaps, or mayhap the blade was twisted and penetrated Sir John's heart. If he fought his assailant the struggle could not have lasted long. I must remember to ask Sir Geoffrey if he had heard a man cry out in the night.

Sir John had not yet begun to stiffen. The stroke which took his life was delivered just before dawn, I thought. Had it come early in the night he would be nearly rigid now in death.

I lifted an arm and examined Sir John's fingernails. I was uncertain if any matter lay under them, for the light was poor. From my pouch I took my smallest scalpel and scraped debris from beneath the nails of the knight's left hand.

I found nothing under his thumb, but under all four fingernails I found stuff which might have been another man's skin, and under Sir John's middle fingernail the detritus was pink. Somewhere a man had a scratch, I thought. If it was upon his face I would have a murderer.

Two of Sir John's fingernails on his right hand had also some unidentifiable substance which was possibly another man's skin, although there was no dark stain which might have been blood.

Sir John's eyes, unlike Sir Henry's, were closed in death. Perhaps after the struggle with his slayer, he sank back upon his pillow and, weak from loss of blood, closed his eyes in endless sleep.

I was about to turn my attention to the blood-spattered wall when I caught sight of a small reddish stain upon the knight's lips. A man's lips are reddish, and a woman's also, so in the dim light I nearly missed the indistinct smudge, faint as it was.

Sir John's lips parted easily enough, rigor mortis only just beginning. I expected to see that he had bitten his tongue in the pain of his wound or in the struggle which had apparently followed. Not so. Sir John's tongue was whole, but between his clenched teeth I discovered a tiny bit of flesh.

Somewhere within Bampton Castle there was a man missing a bit of an ear or a finger or some other accessible portion of his anatomy. If the tiny wound and the scratch were in a visible place my search for Sir John's murderer would end soon, although such a discovery might tell me nothing of who murdered Sir Henry. On the other hand, it might.

I covered Sir John with the blanket and then turned my attention to the wall, where I counted eleven spots of blood surely spattered there when murder was done. Upon the planks of the floor I found five more stains. Was this Sir John's blood, or had he injured his assailant enough that his slayer's blood mingled with his own? I thought not. The reddish tissue I found under a fingernail would not produce a gash large enough to leave even one drop of blood, nor would the tiny bit of flesh I found between his teeth.

I left the chamber, convinced that I had learned what I could, and found Arthur planted squarely before the door. I thanked the groom for his service, and was a little surprised at his reply.

"You'd a' had companions was I not 'ere."

"Oh? Who?"

"Near all the gentlefolk what's in the castle but for Lord Gilbert an' Sir Roger."

"Did any ask of me?"

"Nay. I scowled at 'em, see, so they held their peace and walked on past as like they had some business what took 'em here."

Arthur's scowl is more effective than most, as it comes from the face of a burly man with broad shoulders and stump-like thighs under his cotehardie. My frown is not nearly so effective.

"Lady Margery come past twice, once with Lady Anne," Arthur said.

"'Tis near time for dinner," I said, "and Lord Gilbert will want to know what I have learned. 'Twould be well if you remained here to see that no man enters until Lord Gilbert and the sheriff approve."

Arthur tugged at a forelock and I left him and sought the hall. Grooms had erected tables for dinner, and most of the castle inhabitants were present, their conversations a low hum filling the hall. When I was seen this discourse ended and the hall fell silent.

I did not wish all present to hear my words to Lord Gilbert and Sir Roger, so asked if I might speak to them privily in the solar. My employer nodded, motioned to the sheriff to lead, and we three set off for the stairs.

"What is it?" Lord Gilbert asked when the oaken door was shut.

"Somewhere in your castle there is a man who has been scratched and bitten when he did murder," I said, and explained what I had found in Sir John's chamber.

Lord Gilbert looked to Sir Roger and spoke. "Did you see any man in the hall just now who appeared scratched or bitten?"

The sheriff puzzled over the question for a moment before he replied. "Nay... of course, I wasn't seeking any such wounds. When we return we must be alert. The fellow cannot escape us, I think. Sir John has caught his murderer for us."

The sheriff's optimism was misplaced. We returned to the hall but neither I nor Lord Gilbert nor Sir Roger saw anything amiss upon face or form of any man, gentleman or commons, who took his dinner in the hall that day.

Conversation in the hall was muted, as all who dined there knew that among us was a felon, and perhaps two. Such thoughts lead a man to considering whether or not he might also have unwittingly made an enemy and so become the next victim. Such considerations do little to promote appetite or discourse.

Only Squire William of the castle residents was absent from the meal. Whether that was due to the injury to his nose or to his pride I cannot tell. As in the past few days when I dined in the hall, I watched for some behavior which might indicate a troubled conscience. I saw none.

As the meal ended I saw John Chamberlain escort a man into the hall. The fellow was mud-spattered, as if he had been riding hard upon the roads. The newcomer strode straight to the high table and leaned over to speak to Sir Roger.

Chapter 11

Lord Gilbert required of me that I rejoin him and Sir Roger in the solar when dinner was done. A sergeant, he said, had just arrived with news that on the previous day a brawl between students of Merton College and town folk of Oxford had got out of hand. Such altercations have in the past often become riots lasting for days, with bloodshed and death. King Edward would not be pleased should his realm be so troubled, and would doubtless hold Sir Roger responsible if students and town folk ran amuck whilst he was in Bampton. The sheriff's horse was being saddled at this moment so he might speedily return to Oxford and with a brace of sergeants knock a few heads to bring a halt to the melee.

The sheriff had been of little help, yet I was sorry to see him and his sergeants leave Bampton. But it was as Sir Roger himself had said: he was best suited for enforcing the law at sword point, and seemed elated to mount his beast and be off to a conflict.

Lord Gilbert, Lady Petronilla, and I bid Sir Roger "farewell" and watched as he and the sergeants thundered across the drawbridge and set their mounts toward Shill Brook and Oxford in an easy, ground-consuming canter. The sheriff would be at Oxford Castle by late afternoon and would, I was certain, plunge with enthusiasm into the business of restraining youthful miscreants. I wished the discovery of murderers might bring me as much fulfillment as cracking recalcitrant skulls brought to Sir Roger.

"Well," Lord Gilbert said when the sheriff had disappeared on his way, "we are on our own. Lady Margery continually harps on about returning to Bedford. I have told her that Sir Roger will not permit it until the felon who slew her husband is found. Now we seek two murderers. Truth be told, I'd like to be rid of her." I saw Lady Petronilla nod agreement, then squint as if the movement caused her head to ache. "What do you think?" Lord Gilbert continued. "Are you near to uncovering the truth?"

"Perhaps there are two murderers now to be found," I replied. "Or perhaps one who has slain two. Am I near to exposing the guilty? I suppose so. But how near I cannot say. I am like a man told to travel such and such a road to a destination, which he will recognize when he arrives, but not told how far he must go to reach the place. I have found reason to believe various members of Sir Henry's household guilty of his murder, but then find reason to think my first assessment in error."

"Have you new evidence, other than what you found in Sir John's chamber?"

I remembered the knob-shaped piece of wood and drew it from my pouch. "Yesterday, when we went riding, I saw this in the moat, and fished it out. What do you make of it?"

I wished to learn if Lord Gilbert would draw the same conclusion I had about the object, so allowed him to study the thing without benefit of my opinion.

"Some man has carved away the edges, and there is a hole at the end. Hmmm... and here are four small holes in a row."

Lord Gilbert voiced his thoughts as they came to him, turning the knob in his hands all the while.

"You would not have this in your pouch, nor would you place it in my hands, except that you believe it has to do with Sir Henry's murder. Is this not so?"

I nodded agreement.

Lady Petronilla peered at the knob as Lord Gilbert turned it in his hand. "The bodkin which pierced Sir Henry fit into that hole, did it not?" she said.

"So I believe."

"What of the four small holes?" Lord Gilbert said. "They are little more than pin pricks."

"Perhaps that is what they are," Lady Petronilla said. "Some small tacks were driven in to hold some other thing in place."

"If so, the tacks were small," Lord Gilbert said.

"If I knew what was held in place against the wood," I said, "I might learn to what use the thing was put."

"And knowing that might lead to a felon?" Lord Gilbert asked.

"It might. Have you thoughts as to what might have been fixed to the wood using such small nails? It must have been something which could not pull free easily, or stronger fasteners would have been needed."

Lord Gilbert held the object at arm's length the better to see it, as he is afflicted, like many of his years, with blurring vision when an object is too close before him. I have told him that in London he might purchase bits of polished glass which are made to perch upon one's nose, and with which he might see more clearly when he studies accounts, but he will not. He yet fancies himself a young and virile knight, and believes to use such an aid is beneath his dignity.

As Lord Gilbert continued to examine the knob an image of how this perplexing object might first have been used came to mind.

"Come, m'lord," I said. "Let us visit the marshalsea."

"Something may be learned there of this thing?"

"I believe so."

Lady Petronilla fell in behind us as Lord Gilbert and I set out across the castle yard. There was bowing and tugging of forelocks as pages and grooms interrupted their work to acknowledge Lord Gilbert's presence in their quarter.

We entered the stables. Lord Gilbert swatted away a horsefly, then turned to me. "What do you seek here?"

"Saddles," I replied, and walked past a row of stalls toward the room where saddles, bridles, and such were stored. Nearly two dozen saddles crowded the storeroom, for all those belonging to Lord Gilbert and his household were there as well as those of Sir Henry's retainers. The place smelled of leather and stale horse sweat. Bridles and harnesses hung from pegs fixed into the wall of the storeroom, while saddles rested upon saw-horse-like supports. Newer saddles, and those most likely to be called for use, were nearest the entry. Older saddles, less likely to be needed, sat dust-covered in a darkened corner of the room. It was to these older saddles that I walked, holding the knob before me.

Lord Gilbert followed. Lady Petronilla remained at the entry, the space between the saddles being cramped, her nose wrinkled from the fetid smell.

"What do you seek?" Lord Gilbert asked.

"I wonder if this piece of wood might have been hacked from a saddle frame? The small holes might have been made by nails used to hold the leather cover to the frame."

"Ah, so it might be," he agreed, and he joined me in examining the little-used saddles at the far corner of the storeroom. 'Twas Lord Gilbert who found the damaged saddle.

"Hugh, look here."

I did so. The pommel of an old saddle, likely disused for years, was half gone. The brittle leather which had covered the missing wooden support hung loose. When I held the knob against this dusty leather the tack holes fit perfectly.

"Hmmm, you must question my grooms closely regarding who of Sir Henry's retainers entered this place last week. The man who pried that wood from my old saddle did murder."

"Aye, likely so," I agreed. "Perhaps two murders."

"'Twould be most convenient if it was so... two birds with one stone and all."

Lord Gilbert and Lady Petronilla departed the marshalsea and left me to question the grooms and pages who labored around the horses. This I did, and learned that Sir Geoffrey, Sir John, both squires, and even Sir Henry's valets and grooms were commonly seen about the stables. A knight's beasts are valuable and their condition is important to him. If one of these had spent time in the storeroom, none noticed or remembered. I had discovered the source of the knob likely used to force a bodkin into Sir Henry's ear, but there seemed no way to discover who had hacked it free of an old, dusty saddle.

I crossed the castle yard to the hall, where I hoped to find Sir Geoffrey. His chamber was adjacent to Sir John's, and I thought it likely he might have heard some clamor in the night as Sir John unsuccessfully fought his attacker.

I found the knight in conversation with Lady Margery. My appearance was not welcome. As I approached, the two ceased their talk and glared in such a manner as to bring frost to the hall windows. But a man whose position requires him to sometimes ask unwanted questions becomes immune to hostile scowls.

"Sir Geoffrey," I said, "I give you good day. You awoke this morning to a sorry business."

The knight said nothing, nor did his expression change. My view of Sir John's death seemed agreed upon, so I continued.

"You saw his chamber, and his blood spattered upon the wall. He fought his assailant. Did you hear the struggle? Did Sir John cry out?"

"Nay. Heard nothing. I'm a heavy sleeper. Comes from seizing what slumber I could when marching to battle with Sir Henry, I suppose."

"Who of Sir Henry's household disliked Sir John?"

"Bah," Lady Margery snorted. 'Twas most unbecoming of a lady. "There was no affray in Sir John's chamber last night. You seek to persuade us there was, so to disguise your incompetence." And with that indictment she stood and stalked toward the stairs. But before she reached the end of the hall she turned and spoke again.

"Lady Anne saw a rat this morning running from the brew house. You would be more observant of your duty as Lord Gilbert's bailiff were you to lay traps than to seek murderers where none are so as to hide your unfitness for your position."

And with that she lifted her nose and walked off toward her chamber. I looked back to Sir Geoffrey. His face remained inscrutable.

"Lady Margery," I said, attempting to be as tactful as possible, "is not schooled in herbs nor surgery, and so is mistaken about Sir John's death. He was slain last night. Of that there can be no doubt."

"Then why, if he fought his murderer, did I not hear? I sleep soundly, the walls are of stone, and the doors to the chambers of oak, yet it seems a man in such circumstance would have shouted loudly in his distress. I believe Lady Margery speaks true. You seek to cover your failure. I will speak to Lord Gilbert about this. Lady Margery wishes to be away from this place, and I agree 'tis past time we were gone... before you slay another of Sir Henry's household with your incompetence."

"Sir Roger requires that Lady Margery remain in Bampton until I have found a murderer... or two murderers."

"Hah. We should then never leave, for there are none. And were there felons to seek in Bampton Castle, you are not such a one as could discover them."

Sir Geoffrey rose from his bench and stalked off haughtily. For one baseborn he has mastered arrogance. I contemplated telling the fellow that my father had been a knight, but considered that if a man must tell another that he is of high birth, his manner must not reflect it, and so held my tongue.

But about one thing Lady Margery was correct. If rats had invaded Bampton Castle 'twas my duty as much as any man's to see that they were caught. I left the hall to visit the fewterer. Lord Gilbert's hounds would be of no use catching rats, but there were terriers in the kennels, useful for such a purpose. I could not spend all of my waking hours seeking murderers when there was other castle business to be done.

A man who seeks felons must find evidence of guilt where he can. But what if the evidence is flawed? I mistrusted Sir Geoffrey's words. Perhaps he did hear as Sir John was slain; mayhap he even heard the dying man call out a name. Or perhaps he was the felon, although no man, nor woman either, had spoken of bad blood between the two knights, nor had I witnessed any strife between them.

And what of Walter? He said that he had placed only a thimbleful of crushed lettuce seed into Sir Henry's wine, but what if he lied? How was I to know? And if he did speak falsely, why would he do so? Did he hold some murderous grudge against Sir Henry? If so, no man had spoken of it.

Squire Robert claimed that he sat wakeful all last night, keeping William company in his distress. How could I learn if this was true?

In the matter of Sir Henry's death all men proclaimed innocence and ignorance, but one, or perhaps more, lied. So it had come to this: that I must trust no man, and assume all were dishonest until I could prove them otherwise. When I had proven the honesty of all but one or two, those must be the felons. But confirming the truthfulness of the innocent may be as difficult as finding out the guilty.

I returned to the solar. Lord Gilbert must know that, with Sir Roger away, his guests were considering departing Bampton.

"Hah," he said when told. "I'm of two minds. I'd be pleased to see them away, and be rid of the lot. But Sir Henry, for all of his faults, was a valiant knight and 'twould be a disservice to him to allow his murderer to escape justice. Be at ease. I will speak this hour to Lady Margery and whether she likes it or not she will remain my guest until you have found who murdered Sir Henry. How much longer, you think?"

"I cannot say, m'lord."

"Well, do be quick about it. Lady Margery and I think alike. We would both prefer her gone from here."

Lord Gilbert's kennels lay beside the marshalsea. I found Gerald the fewterer brushing matted fur from one of Lord Gilbert's hounds and told him to put his terriers to work near to the brew house and bake house. He tugged a forelock and promised to do so as soon as he had completed the task at hand.

The gloomy weather was beginning to lift. The sky was yet clouded, but here and there a glimpse of blue sky was visible as the wind from the north broke and tattered the clouds. The breeze would soon dry the roads, and I might enter Galen House this evening with shoes free of mud.

The thought of my home was appealing, and as I

had no plan in mind to advance the search for Sir John's murderer, I set out for Mill Street.

Shill Brook ran high, its water muddy from the dirt of the fields washed into its flow by the recent rain. Too much water obscured the stream bed. So it was with the murders in Bampton Castle. There was evidence everywhere I looked; so much that it seemed but to obscure the truth of the matter.

Kate was eager to learn of Sir John's death, and when I told her of the business she cast her eyes down to her hands, which lay folded in her lap, and said, "So much evil is come upon the castle. Who next will die, I wonder?"

Here was a thought that I had not entertained. Resolved as I was to find who had murdered Sir Henry and now Sir John, I had not considered that there might be others in Sir Henry's household whose lives were at risk. But how could I know who these might be if I did not know why Sir Henry and Sir John had been slain, so as to seek some commonality?

"You believe two deaths may be followed by a third?" I said. "Why do you say so?"

I wondered if the Lord Christ had given my Kate some insight which He withheld from me, or if she saw matters in Bampton Castle more clearly from watching from a distance.

Kate shrugged and pursed her lips. "No reason," she said. "But my father says misfortunes always come in threes."

I had no wish to contradict my father-in-law, and as he had the wisdom of years, considered that he might speak true. I made no reply, but thought on this new and unappealing notion. Was there another man, or perhaps a woman, lodged in Bampton Castle, whose life was in danger? So far death had come only to Sir Henry and a knight in his household. Did danger lurk within the castle walls for Lord Gilbert and Lady Petronilla and their retainers also?

I had thought that Sir Henry's death involved some dark matter within his household; his debts, perhaps, or his unhappy wife and daughter foremost in my considerations. But what if none of these were so? Perhaps some other wickedness was hidden in Sir Henry's retinue.

While I considered this new and unwelcome notion Kate set a footed pan upon the coals of the hearth and began preparing hanoney for our supper. She continued her part of the conversation but I confess to inattention, being lost in apprehension of more deaths at Bampton Castle. Her words finally penetrated my musing, and I asked her to repeat what she had said.

Kate frowned in exasperation. "Something is at the eggs. I found three this morning broken and eaten."

"Nothing has taken a hen?" I asked.

"Nay, they are all accounted for."

"Then 'tis no fox or badger that has been in the henhouse, or a hen or two would be gone. I will see to the coop after supper. Perhaps a board has come loose and a rat has got in. A rat was seen in the castle not long past."

"There will be more eggs in your hanoney if you can stop the thief."

Chapter 12

"Sir Geoffrey wishes to bury Sir John this day," Lord Gilbert said when I greeted him next morn. "What say you? Have you any objection?"

I had none. John Chamberlain was in attendance upon Lord Gilbert when I arrived at the solar, and he was sent to tell Sir Geoffrey that there were no objections to burying his companion this day.

When the chamberlain had departed the solar Lord Gilbert turned to me. His face was unreadable, but his silence spoke as well as words might. He was not pleased.

Few nobles can contain their ire for long, being accustomed to seeing retainers act to satisfy them when they are vexed. We did not face each other mute for more than a few heartbeats. "How many more men will die in Bampton Castle before you seize the felon?" he said.

I dared not tell Lord Gilbert that the same question had filled me with dread since last evening. Perhaps a calamity feared may be more likely to occur. On the other hand, to ignore an approaching evil will not deflect it. I was much torn.

"Sir Roger would have had Squire William off to Oxford Castle dungeon by now," I said. "But that would not have prevented Sir John's death."

"Oh? Did not Sir John and the squire quarrel? And did that not lead to Sir John being weak and abed when he was slain?"

"Aye, it did. But whoso wished to do away with Sir John would have found opportunity even had he not lain wounded in his bed. A man who seeks to do harm to another will find his chance sooner or later. And Sir Roger's rash arrest of William would have served only to do an injustice."

"William had nothing to do, then, with either death?"

"I do not know. I think not. I have an aversion to seeing an innocent man sent to Oxford Castle dungeon."

"Ah, no wonder, as you were sent there yourself. But do you think I wish to see an innocent man do the sheriff's dance? Not so."

"Then yield me time to do justice. If you demand haste you may compel me to error."

Lord Gilbert chewed upon his lip, then spoke. "My wits are clouded. I wish Lady Margery and her household away, which cannot be if you are to find a murderer. I want two things, but can have but one."

"One at a time," I said. "I will be diligent. Discovering a felon, or two, must come first, and then Lady Margery may be away. She wishes it as much as you, I believe."

"We agree on few other things," Lord Gilbert muttered.

John Chamberlain reappeared at the door to the solar and announced that all was ready for Sir John's funeral, and would Lord Gilbert and Lady Petronilla be pleased to walk with Lady Margery and Lady Anne in the procession to St Beornwald's Church?

Lord Gilbert turned to me. "That was swift." To John he said, "Lady Petronilla is with the nurse and our children in the nursery. If she is at leisure, tell her to join me here."

She was, and appeared a few moments later. Together Lord Gilbert and Lady Petronilla descended the stairs to the hall and I followed. I had no obligation to Sir John, to mourn at his funeral, but thought attending the burial could do no harm and might be an occasion for learning something which might resolve the puzzles cast upon me.

No one spent even a farthing to hire mourners for Sir John, so only the Lady Margery's household, Lord Gilbert, Lady Petronilla, and I would follow the bier to the churchyard. Sir John lay upon two planks, shrouded in black linen. Lady Margery did not even rent a coffin to see him to his grave.

Walter and three of Sir Henry's grooms lifted Sir John, and the small procession set off for St Beornwald's churchyard. Lady Margery set up a wail, which lady Anne copied, but 'twas plain their hearts were not in it. By the time we passed Galen House their lament had faded to a whimper.

When the funeral mass was done, I was no closer to discovering the guilty than when the day had dawned. No man showed any indication of pleasure or satisfaction when Sir John was lowered into his grave, there to await the Lord Christ's return beside Sir Henry. No man gave much evidence of grief, either. Not even Sir Geoffrey.

I took my dinner at Galen House, having grown weary of dining in Bampton Castle hall, watching others to see if I could detect some guilt in their eyes or actions. This exercise came near to ruining my appetite, which, as Kate would tell you, is not easily done.

Kate had not known whether or not to expect me at our table for dinner, so had prepared but a simple repast for herself and Bessie. But I did not regret my absence from the castle hall. The pottage I consumed that day was improved by the companionship of my wife and child, which was much to be preferred over that of a shrewish woman, a haughty knight, and a covetous maid.

But I would discover no felons at Galen House, so when I had eaten my fill I kissed Bessie and my Kate and set off for the castle. I had in mind to seek Isobel, Lady Margery's lady-in-waiting, to gather more knowledge of Sir Henry's family and retinue.

Lady Petronilla, Lady Margery, Lady Anne, and their ladies and servants were all together in Lady Petronilla's chamber when I returned to the castle. So John Chamberlain said. He did not appear pleased when I told him to visit the chamber and pluck out the maid Isobel.

I awaited Isobel in my old bachelor chamber off the hall, where I had earlier questioned her before William and Sir John shattered the castle's peace. Isobel seemed less apprehensive than when she had entered the room on Sunday. Perhaps I did not seem the ogre she had first feared.

I bid her be seated upon the bench. She peered at me with some suspicion as she did so, but I did not see fear in her glance. Whether or not this was a good thing I could not decide. Most bailiffs believe their task of keeping order upon their lord's estate to be best accomplished if those who live upon the manor have a healthy fear of displeasing them. Some years past, when I was newly come to Bampton, a villein who owed four days' week work claimed illness and would not do the ditching the reeve required of him. I told the man I might cure his complaint with surgery. It was remarkable how readily he regained his health. But in the case of Isobel I could see no cause for surgery so could but trust her honesty.

"You who serve Lady Margery must speak of the deaths of Sir Henry and Sir John," I began. "What is said of these felonies?"

Isobel shrugged. "There are as many opinions as there are maids in Lady Margery's service."

"Very well. What are these theories?"

"Lady Margery has convinced Hawisa that Sir Henry and Sir John are dead of your incompetence. Judith believes that Sir Geoffrey must have had a hand in one of the murders. Perhaps both. But she does not speak of this before Lady Margery. Philippa thinks William, mayhap with Robert's assistance, and Lady Anne's knowledge, is guilty."

"What say you? You believe me guilty of malfeasance?"

Had Isobel feared me I would have no straight answer from her. She looked at me for a moment and evidently decided that she had no cause for worry, not being suspected herself, and apparently no longer concerned that she was suspect in the taking of Lord Gilbert's silver.

"I know nothing of wounds and remedies and such," she said.

"I may be responsible, then?"

"I think not. I saw Sir John's blood spattered upon the wall."

"Which of Lady Margery's attendants then do you believe closest to the truth?"

Isobel thought on the question for some time, then spoke. "None," she said softly.

"Then you must suspect some other man... or woman."

Isobel did not respond. I spoke again. "Who did Sir Henry and Sir John so anger that the angered person would do murder?"

"Many folk," Isobel finally said.

"How so?"

"Sir Henry served as Commissioner of Laborers."

I wondered how, insolvent as he was, Sir Henry had found funds to purchase the post from the King. Borrowed, probably.

"Many men serve the King's justice," I said. "Few are done to death."

"Few enforce the Statute of Laborers as did Sir Henry," she said.

"Ah... he was rigorous in preventing the commons from seeking to better themselves?"

"More than that."

"More? What do you mean?"

"He was known to extort unjust fines from tenants and laborers, and would send any who would not pay to the stocks or his dungeon."

"Is this more than rumor?"

"Aye. There were always men jailed in his manor. Some for a few days, others for a fortnight or more, 'til they paid their fines."

If Sir Henry had indeed borrowed to buy his post, here was another reason, in addition to his poverty, for him to deal harshly with any who might come before him charged with violating the statute. And if few were charged, a reason for extorting fines from laborers who had done no wrong.

"What of Sir John?"

"He and Sir Geoffrey apprehended those who were accused and brought them before Sir Henry."

"They profited from Sir Henry's extortions?"

"Aye, so it is said."

"Do you believe this to be true?"

"Aye. Many times I saw Sir Geoffrey and Sir John bring men to Sir Henry. Some had fled as far as St Albans and Northampton where they thought to find employment at better wages. Others were those who would not or could not pay the fines which Sir Henry demanded."

"Who, then, of Sir Henry's retinue with him in Bampton suffered loss because of his extortions?"

"I know not. I heard from Hawisa that Walter's father was fined for charging too much for his labor, but that was before I came to serve Lady Margery, six years past, or seven."

"What work does Walter's father do?"

"A smith, I believe."

"So you believe Sir Henry's death due to the abuse of his authority?"

"I know not what to believe. I know only that he made enemies and none with him in Bampton were among them, I think. Rather, they were his aides."

"William and Robert? Did they assist Sir Geoffrey and Sir John in seizing men who would gain more from their labor than the statute permitted?"

"Aye. Several times I saw all four ride out together."

"And they returned with men who were imprisoned 'til they could pay their fine?"

"Sometimes."

"And sometimes they returned with the coin Sir Henry wished taken from those charged with violating the law?"

"Aye. So it was said."

"But none of these folk would have come with Sir Henry to Bampton?"

"Nay. Who would wish to do so? And he would not prey upon his own retainers."

"He would not," I agreed. "But there are surely many men who, did they know of Sir Henry's murder, would not grieve."

Isobel nodded agreement.

"Is there talk of who may replace Sir Henry as Commissioner of Laborers?"

"Lady Margery says Sir Geoffrey will have the post."

"That's not all of Sir Henry's possessions he is likely to have, eh?"

Isobel blushed. "Nay," she replied.

"Will he be as rapacious of the commons as Sir Henry? He is baseborn, I am told."

"Aye, but few speak of it. Not when he or Lady Margery are close by. And he has little compassion for the commons when their money is at issue."

"Before Sir John was found dead, did Lady Margery

speak then of Sir Geoffrey replacing Sir Henry as Commissioner of Laborers?"

"I daresay. Don't remember clearly. All is a muddle. Can't remember who said what and when."

"Did Sir John seek the office also, you think? The post is not for Lady Margery to give, nor is it inherited."

"Why not? 'Twas a source of income he could have no other way."

"So with Sir Henry dead, and then Sir John, Sir Geoffrey might have two things he wanted – Lady Margery and a position he might use to extort pence and shillings to fatten his thin purse."

"Aye. And he'd not overlook even a farthing from the meanest sort. Sir Henry didn't."

"Yet 'tis said Sir Henry was needy. If he used his position to take unjustly from the commons, why did he lack funds?"

"Don't know. He had debts, and Lady Margery likes her jewels. She was much angered last year when Sir Henry sold an emerald ring without her knowledge."

"When you return to Lady Margery she will want to know of our discourse. On no account must you tell her of my questions or of your replies."

"What am I to say? She will surely ask, and so will her other ladies."

"Say that we spoke of William. 'Twill be no lie. His name was mentioned. Say I had many questions about the quarrel between William and Sir John. This also is true."

Isobel arose from the bench, but as she turned to leave the chamber a last question occurred to me.

"Can Sir Geoffrey read and write?"

"Aye. Not well, I think."

"You have seen examples of his pen?"

"Nay. Just heard Sir Henry speak to him of it once. Sir

Geoffrey was rueful that he lacked knowledge. Didn't learn to read and write 'til he entered Sir Henry's service."

Isobel departed the chamber. I remained, considering what I knew, and what I had just learned. Sir Geoffrey, I decided, had slain Sir Henry to gain a wife and an income, and when he saw these prizes threatened by Sir John, took the opportunity of Sir John's wound and quarrel with William to do another murder.

Sir Geoffrey would have access to the marshalsea, where he might have hacked a knob from an old, little-used saddle, and he had enough skill with a pen that he could write a message to Sir Roger designed to set askew any investigation.

How the knight got his hands on the pouch of crushed lettuce seeds I did not know, but thought that either Walter or Lady Margery might know something of the business. But if I asked, they would deny it, so there was no point in doing so.

And the portpain was also a puzzle. Did Sir Geoffrey have it from Lady Anne? Why so? Or from Lady Margery? This was more likely. But how would she have got it from the pantry? Was I of Sir Roger's disposition, I would have suggested that Lord Gilbert rack the knight until he told all.

There were two problems with such a business. Lord Gilbert has no rack at Bampton Castle dungeon, and a man whose arms and legs are being drawn from their sockets will say whatever is needful to end his suffering.

I climbed the stairs to the solar, where I found Lord Gilbert reading his book of hours. He looked expectantly from his devotional. When I had sought him in the past five days it was usually because I had questions or answers. Mostly questions, few answers. He waited to learn which it would be this day.

Lord Gilbert pointed to a bench near the cold hearth and invited me to sit. I did so, then told him of what I had learned from Isobel.

"The Statute of Laborers has caused much enmity," he said when I had finished. "If a gentleman pays only what the law permits, his laborers will go elsewhere, but if he pays enough to entice men to remain in his employ he will run afoul of the ordinance and be fined for his infraction."

Trust Lord Gilbert to see the matter from a gentleman's perspective, rather than that of the commons.

"Did Sir Henry fine any gentleman for paying wages above what is allowed?" he continued.

"Isobel did not say."

"Probably did," Lord Gilbert said. "He was in great want, I think. A penny is a penny, no matter whose purse it may be plucked from."

Lord Gilbert closed his book, gazed thoughtfully at the window, then continued. "Sir Geoffrey is the felon, then?"

"So it seems."

"I am sorry to hear it. He was valiant in battle."

"So was Sir Henry," I said, "but his courage did not prevent him dealing unjustly with men who deserved better."

"Will you arrest him this day? If you do so, Lady Margery can be away tomorrow."

"You believe that you have heard enough evidence against Sir Geoffrey to satisfy the King's Eyre?"

"You think not?"

"I would like to be more certain."

"Bah... you are too precise. There are few certainties in life."

"Aye. Nevertheless, I would like another day or two to seek more evidence against the man. Now that I know better where to seek for it, the proof of Sir Geoffrey's guilt may be more readily found."

"Very well. Where will you search first?"

"It may be time to press Walter."

"Sir Henry's valet? Why him?"

"He gave the sleeping draught to Sir Henry. It was his duty and he admits that he did so."

"If he admits this, why seek more from him?"

"Sir Henry was given more than a thimbleful of the stuff. Perhaps Walter did so at some other man's urging, told that it was all for Sir Henry's good."

"Sir Geoffrey?"

"Aye. It may be that Sir Geoffrey hoped the greater dose would send Sir Henry to an endless sleep. He was, nevertheless, prepared with other measures if it did not."

"Hmmm. I can see how it might have been. But what of the bodkin and bloody linen found in the squires' chamber?"

"How Sir Geoffrey got the portpain I cannot guess, but it would have been no great trouble to enter the squires' chamber and leave the incriminating stuff behind whilst they were out."

"Did the Lady Anne take the portpain with the silver, and give part of it to Sir Geoffrey?"

"If I have the wit to ask the proper questions of the proper people, we will soon know."

"Seems unlikely," Lord Gilbert said. "More likely Lady Margery might have given it to him. But that would make her complicit in her husband's murder, would it not?"

"Mayhap."

"And how did Lady Margery come by the portpain? Would she steal my linens?"

"Who can say?" I shrugged.

"You are off to see the valet, then?"

"Aye. I have heard that he and other of Sir Henry's grooms and valets play at nine man's morris in the gatehouse anteroom with Wilfred the porter and his assistant, when they have no duties to attend to. I'll first seek him there."

I bowed to my employer and backed to the door of the solar. A few moments later I stood under the portcullis and watched as Wilfred and his guests attempted to relieve each other of farthings and ha'pennies. The game ceased when my shadow darkened the door. Lord Gilbert has not forbidden his grooms and valets from gambling, but there were yet guilty expressions on five faces. No man likes his lord's bailiff to find him at some questionable business. And Sir Henry's servants surely knew the consequence of unwisely putting one's coin at risk.

The men had been kneeling upon the flags of the anteroom, but scrambled to their feet when they saw who it was who looked down upon their sport.

"Master Hugh," Wilfred said, tugging a forelock. "I give you good-day. How may I serve you?"

"'Tis Walter I seek." I motioned to the valet to follow me from the gatehouse and saw his companions exchange questioning glances as he fell in behind me.

I wished to speak privily to the valet, so took him also to my old bachelor chamber off the hall. I did not want Sir Geoffrey to come upon us suddenly and see me in serious conversation with Walter. He might assume what I was about.

Silence may be as great a menace as threatening words to those who hold secrets. I did not speak to Walter as we crossed the castle yard from the gatehouse to the hall. When we entered my old chamber I motioned for him to sit upon the bench, then walked behind him to the window, where I gazed out upon the castle yard and made pretense of collecting my thoughts. After a few minutes of this sham I faced him and spoke.

"You told me that you prepared Sir Henry's wine with a thimbleful of the sleeping draught I provided. Is this not so?"

"Aye."

"But when I inspected the pouch, much more than that was missing... Who told you to give Sir Henry a greater dose? Sir Geoffrey? Lady Margery? Sir John?"

Walter glared at me indignantly. "I provided only what you required. A thimbleful. No man told me to increase the dose."

"'Twas your own choice, then, to give Sir Henry more of the crushed lettuce seeds than was meet? Did he request it?"

"Nay. 'Tis not what I meant. No man, nor woman either, told me to give him more than was asked, nor did I do so."

"Someone did. If not you, who would do so?"

"Don't know. After Sir Henry drank the draught I left his chamber."

"Leaving the pouch of crushed lettuce seeds upon his table?"

"Aye. Just so."

"And you saw no man nearby, in the corridor outside Sir Henry's chamber, perhaps?"

Walter was silent. Here is a question he does not wish to answer, I thought at the time.

"Who did you see?"

Walter studied the back of his right hand, evidently considering his words and his fingernails. The silence grew oppressive, but I said no more, allowing the valet to soak in his discomfort.

"Sir Geoffrey was there," he said finally.

"He saw you leave Sir Henry's chamber?"

"Aye."

"Did he speak?"

"Aye. Asked if Sir Henry slept. I told him, 'Nay,' but should do so soon, if your potion was successful."

"What did Sir Geoffrey say then?"

"Said no more. Went to 'is chamber an' I went to the stairs and sought my own bed."

"You saw no more of Sir Henry, or Sir Geoffrey, 'til next morning?"

"Aye."

"Has Sir Geoffrey spoken privily to you since Sir Henry was found dead?"

Once again the valet seemed reluctant to answer. I took his silence as answer enough, and continued.

"What did he say?"

"Said as how I was not to tell you or Sir Roger that I saw 'im after I'd given Sir Henry the potion. An' if any man pressed me on the matter I was to say 'twas Sir John I met in the corridor."

"Why would you do so if it was not so?"

"Sir Geoffrey said 'e'd make it worth my while to do so… but if I said 'twas 'im I saw, I'd suffer for it."

"Why do you speak of it to me, then? Sir John is dead, and cannot refute the allegation if you tell me it was him you saw outside Sir Henry's chamber. Sir Geoffrey is hale and healthy. Do you not fear his vengeance for speaking of this?"

"I did. That's why I would not tell of it before. But I see now 'tis a coward's part I've played. Sir Henry wasn't a bad master, an' didn't deserve to die as 'e did."

"At Sir Geoffrey's hand, you think?"

"Suppose so. Been tryin' to think who else could've done the murder."

"And…?"

"Don't see anyone else as havin' reason or chance to do it."

"Not Squire William?"

"Thought at first it might be 'im as slew Sir Henry. Sir Henry was about to dismiss 'im, I think."

"Because he was unhappy that Lady Anne esteemed the lad?"

"Aye. An' was he away there'd be one less retainer to provide for."

"And a loss of reputation in the eyes of his peers. No knight would willingly keep fewer knights and squires in his household."

"Suppose so. Don't know much of that sort of thing amongst gentlefolk."

"I am told that Sir Henry angered many folk around Bedford. He was a Commissioner of Laborers, charged with enforcing the Statute of Laborers, as you will know. 'Tis said he was unjust in the fines he levied."

"Don't know about that," Walter said. "Wasn't my business. Who said so?"

I made no reply, but thought it odd that Lady Margery's ladies-in-waiting would know more of Sir Henry's affairs than his valet, and that Walter would not speak of the fine his father had been required to pay some years past.

"Will the sheriff arrest Sir Geoffrey?" Walter asked.

"If there is evidence of his guilt," I replied.

"Does evidence point to any other?"

"Some does," I said. I did not wish for the valet to think the matter resolved, when I was yet uncertain myself. At that moment I did not believe Sir Geoffrey guiltless, but thought another might be involved. Who, I could not say. And without more proof the King's Eyre would likely set him free. I might send a commoner to the gallows with the evidence I had, but not a gentleman. Not even a gentleman who was once of the commons.

Chapter 13

I sent Walter on his way and returned to the solar. For what I wished to do next I would need Lord Gilbert's aid. I wanted to interrogate Lady Anne.

"What did you learn from the valet?" Lord Gilbert asked.

"He saw Sir Geoffrey in the corridor outside Sir Henry's chamber, just after Sir Henry had consumed the sleeping draught."

"Sir Geoffrey's chamber is there. Where else would he be if he was going to his bed?"

"He told Walter to say, did anyone ask it of him, that 'twas Sir John he saw... said he would do well by him if he did so, but the valet would find trouble if he told the truth."

"Why, then, did he do so? Does he no longer fear Sir Geoffrey's wrath?"

"My thoughts also," I replied. "Walter said Sir Henry was a good lord and deserved better."

"So he will now speak the truth when he would not six days past?"

"So he said."

"You believe this?"

"I've no reason not to."

"And what of the sleeping draught? You said much of the herb was missing from the pouch. Did Walter provide it to Sir Henry?"

"He said not."

"Then who did?"

"Perhaps Sir Geoffrey went to Sir Henry, found him yet awake, and offered to fetch more wine so he could take more of the potion."

"Would Sir Henry take this act of kindness from a man he knew wished to steal his wife?"

"Why not? He had already perhaps consumed some of the crushed lettuce seeds, to no effect, good or ill, so would have seen no reason to reject such an offer."

"What if, when Sir Geoffrey returned with the wine, he had put some other substance into it?"

"Poison?"

"Aye."

"When I tasted the dregs in Sir Henry's cup I could detect no off flavor."

"Are there no poisons which are tasteless?" Lord Gilbert asked.

"There are some. But if he poisoned Sir Henry's wine, why pierce him with a bodkin?"

"Wanted to be sure of Sir Henry's death, I suppose. But you think poison unlikely?"

"Aye," I said. "I do. The increased dose of my potion would have sent Sir Henry to a deep sleep, so that a man might do him to death without awakening him."

"Then arrest Sir Geoffrey and let's be done with this matter. Send him to Sir Roger and let the King's Eyre sort out the details."

"I have yet a few questions."

"For whom?"

"Lady Anne. Would you send John Chamberlain to request that she join us here?"

"What do you expect to learn from her?" Lord Gilbert asked.

"If I knew her replies I would not need to ask of her."

"Oh… aye, just so. Very well. Seek John and tell him to request Lady Anne's presence in the solar."

I did so. John was easily found, but he must have had some difficulty locating Lady Anne, for I returned to the solar and with Lord Gilbert waited nearly an hour before Lady Anne appeared.

Wealth can stiffen a man's spine, and a maid's also, I think, but poverty will undermine confidence. Sir Henry and his daughter were needy. John Chamberlain ushered Lady Anne into the solar and her apprehension was clear.

Lord Gilbert and I stood, and my employer motioned to Lady Anne to take the best chair. He dismissed John, and I seated myself on a bench while Lord Gilbert resumed his place.

Lady Anne had stolen the silver of one of the great barons of the realm, and even though the goods had been returned, was now facing him and his bailiff. Neither I nor Lord Gilbert had spoken a word but in greeting, yet a tear appeared upon her cheek, glistening in the light as the afternoon sun slanted through the solar windows.

Lord Gilbert looked to me and folded his arms across his broad chest. No doubt he also saw Lady Anne's reaction to this encounter. Good. Fear may be, in my experience, a great encourager of truth, especially if one fears being caught in a lie by a powerful lord, or even his bailiff.

"Six days past," I began, "you helped yourself to Lord Gilbert's spoons and knives. When you were found out, and the return of the silver was demanded, you wrapped them in linen and left them in the screens passage, near the pantry, as was demanded."

Lady Anne made no reply to this review of the matter, which I took to mean that she had no objection to the truth of the accusation. Lord Gilbert must have thought the same. He spoke next, and bluntly.

"Why did you take my silver?"

Tears coursed down both of Lady Anne's cheeks. She bit her lip, and then answered.

"I did not plan to do so."

"Then why?" Lord Gilbert said.

"I went to the screens passage to seek the butler," she sniffed. "Lady Margery wished an ewer of wine in her chamber and her ladies were all about other duties. I saw the pantry open, and a box there with silver, and no other person about."

"So you took the opportunity to seize m'lord's silver," I said, "but a page saw you leave the pantry."

"Aye," she agreed.

"You were found out. Why did you not return my silver then?" Lord Gilbert asked.

Lady Anne hesitated. "Thought as he who saw me was but a youth, and I a lady, he might not be believed if he did accuse me. I was ready to charge him with the theft."

"Why did you not do so?" I asked.

"My conscience troubled me. If Lord Gilbert was like my father, the page would hang if I was believed."

"If you thought Lord Gilbert might be like your father, why risk such a theft?"

"I am a knight's daughter, but have nothing. I once owned jewels. Not many, but I had some. Father sold them all to pay against his debts. Since the great death, crops fetch little and tenants demand reduced rents. I've had no silk or linen for a new gown these two years... nor even wool."

"Your want overcame your fear of discovery?" I asked.

"Aye. I'd no sooner returned to my chamber with the silver than I regretted the deed. But I did not know what I was to do."

"So when Walter told you that your theft was discovered, and the silver must be returned," I said, "you were not surprised that your guilt was known?"

"Nay. I expected so."

"You wrapped the spoons and knives in a portpain and left them in the screens passage, as Walter told you to do. I had promised that no man would be present to see you return the silver, and none was."

"Nay," she said. "'Twas not like that."

I looked to Lord Gilbert, and he returned my gaze, one eyebrow lifted, as is his custom when puzzled.

"How was it, then?" I asked. "How did you come by Lord Gilbert's portpain? Don't deny it. One of his portpains is missing from the pantry."

"I did not return the silver. Walter did."

"Ah," I said. "But there is yet the matter of the portpain the silver was wrapped in. How did you have that?"

"I had no portpain. When Walter told me I was found out, and if the silver was returned the matter would end, I begged him to return it for me. He refused at first, but Lady Margery heard us quarrel and demanded the cause. I said I wished Walter to perform some service for me and he would not. Lady Margery demanded that as he valued his position, he do as was required."

"Lady Margery did not ask what it was you desired of Walter?" I asked.

"Not at first."

"When, then?"

"She did not leave us. Stood planted, hands on hips, waiting for Walter to do as I wished. We stood thus until I could bear it no more. I went to my chest, withdrew the silver, and gave it to Walter."

"'What is this?' Lady Margery demanded of me. 'Whose spoons and knives are these, and what is Walter to do with them?'"

"I told Lady Margery all; that I had taken the silver in hopes that I could sell it for enough to buy silks and fine new shoes, but must return it as I had been found out."

"What did Lady Margery then say?" Lord Gilbert asked.

"Called me foolish."

"I don't often agree with Lady Margery," he said, "but she spoke true. 'Twas foolish indeed to steal my silver. Could you not guess the stuff would be missed?"

Lady Anne did not reply for some time. When she did her words stunned us both. "She said if I wanted to take Lord Gilbert's chattels I should be certain of not being discovered."

"She was angry that your theft was revealed, rather than that you had stolen goods from your host?" I said.

"Aye."

"What then?" I asked. "Did Walter then do as you wished?"

"He did. Took the silver from my hands, but dropped a spoon. 'Twas then Lady Margery told him to wait."

"For what?"

"She left the room. Don't know where she went. Returned soon enough with a length of linen cloth. Must have gone to her chamber for it. Told Walter to wrap the silver in it so no one would see what it was he had when he took it to the screens passage. Lady Margery did not know that no one was to be nearby to see the return of the silver."

Here was an interesting tale. The missing portpain in which the silver was returned had been in Lady Margery's possession. Had the bloody fragment in the squires' chamber also been in her hands before it was used to absorb Sir Henry's blood?

If so, was it to Sir Geoffrey that she had given a scrap? Or did Sir Geoffrey have the linen first, and give the remnant to Lady Margery?

The more I learned the more confused I became. I began to wish that I had never seen the small drop of blood on the floor of Sir Henry's chamber. Had I not, I would never have examined Sir Henry's ear and discovered a murder. I would have, for want of any contradictory knowledge, proclaimed the death as common to a man of Sir Henry's age. Lady Margery's accusation that my potion was at fault would have gone unchallenged.

Even I might have thought the accusation just.

I dismissed the thought. What kind of man am I to accept injustice if to struggle against it brings inconvenience? Is a calm, peaceful life worth such a price? Can a man see harm done to another yet go to his bed and rest easy of a night? Mayhap some men can, but I would be loath to think myself one of them. Where would men be if the Lord Christ had decided that being nailed to a cross was too inconvenient, and rather than offer His life for the salvation of all who believe, preferred a life free of sorrow and pain?

Lord Gilbert studied me in the silence which followed Lady Anne's revelation. An eyebrow, as usual, was raised.

"You will speak to no one of this interview," I said.

"But the chamberlain drew me from Lady Margery. She will ask where I went."

"Very well," I sighed. "If she asks, tell her all. Tell her I know of the portpain, and how a fragment of it was used. Tell her I know of her dalliance with Sir Geoffrey. Tell her I am about to seize a murderer and take him to Sir Roger to appear before the King's Eyre."

Lady Anne curtsied to Lord Gilbert, backed to the door, then fled from our presence. I heard her footsteps echo in the corridor as she hastened from the scene of her discomfort.

"What do you make of that?" Lord Gilbert asked. "The daughter steals my silver and the mother – well, stepmother – steals my linen. Find a murderer, so I may be rid of them. Lady Petronilla's jewels may vanish next."

"Perhaps Lady Margery did not take the portpain."

"Why, then, did she have a part of it? Did some other steal it and give part of it to her?"

"Perhaps... or 'twas the other way round. She took the portpain and gave a fragment to another."

"To Sir Geoffrey? To wipe away her husband's gore when murder was done?"

"Mayhap."

"Well, then, you told Lady Anne that you were about to arrest a murderer. Do so."

"I did not tell Lady Anne that I was ready to seize a murderer. I told her to tell Lady Margery that I was. There is a difference."

"Oh... aye. You play games with me."

"Nay. I attempt to do right. When felons use trickery to escape the penalty due them, it is sometimes needful to use deception to trip them up."

"Who do you deceive? Sir Geoffrey?"

"Aye. If he is the murderer, and is told that I am soon to arrest him, he may attempt some deed to avoid capture, or perhaps try to flee. I am going to find Arthur and Uctred and set them to watch at the marshalsea. Sir Geoffrey may send a page to saddle his horse, as if to go riding in the country. If he does so it will be another bit of evidence for his guilt. He will likely be attempting to escape capture."

"Be careful. If he believes you are ready to accuse him, the deed you speak of may be a third murder... if 'twas he who plunged a dagger into Sir John. A man cannot be hanged three times for three murders."

"I believe he did so, and I will heed your warning."

I found Arthur and told him to seek Uctred and together keep watch over the marshalsea. I hoped, when Lady Margery learned from Lady Anne what I knew, that she would go to Sir Geoffrey and set him to flee, or do some other thing which might confirm his guilt. I told Arthur to keep the marshalsea under close study, but not to appear to be doing so. He rolled his eyes at this instruction, being directed to do a thing whilst appearing to do another.

I wandered about the castle for the remainder of the afternoon, awaiting some incriminating act from Sir Geoffrey after he learned from Lady Margery what I knew. Lord Gilbert's grooms began to erect tables in the hall, but there was no sign of Sir Geoffrey. I walked to the marshalsea to question Arthur, and learned that the knight had not been near the stables, nor had any of Sir Henry's pages, either. Had he hidden himself away in his chamber? Or already fled castle and town? I entered the stables and went to the stalls where his beasts were kept. They were both present, his page evidently having returned them from the meadow for the night before I set Arthur and Uctred to watch the place. If Sir Geoffrey had fled to save his neck he did so afoot, which no knight would do.

Lord Gilbert must have thought it unseemly to serve an elaborate supper on such a day. The removes that evening were simple, even though 'twas not a fast day. His cook prepared capons farced, cormarye, rice moyle, and cabbage with marrow. And parsley loaf with honeyed butter. For the subtlety a simple chardewarden sufficed.

I had spent many hours in the past week watching Sir Henry's household at their meals in the hall, seeking, but not finding, some sign of guilt in expression or behavior. Why should this supper be any different?

It did seem to me that most of Sir Henry's retainers and family had little appetite, but that could not mean that they were all felons. Perhaps they worried that another death might be expected, and they might provide the corpse.

Lady Margery, who in the past had not hesitated to glare at me frequently from the high table, did not look even once in my direction during the meal. At least, not when I was observing her. She spoke little to Lady Petronilla, and seemed often to glance at the empty place to her right where Sir John had taken his meals.

Sir Geoffrey, to my surprise, took his normal place at the high table. Like all in the hall that evening, he was quiet and ate sparingly. But he did not look away when our eyes met. Either Lady Margery had not told him of my words to Lady Anne, or he believed he had nothing to fear, or he was a skilled player.

When the meal was done I joined Lord Gilbert in the solar, and together with Lady Petronilla we reviewed the week past, seeking some insight which had escaped us. We failed.

Lady Petronilla complained of feeling unwell, called for one of her ladies, and went to her chamber. I could think of nothing more to be done this day, so bid Lord Gilbert a good evening and departed for Galen House.

But before I left the castle I called upon William. The squire had not appeared this day for dinner or supper, and I wished to reassure myself that his nose was mending as should be.

The door to the squires' chamber was open, allowing a breeze to cool the room on this warm summer evening. I found William seated at his table, which he had drawn to the window, writing upon a sheet of parchment. The fading light was yet enough to illuminate his work and at a glance I saw that he wrote well, with a hand as skilled as any monk's.

The squire's eyes were yet purple, beginning to turn to green and yellow. The effect was quite loathsome, together with his swollen nose, and I understood why the youth did not wish to present himself to Lady Anne in such a state.

It was no business of mine to whom William wrote, but my eyes fell upon the document and I saw that Lady

Anne's name was inscribed across the top of the leaf in a large, flourishing hand, easily readable from where I stood.

William had turned from his writing when he heard me enter his chamber, but returned for a moment to his work, completing a thought before he stood to greet me.

"You did not take supper in the hall," I said by way of explaining my presence. "So I thought to see that all is well with you before I leave the castle for the night."

"As well as might be," William shrugged. "But I will be pleased when the linen plugs you thrust up my nose may be removed."

I agreed that having to breathe through one's mouth for a fortnight was not a pleasant prospect, but told William that he must resist the temptation to remove the wads before the time had expired. "If your nose should heal badly, skewed one way or the other," I explained, "it might cause such an obstruction that you never again take a breath through your nostrils, and your nose may forever point to one side of your face or another."

William said nothing while he contemplated such a fate.

"You write a fair hand," I said, nodding to the parchment upon the table.

The youth would have blushed, I think, but for the pageant of colors which already marched across his face.

"Sir Henry's chaplain taught us well," he said.

"You and Robert?"

"Aye, and all who needed instruction."

"Sir Henry wished his squires to be able to read and write?"

"Not only squires. Pages, grooms, valets, all in his service must be instructed. Sir Henry said times are not like as of old, when men needed only to work or fight, as their station demanded, and writing could be left to churchmen and scholars."

"Was there no unlettered man in Sir Henry's service?"

"Not that I know of. He'd not have it. Required Sir Geoffrey to learn when he entered his service."

"I have heard that Sir Geoffrey was low-born," I said. "Does he read and write with competence now?"

"Aye. Nearly as well as any man, though 'tis said learning letters is a thing best accomplished when young."

"So 'tis said," I agreed. "If you have no complaints I will leave you to your letter."

William bowed, then turned back to his parchment, no doubt eager to complete his work before the light failed.

Here was perplexing news. The note Sir Roger found slipped under his chamber door was written in a poor hand. It was yet in my pouch, so I withdrew it as I crossed the castle yard and once again inspected it. The light was poor, but it was adequate to see that whoso wrote the message could not be said to write nearly as well as any man. Did Sir Geoffrey then not write this? Some man, or woman, did. Perhaps, if Sir Geoffrey was right-handed, he took quill in left hand to scrawl a message that would disguise its composer.

If 'twas not Sir Geoffrey who wrote Sir Roger's note, who did so? Someone wished me to think Squire William guilty of Sir Henry's murder. If Sir Geoffrey was the felon, why would some other try to set the sheriff after an innocent man? Would Lady Margery do so, perhaps being complicit in her husband's death?

I studied the note again as I walked Mill Street toward my home. The letters were crude, and seemed to me not written in a feminine hand. They were large, square, and whoever had inscribed the letters had pressed the quill forcefully upon the parchment. I thought it likely a man had written the note, but if not Sir Geoffrey, then who? Surely the hand that held pen to this parchment also slew

Sir Henry. Unless Sir Geoffrey commanded some other to write for him. This thought occupied my mind until I arrived at Galen House and Kate greeted me. Her embrace drove other considerations from my mind.

Bessie was tucked into her cot, and Kate's hens had retired to the hen house, so all was quiet at Galen House. Kate covered the coals upon our hearth and we sat upon a bench in the fading light of the toft in companionable silence.

But Kate was unwilling to remain ignorant of the day's events, and so after allowing me a time with my thoughts, asked of the news. I told her.

"Sir Geoffrey is the murderer, then," she said.

"So it seems. He used the note to Sir Roger to turn suspicion to another when he learned that I had discovered the cause of Sir Henry's death."

"You think Lady Margery knew of his felony? Perhaps aided it?"

"She had the portpain in her possession, and Sir Geoffrey used a fragment of it to wipe away Sir Henry's blood."

"Will you charge them both?"

"Probably."

"Probably? You have some doubts?"

"I can understand Sir Geoffrey doing Sir Henry to death... and Lady Margery aiding in some way. But why slay Sir John?"

"Did not the squire say that Sir John was also fond of Lady Margery? Perhaps Sir Geoffrey wished to be rid of a rival."

"'Tis the only answer which makes sense," I agreed. "But if I knew or understood more, perhaps another explanation would also make sense. Or make better sense."

"What more do you need to know?"

"I would seek it if I knew. There is the problem of ignorance. I do not know what it is that I do not know."

"You speak in riddles."

"This business has been a riddle from first to last. I will be pleased to place it in Sir Roger's hands. He can lay Sir Geoffrey's fate before the King's Eyre."

"Will he hang?"

"Probably. The King's judges generally assume that if a sheriff seizes a man and presents him before the court there must be warrant for the accusation."

"So Sir Henry will be avenged."

"Aye, although the folk he wronged will never be so."

"What wrongs did Sir Henry do?"

I told Kate about Sir Henry's misuse of his office.

"Near Bedford there will be many folk, Isobel said, pleased to learn that Sir Henry now sleeps in St Beornwald's churchyard."

"And one of them," Kate said, "serves in Sir Henry's household."

"Aye. And the maid said that Sir Geoffrey and Sir John, and even the squires, aided Sir Henry, going about the countryside, seizing those accused of accepting higher wages for their labor than the statute allows. Even taking those against whom no complaint had been made, and demanding fines of them."

"Such a man would make many enemies," Kate said.

"Aye. But with swordsmen to defend him and a strong house to shelter him, his foes could do little."

"Until he left his house and traveled to another, and his knights were not close by," Kate said.

I did not reply to Kate's remark, but I thought on her words there in the darkening toft. What if some man, wronged in the enforcement of the Statute of Laborers, had accompanied Sir Henry to Bampton Castle, and struck him down here for his unjust governance, where he thought himself safe? Such a man would perforce be a valet or groom or page to Sir Henry. Both his knights and squires benefited in his employ from his sharp practice. Unless the benefit was thought too puny and a knight – it could not be a squire – wished to advance from employee to employer. Might this be why Sir Geoffrey pierced Sir John? Eliminating competition of a different sort? But if some malcontent valet or groom did murder Sir Henry, why then attack Sir John also? Kate's thought appeared at first to open new paths toward a felon, but soon enough these closed.

Kate rested her head upon my shoulder. Odd how such a simple thing can drive other thoughts from my mind. 'Twas not until later, when I lay abed, moonlight from a waxing gibbous moon illuminating our bed chamber, that my thoughts returned to Sir Henry's misuse of the Statute of Laborers and the enemies he might have made. 'Twould not take long, I decided, to seek information of Sir Henry's valets and grooms and pages. He had brought with him to Bampton three of the first, four grooms, and but two pages. I might have guessed the thinness of his purse when first we met from the few retainers who served him on his journey.

Chapter 14

A babe serves as well as a rooster to announce the dawn. Bessie did not wail loudly, but she made plain her displeasure at an empty stomach. Kate rose from our bed to deal with the starving infant. On a cold winter morn I might have been content to remain warm under the blanket, but the morning was pleasant and I was determined that this day would see Sir Henry's murder resolved.

Kate had set a kettle upon the hearth to warm water. I filled a bowl and washed my face and hands. Bessie laughed and clapped to see me splashing about.

Kate set half a maslin loaf and a wedge of goat's cheese before me. I hurriedly broke my fast, swallowed a cup of ale, which was quickly going stale, kissed Kate, and set off for the castle.

Wilfred tugged a forelock by way of greeting when I passed through the gatehouse but I saw few other folk about. I turned from the hall to the chapel, assuming that Lord Gilbert's chaplain had not completed morning mass.

Lord Gilbert led folk from the chapel as I approached. I noticed that Lady Petronilla did not accompany him this morn and assumed she was yet unwell.

In the small hours of the morning, awake in my bed and listening to Kate breathe and to the sounds of the night, I had determined that I would seek Lady Margery's servant Isobel again. The woman no longer seemed to fear me, but was willing to provide answers to my questions even so, apprehension for one's personal security being perhaps overrated as a tool with which a bailiff may pry truth from an obstinate witness. Nevertheless, 'tis a tool I will not discard.

I waited by the chapel door until she appeared, with other of Lady Margery's servants, walking behind her mistress. Lady Margery, being past me and in conversation with Sir Geoffrey, did not see me approach Isobel, nor did she hear my words to her, nor did she see Isobel follow me to the hall.

There was no need to seek the privacy of my old bachelor quarters, as the hall was empty at such an hour. I motioned to a bench beside the wall to indicate that Isobel should sit. I joined her upon the other end of the bench, desiring that the young woman think of me as a confidant rather than an inquisitor.

"Sir Henry," I began, "was not eager to return to Bedford. He was a guest here for nearly a month. You said he was rigorous in collecting fines from those who abused the Statute of Laborers, but he could not do so while here, in Bampton. Why was he not eager to return to his home and resume collecting fines? Did Lady Margery never speak of this?"

"Feared for his life, I think," Isobel said.

"There was a man Sir Henry had wronged who threatened him?"

"Not one man. Many. Squire William overheard a conversation at an ale house. Men were plotting to do away with Sir Henry for his avarice."

"Sir Henry thought this threat grave enough that he left his home?"

"Two knights, two squires, and a few valets, grooms, and pages would make a thin defense against an angry mob," she said.

"There was a plot to attack his house?"

"Aye. William overheard them speak of the day. St Boniface's Day."

"How did you learn of this?"

"William told Lady Anne," Isobel said.

"Ah... the lad hoped to win Sir Henry's favor."

"I suppose. Gossip was that Sir Henry was ready to send William from his house."

"Because he and Lady Anne..."

"Aye."

"But William accompanied Sir Henry to Bampton."

"Perhaps he softened toward the squire after William did him good service."

"Did William really overhear such chatter, I wonder, or did he say so to cause Sir Henry to look upon him more favorably?"

Isobel shrugged. "Who can say? Sir Henry believed the report. He sent to Lord Gilbert next day seeking a visit, and a week later we were upon the road."

"I learned yesterday that Sir Henry wished all of his household to read and write."

"Aye."

"Even the women?"

"Aye. All in his household. Lady Margery thought it foolish, but he would have it no other way. Said 'twas new times we lived in, and all must realize it."

"So even women and grooms and pages received instruction?"

"All."

Here was intriguing information. The message Sir Roger found slid under his door had been scrawled in an unskilled hand. Sir Henry demanded that all of his retainers be literate, but perhaps that requirement did not exceed a rudimentary knowledge. In Bedford both Sir Geoffrey and Sir John would have been nearly as despised as Sir Henry for their part in unjustly enforcing a hated law. Was that why Sir John had died, and why evidence pointed to Sir Geoffrey as one who had murdered two? Was I, I wondered, intended to be the dupe of some plotter? Was I to seize Sir Geoffrey and see him hang for murders he did not do? If Sir Geoffrey died upon a scaffold, then Sir Henry and his chief agents would all be dead, two murdered by the other, or so men would believe. But if Sir Geoffrey were not the felon, then he who did the murders would forever be free of suspicion, so long as he took no other life.

But why, then, the note sending me and Sir Roger to the squires' chamber? Isobel said that the squires did from time to time assist Sir John and Sir Geoffrey in apprehending those who may have sought more for their labor than the law allows. And it was William who learned of the plot against Sir Henry and warned him of the danger. Did the commons about Bedford learn that their plot was discovered, and who it was who had betrayed them? Was I then to be the unwitting tool of those who did murder, thinking if and when I seized William that I had collected a felon? If so, I have been a great disappointment to some man. Or men. They must believe me so dull of wit that I cannot follow a path so clearly set before me. Perhaps they are correct.

'Twas Walter who told me that Sir Geoffrey was outside Sir Henry's door the night he died. 'Twas Walter who had access to the pouch of crushed lettuce seeds, and who could have increased Sir Henry's dose. Walter was of the commons. He would not have run afoul of Sir Henry's enforcement of the Statute of Laborers, but he knew a man who had. His own family had suffered, according to Isobel. Was this reason enough to do murder? Walter's father had been fined many years in the past. But Walter had said Sir Henry was a good lord.

I had suspected at various times Squire William, Lady Margery, Sir Geoffrey and Sir John of doing Sir Henry to death, because with each I saw a motive. That Walter the valet might have done murder had not seemed likely, as I at first saw no reason he would do so.

I bid Isobel "Good day," and sent her off to her duties with Lady Margery. From the hall I climbed the stairs to the solar, where I hoped to find Lord Gilbert. I did. He was alone.

My employer sat behind his desk, a parchment before him, but I think he did not heed the document, for his head rested in his hands. He saw my shadow in the doorway, looked up, and invited me to enter.

"What news, Hugh?"

"I had hoped to tell you the conclusion of the matter of Sir Henry's murder this day, but I cannot."

"When will you do so? Foolish question... I must not vex you about your duty. You know it as well as I do."

"I believe that next week at this time I may know who has killed Sir Henry and Sir John."

"Next week? One man slew both?"

"So I believe, but the evidence I seek I am not likely to find here. I must travel to Bedford."

"But murder was done here. You think some man from Bedford came here, did the felony, and then returned to his home?"

"Nay. But the evidence I seek, if it is to be found, will tell us which of Sir Henry's household did the murders."

"Bedford is a long way – two days' hard travel."

"So I have heard. I will return in five days. One day at Bedford will suffice, I think. I would take Arthur with me."

"Very well. 'Tis always good to have a companion when upon the roads. When will you leave?"

"This day."

"Sir Henry's manor was at a village near to Bedford. Wootton, I believe. What do you seek there?"

"Sir Henry did harm to many men in the course of his duties as a Commissioner of Laborers. But few traveled with him to Bampton."

"You believe his office led to his death? You suspected Sir Geoffrey, I thought."

"It may be that he is guilty. He had cause."

"Aye. And with Sir Henry dead, he might assume the post of Commissioner of Laborers. Will you take Bruce?"

"Such a journey will be too difficult for the old horse, I think. You have several palfreys in the marshalsea."

"Take whichever you wish. Just return with these murders solved."

Such an admonition was unnecessary. I was as anxious as my employer to see the business ended. I bowed my way from Lord Gilbert's presence and sought Arthur. The groom always seemed ready to travel when I needed his company, and when I told him to prepare two of Lord Gilbert's palfreys for travel, and to tell Cicily that he would be away for five days, he smiled and set immediately to the work. I told him also to bring a sack with an old, worn cotehardie, and a tattered pair of shoes. Arthur lifted an eyebrow at this instruction, but he has known me for such a time that odd requests from me no longer surprise him much. I left the castle and hurried to Galen House.

Kate was not pleased that I would be away, but her displeasure softened when I told her that I hoped to learn the identity of a murderer by leaving Bampton for a few days.

"A murderer?" she said. "You believe one man killed both Sir Henry and Sir John, then?"

"I believe it possible... no, I believe it likely."

"Then godspeed, husband. I am pleased that Arthur will accompany you."

"He is a good companion, and no fool. And has an arm as thick through as a gate post."

I took Kate in my arms, kissed Bessie upon her head, and returned immediately to the castle. Arthur had two palfreys saddled and ready, the grey which he often rode, and a chestnut mare which Lord Gilbert had recently purchased. We would seek an inn at Oxford for our dinner, and continue east until we might find an abbey or priory where we would be made welcome when night fell.

Our beasts were well rested and young, so we passed Osney Abbey and entered Oxford by way of Bookbinders' Bridge by the time our stomachs demanded dinner. We left the palfreys at the stables behind the Fox and Hounds, with instructions that they each be fed a bucket of oats, while we entered the inn and consumed a roasted capon and several maslin loaves.

Days in late June are warm and long. I nodded drowsily upon the mare as she carried me from Oxford across the verdant countryside. Men, and women also, were busy in the fields. The last of the hay was being cut, and as men swung their scythes, their wives turned the hay so it would dry evenly. In some fields hay which had been cut some weeks past was being raised into tall stacks. Children were busy in pea and bean fields, cutting thistles and dock, and in a few fields plowmen were at work behind oxen and horses, turning the soil for the second plowing of the summer.

We did not press the palfreys, the better to save them for the long day's travel, and the next. Nevertheless, we found ourselves near to Buckingham when night drew nigh. Across a field from the road we saw an abbey, nearby a small village called Chetwode.

I pointed to the abbey rooftops, and told Arthur we would seek lodging there for the night.

Chetwode Abbey is a house of Augustinian Canons, and is not large or wealthy. We received what hospitality the place was prepared to offer, which was a bowl of pottage and a bed, and hay and a small measure of oats for our beasts. I think the abbot was not over pleased to learn that we would return to enjoy their hospitality in a few nights.

Next day, as we neared Bedford, I drew Arthur to the side of the road. The sack of his worn clothes I had slung across my palfrey's rump. This I now took a few paces into a wood, and exchanged the old clothes for my fine chauces and cotehardie. Kate had not cut my hair for several weeks, nor had I trimmed my beard for many days, so with Arthur's tattered garments I looked the part of an unkempt laborer seeking employment.

A half a mile beyond this place we found a lad weeding a bean field. I sent Arthur to ask him of Wootton. I saw the youth gesture in response, and soon Arthur returned.

"A mile ahead we will come to a way which leads to the manor of Lower Shelton, the lad said. A mile beyond that we will see a path which leads left to Wootton."

The day was far gone when we came to the place where the path to Wootton diverged from the main road. I dismounted and told Arthur to do the same. It would not do to be seen entering the village upon two well-fed horses. Not if the subterfuge I had in mind was to succeed.

A small wood bordered the track to Wootton. We led our beasts into this grove until they were well hid from any traveler who might pass this way. We removed their saddles and tied them to trees a few paces apart, so they should not entangle themselves, then set out afoot for the village and manor of Wootton.

Sir Henry's manor house was in great need of repair. Daub had peeled away from the wattles in several places, and the thatch was rotting and thin. Had I not before known of his impoverished state, I would have learned of it upon seeing his house. I wondered what Lady Margery thought when she laid eyes upon the place for the first time.

Beyond the manor house the single street of the village extended perhaps two hundred paces to a small church. Between the church and Sir Henry's house this street was lined with the homes of tenants and villeins. A few of these houses were in disrepair and uninhabited. Sir Henry would not reduce rents upon his lands to attract men to take up holdings abandoned due to the pestilence. Near the church I saw a thing which brought me great pleasure. A pole was erected before one of the houses, and atop it there was an upturned basket. Some ale wife had fresh-brewed ale and was advertising her supply. I pointed toward the place and Arthur and I made our way there.

A child played in the toft before the house, and within the place I heard a babe voice its displeasure over some matter probably having to do with food. I knocked upon the jamb, for the door was open, and a moment later a wary female face peered suspiciously at me from the dark interior of the house. There are surely few visitors to a place like Wootton.

"You have ale for thirsty travelers?" I said, and nodded toward the pole and basket.

"Aye... fresh-brewed yesterday." The hard look upon the woman's face softened as she realized she had customers. "A ha'penny for a gallon," she continued.

The woman invited us to sit upon a crude bench at her table, and produced two wooden cups of dubious cleanliness. I hope Lord Gilbert appreciates the afflictions I endure in his service.

The squalling babe fell silent and peered at us. I took a swallow of ale, which was not watered and was well brewed. Then I spoke to the woman.

"Does your lord require laborers? We seek employment."

"Hah," she snorted. "If you'll work for naught and be pleased for the chance."

"Your lord has enough men that he does not need to find more?"

"Nay. He has few enough. But Sir Henry's a Commissioner of Laborers. Won't pay a farthing more than the Statute of Laborers requires, an' will seek out an' fine them as disobeys the law."

I allowed my face to express what I hoped the woman would take as sorrow. "Do men not flee his lands?" I asked.

"As you have fled from your lord?" she winked.

"We be just honest men seeking a decent living," Arthur said.

"Some have fled, but many Sir Henry has sought out and brought back... an' he levied great fines upon 'em, too."

"Not a popular man, then, I'd guess."

"Oh, aye," the woman chuckled. "That's why you'd not find 'im home did you seek him to ask for work."

I said nothing, but cocked my head as if perplexed by her words. She continued.

"Sir Henry an' his household set out for some place beyond Oxford, so I heard. One of 'is squires learned that some folk hereabout was plottin' to kill 'im, an' the knights an' squires what serve 'im, also."

"He is a cruel lord?"

"Aye," she spat. "A few months past, jus' before Candlemas, I b'lieve, Arnald Crabb set 'is goods in a cart an' went off to another manor. Near to Wolverton, I heard. Sir Henry knew it must be that the lord he was to rent land from must've reduced rents to seek new tenants, so sent men to discover was it so, an' bring Arnald back if it was true."

"Arnald was a tenant of this place?"

"Since 'e was born. His kin live 'ere yet... uncle is smith in the village."

An alarm bell rang in my mind. Walter's father had been a smith.

"Smiths often seek better wages, I hear. Has your smith ever sought to better 'imself?"

"Once, years past, it was. I was but a wee lass. Charged folks more for hinges an' nails and such stuff than the statute allowed. Sir Henry put a stop to that, right enough."

"So this Arnald was fined for daring to take up lands of another for lower rent than permitted?"

"Nay... 'e's dead. Can't fine a dead man. Sir Henry sent men to bring 'im back, but folks at 'is new place fought to stop 'em, so I heard. Arnald got hisself pierced in the fight an' died next day."

"And his family lives here yet?"

"Aye... well, not 'is wife. She wouldn't return an' Sir Henry thought it best to leave 'er be. Lots o' cousins, though."

"These were not angered when Arnald died?"

"Oh, aye. That's why Sir Henry fled the place, you see. They was plottin' to do away with 'im. Him an' 'is knights an' the two squires, as well, like I said."

"You said Sir Henry was visiting a place beyond Oxford? Was his name Sir Henry Burley?"

"Aye," she said, with some suspicion furrowing her brow. "How'd you know of 'im?"

"He's dead. We were in the town of Bampton a few days past, an' learned of the death."

"He tried to flee the revenge of them he'd plundered, but didn't travel far enough. Was 'e murdered?"

"So men there said."

A look of satisfaction crossed the ale wife's face, but this rapidly faded. "'Is wife'll be as hard as Sir Henry ever was, an' Sir Geoffrey'll no doubt have the post Sir Henry had... an' Lady Margery, too."

"Sir Geoffrey?"

"One of Sir Henry's knights, an' a favorite of Sir Henry's wife, if you know what I mean." The woman winked.

"Who else of Arnald's kin live nearby, that they could plot against Sir Henry?"

The woman's eyes narrowed. "Why'd you want to know? Half the village knew of the plan, not just Arnald's family. Only cousin what didn't know of what was to happen was Walter, I'd guess."

"Walter?"

"Aye. A valet to Sir Henry. Don't think 'e knew of the scheme. Folks didn't trust 'im, you see, bein' Sir Henry's valet."

I had consumed nearly half the ale from the crusted wooden cup, and thought I need drink no more. Walter was a cousin to a man slain by Sir Henry's men. I knew that Walter had had opportunity to murder Sir Henry. Now I knew he had reason, as well.

I thanked the ale wife for the drink, and nodded toward the door. Arthur saw and rose from his bench. Together we left the hovel and set off toward the decrepit manor house and the east end of the village.

Arthur had heard all of the conversation, and spoke as we approached Sir Henry's dwelling.

"'Twas Walter, then, who did murder, an' not Sir Geoffrey?"

"It may be. But I have no proof of it, nor can I think of a way to confirm it to be so."

"It's a long way back to Bampton. You'll think of somethin'."

I might have wished for Arthur's confidence.

We had seen no village large enough to have an inn while on the way to Wootton, so were required to sleep that night upon piles of leaves in a wood nearby to a place called Cranfield. I discovered the name when, next morn, I smelled the village baker at his work and sought fresh loaves of him. We halted in the journey that day to allow the horses to feed in a meadow beside the road, but even with this delay we arrived at Chetwode Abbey while the sun was yet well above the trees. The abbot did not seem much pleased to see us again. We left the place next day at dawn, paused once again in Oxford to seek a meal, and entered Bampton shortly after the ninth hour.

Arthur was correct. Whilst swaying upon my palfrey's back a plan had come to my mind to discover if Walter the valet had slain his lord. If he had not, my scheme would tell that, as well.

I halted my journey at Galen House and sent Arthur on to the castle with the horses. I had been four days away from my Kate and Bessie. Solving Sir Henry's murder could wait another day. He would not mind.

Next morning I rose early and arrived at the castle before Lord Gilbert's chaplain had concluded mass. I waited at the entrance to the chapel, and when the service was done approached Walter as he departed the chapel with the other valets and grooms of Sir Henry's household, following the folk of quality. I beckoned to the valet and nodded toward the hall, indicating that I wished for him to follow. He did so, and a moment later I sat upon a bench pushed against the wall and motioned for him to do likewise. In a voice barely above a whisper, so as to cause the fellow to believe us conspirators together, I told him that I had returned the day before from Wootton, and laid out a case against Sir Geoffrey.

"I am not surprised," Walter said when I had done. "The man was baseborn and baseborn he remains, for all his airs. When will you arrest him?"

"Soon. Perhaps this day. But I would be well pleased to have more evidence against him. Testimony which might send the commons to a scaffold is often not enough to convince the King's Eyre of a knight's guilt."

"You wish my aid in the matter?" Walter asked, seeing where the conversation was going. Or thinking he saw its direction.

"Aye. 'Tis my belief that Sir Geoffrey also slew Sir John. Sir John awoke and fought when his attacker pierced him, and this I know for his blood spattered upon the wall of his chamber. Some of that gore must have sullied Sir Geoffrey's clothing when he did the murder, but although I've closely examined his cotehardie whenever he is near, I see no evidence that blood has ever spotted it."

"What, then?" Walter asked. "Has he another garment?"

"Surely. But I think it more likely that he wore only chauces and kirtle when he stabbed Sir John."

"How will you discover this?"

"With your aid."

"What must I do?"

"When all castle folk are at dinner you must go to Sir Geoffrey's chamber and seek a bloody kirtle. Look in his chest and under his mattress. It has been three days since Sir John died. Perhaps he has discarded the stained clothing, but if not, if your search is fruitful I shall have him. I ask you to do this because, as you are of Sir Henry's household, 'twould not appear odd to see you enter Sir Geoffrey's chamber, as it would for me or some other man in Lord Gilbert's employ. You will miss your dinner, but 'tis a fast day and stockfish will be your meal. I'll see that the cook holds some back for you."

"Aye," Walter said without hesitation. "I have told you, Sir Henry was a fair master and I would see his murderer punished for the deed."

"Excellent. With your aid, before this day is done, I may have a murderer in hand. Now, you must not go near Sir Geoffrey's chamber this morning. I would not have him see you loitering about and take fright."

"Does he suspect that you think him guilty?"

"He may. I do not wish this bird to take flight and escape my snare."

"I will do as you ask," Walter said, then bowed and bid me "Good day."

"And a good day to you, also," I said. If my scheme succeeded, and my new suspicion was just, it might be the last good day the valet would ever know. Justice is a beautiful thing. Seeking it may be ugly.

I sought Sir Geoffrey next. He and Lady Margery had followed Lord Gilbert from the chapel, so I thought perhaps they had joined him in the solar, there to await dinner in light conversation. As light as conversation may be with two corpses hanging over it.

Lady Anne was present in the solar also, but not Lady Petronilla. Lord Gilbert sat with his back to the door, but when he saw Lady Margery glance in my direction and curl her lip in distaste he turned to see who it was who had annoyed her. Annoying Lady Margery does not require great effort. Nearly anyone is capable of doing so, but I have special talents in that regard.

"Master Hugh," Lord Gilbert greeted me, "I give you good day. How may we serve you?"

That gentlemen and ladies might serve a mere bailiff is a fiction, but gentlefolk do have their pretensions of duty to the commons, and this serves, I suppose, to justify to them their position. Well, we all seek to vindicate our deeds.

If we found that we could not, we might behave otherwise. But as men generally refuse to change their ways through many years, it must be that we have discovered means whereby to excuse ourselves for the evils of this world in which we share.

"I would speak privily to Sir Geoffrey," I said.

The knight looked to Lady Margery and she rolled her eyes in disgust. What the woman thought of me was of no consequence. Another woman, whose shoes Lady Margery was unfit to lace, thought well of me, and that was all that mattered. But her display of disrespect did anger me, I must admit. The Lord Christ said that we will know the truth, and the truth will set us free, but mayhap knowledge of the truth may upon a time make us angry as well.

Sir Geoffrey was not pleased to be asked to leave the solar, and of this his countenance left no doubt. He knew, I believe, that he was suspect in two deaths and surely had some concern that I intended to question him sharply. Five days past I would have done. I might yet.

When we were safely away from the solar I stopped to face the knight, who had followed me from the chamber. The corridor was dim, but I could see Sir Geoffrey's lips drawn thin below scowling brows.

"What's this about?" he said.

"I wish to inspect your chamber," I replied.

"What? Absurd. What do you expect to find?"

"If I knew that I wouldn't need to examine the room, would I? Actually, it is what I do not expect to find that should concern you."

"You wish to inspect my chamber for something you believe is not there? Bah, you speak in riddles."

"I have been told this before."

"Just what is it you think you will not find in my chamber?"

"Evidence of murder," I said.

This concentrated Sir Geoffrey's thoughts and I saw his jaw work as he clenched his teeth.

"Whose murder?" he said after a pause.

"Sir John's."

"So you will inspect my chamber for things you do not believe you will find?"

"Exactly. Shall we go?"

I turned from Sir Geoffrey and led the way to his chamber where I stopped and waited for him to open the door and enter. He did so.

The space was well lit, the window admitting the morning sun, now bright and warm over Bampton Castle's south wall. Sir Geoffrey's face was full of anger as he stood aside his door and waited for me to enter the room.

"You believe I slew Sir Henry and Sir John?" he asked. "Many do, I know. Lady Margery has heard the talk."

"Nay. A week past I thought differently. Today I believe you to be foolish, greedy, and corrupt, but no murderer."

"Then why seek evidence of murder here, in my chamber?"

The knight made no defense of my accusation that he was foolish, greedy, and corrupt. Perhaps he thought these were minor infractions when compared to murder, which he had worried might be the charge against him. Or perhaps he agreed with my judgment.

"Because what is not here now may be so before this day is done."

Sir Geoffrey's mouth dropped open. "You will find no evidence of murder in my chamber, now or later, this day, or any other."

"I believe that you are mistaken. But we shall see. Will you open your chest?"

The chest was grand, as one might expect of a knight,

217

more than a yard long, made of polished oak, and bound with iron. Sir Geoffrey sighed, drew a key from his pouch and unlocked the chest. When he opened it I said, "Do not lock the chest when we are done here."

I had not considered that he might own a chest with a lock, and that he might keep it locked. My plan might be tossed askew if no man could gain access to the box.

Sir Geoffrey stood back and folded his arms while I examined the contents of the chest. There I found extra kirtles and braes, as one might expect, and a fine new green cotehardie reserved, I suppose, for special feasts and such. Two caps were there, one red, the other green, with fashionably long liripipes as young men like to wear. Although Sir Geoffrey is no longer young.

I was surprised to find amongst the clothing a book of hours. It was a thing of beauty, and worth thirty shillings, I think.

Sir Geoffrey watched as I examined the book. "A gift," he said.

"From Sir Henry?"

"Nay. He'd not give up a thing so fair as that. Sell it, more likely."

"From some gentleman, then? A man you would have taken to Sir Henry charged with demanding too little of his tenants in rent for their lands in order to keep them in their place?"

Sir Geoffrey looked as if I'd swatted him with the book. "Nay," he said. "From the Black Prince himself."

"Oh yes, I've heard that you distinguished yourself in battle."

The knight did not reply, so I replaced the book and resumed a plunge to the bottom of the chest. I found a pair of shoes, old and well-worn, and a pair of riding boots of good quality. Two pairs of gloves were also there, one pair fur lined for winter use. All was as I expected. I did not find any garment with bloodstains upon it.

I stood from the chest, faced Sir Geoffrey, and said, "Remember, do not lock your chest. 'Tis now nearly time for dinner. We will return here after the meal and see if your chest is then as 'tis now."

"Why should it not be?"

"Because there is a man who will also seek evidence of murder in your chamber while we are at dinner. But unlike me, I believe he will find it."

"What? How so? What will he find, and where can it be?"

"Unless I am much mistaken – which is surely possible, for I have much experience in being mistaken – he will find a bloodied garment in your chest."

"Bah. You have just now been in my chest. You saw for yourself there is no such thing there."

"Aye, so I did."

I saw the light of understanding flash in Sir Geoffrey's eyes. "The man who will find bloody clothing in my chest will be one who has put it there."

"So I believe."

"And he will have such a garment because he slew Sir John?"

"Aye. Sir John, surely, and likely Sir Henry as well. Sir John resisted his attacker and his blood spewed out upon the wall of his chamber and likely upon his assailant as well."

"Why not seek a bloody garment amongst the fellow's possessions?"

"It is likely well hid, and I do not want the man to know that I suspect him until I have proof of his guilt."

"Who is this man?"

"Walter."

"The valet? But why... ah, I see."

"What do you see?" I asked.

"Why the man would do these murders."

"Tell me. I believe him guilty, as a few days past I thought it likely you were the felon. But I would like to know why you think he may be the murderer."

Sir Geoffrey looked from me to his chest as if he expected to see some new thing there, then clasped his hands behind his back and spoke.

"'Twas the fines, I think, and his kinsman's death."

"Fines? Death? Sir Henry was charged with enforcing the Statute of Laborers, which duty you, Sir John, and the squires assisted. These are the fines you speak of?"

"Aye."

"Why should Walter be so angered about fines? He was Sir Henry's valet and would not be charged with violating the statute... unless it is his father you speak of. And what of death?"

I knew the answer to that question, but wanted to hear from Sir Geoffrey his account of what had happened to Walter's cousin.

"His father and cousin were accused of violating the statute."

"The father I know of. A smith accused of charging more for his labor than the statute permitted."

"Aye. Walter's father was the only smith in Wootton an' the villages nearby after plague returned seven years past."

"And Sir Henry charged Walter's father for violating the statute," I said, "demanding more for his labor than the law allowed?"

"Aye."

"What was his penalty?"

"Don't know. Sir Henry sent me an' Sir John to collect 'im, and take the fellow back to his home when Sir Henry was done with 'im."

"I am told that Sir Henry levied heavy fines, and sometimes awarded penalties when none was warranted, no law broken."

"Who told you that?"

"No matter. What of Walter's cousin?"

"He was a tenant of Sir Henry's lands at Wootton. Bein' a Commissioner of Laborers, Sir Henry wouldn't reduce rents, as many gentlemen do, so Arnald went elsewhere. Took 'is family off to a manor near Wolverton, where so many folk had died of plague the lord was willing to reduce rents to attract tenants. By half, I heard."

"Permit me to complete the tale," I said. "When Sir Henry learned where the fellow had gone – perhaps he stole away in the night – he sent you and Sir John to fetch him back, and levied a great fine as well."

Sir Geoffrey did not reply.

"If I am wrong, what did happen?"

"Arnald would not come. We seized 'im, but he fought us, and raised such a tumult that other tenants soon gathered. We were overmatched three or four to one, though we had swords and Arnald and his friends had but spades and scythes and clubs. One had a dagger, I think."

"What then?"

"They who set upon us were not content to drive us off. Their blood was up, and all the grievances of the Statute of Laborers which they had borne for many years incited them. They sought to slay us."

"The commons are resentful of the Statute of Laborers," I agreed. "But you escaped?"

"Aye. Sir John was knocked about when a man caught him across the ear with a stave, but we fled safely enough."

"Without Walter's cousin."

"Aye. Sir Henry would have sent us back for him, but

'twas no use. Arnald was sore wounded and died next day, so we heard."

"Did William and Robert accompany you when you went to seize Arnald?"

"Aye, they did. 'Twas likely William who ran 'im through."

"Who else of Sir Henry's household knows of this?"

"Don't know."

"Did you speak of it to Lady Margery?"

"Nay."

I began to see what Walter had done, and why he had done it. He wished Sir Henry dead for the penalties he had inflicted upon his father and the murder of his cousin, honest men seeking to better themselves. When I sent crushed lettuce seeds to aid Sir Henry's sleep the valet had given his lord a larger measure than called for, probably hoping the dose would end Sir Henry's life.

Some time in the night he had crept back to Sir Henry's chamber to learn if the potion had done the work he intended. It had not. So Walter fell back upon an earlier scheme: the bodkin through Sir Henry's ear. My sleeping draught was but a coincidence, and an aid to a murder Walter had likely already planned.

The valet trusted that his felony would not be discovered, but if it was, hoped that some other man might be assumed guilty. Thus the note under Sir Roger's door. Perhaps Walter knew that it was William's thrust which had mortally wounded his cousin, so hid the awl and bloody linen in his chamber in hope that William would be implicated in Sir Henry's death. Mayhap Walter thought that Sir Geoffrey and the squires would be accused of plotting together against Sir Henry, for they had all been involved in the attempt to return Arnald to Sir Henry's lands, and Walter would have wished calamity upon them all.

Sir John's death was not planned, I thought, until the fight with William left him wounded and less able to defend himself. And as neither of the squires nor Sir Geoffrey had yet been accused of Sir Henry's murder, Walter saw a way to slay Sir John and have the sheriff and King's Eyre do away with William.

The stolen silver and portpain, I was convinced, had nothing to do with murder, but the coincidence of their theft at such a time had served to complicate matters and draw me down unproductive paths.

From a distance I heard the bell sound to call us to our dinner. I looked to Sir Geoffrey and nodded toward the chamber door, then led him to the corridor. He followed, and closed the heavy door behind him.

As this was a fast day, no meat, eggs, or cheese were served. The first remove was stewed herring, sole in cyve, and boiled plaice. For the second remove there was charlet of cod, and roasted salmon in spiced sauce. For the third remove the cook presented cyueles, crispels, mushroom tarts, and a fruit and salmon pie. For the subtlety there was pears in compost. It is sometimes difficult to enjoy such a meal when I know that my Kate is home in Galen House consuming a pease pottage with no pork to flavor the dish. Well, some discomfort must be accepted to do the work Lord Gilbert asks of me.

Walter's place near the foot of a side table was vacant. Sir Geoffrey saw this also, and gave me a knowing glance as Lord Gilbert's chaplain said a prayer for the meal and the valets served the first remove. Those who sat low at the tables received only some of the stewed herring with their stockfish and maslin loaves.

Chapter 15

There was another empty chair at dinner this day. Lady Petronilla's place was vacant. I am a surgeon, not a physician, but I thought it likely that Lord Gilbert would soon approach me regarding his wife's indisposition.

I was eager for the meal to end, to learn if my ruse was successful. No one, of course, could leave the hall until Lord Gilbert indicated that the meal was done by rising from his place. This he did without lingering over the subtlety, perhaps concerned for his wife.

As soon as Lord Gilbert stood I glanced to Sir Geoffrey, nodded toward the stairs, and left my place at the head of a side table. On my way to the stairs I passed behind Arthur, tapped the groom upon his shoulder, and bid him accompany me. A bailiff almost never gets in trouble by having too much muscle to enforce his authority.

The three of us approached Sir Geoffrey's chamber and found the door closed as when the knight and I had left it an hour and more past. I waited for Sir Geoffrey to enter his chamber, then followed and went straight to the chest.

We had approached the room in silence, so Arthur knew nothing of my plot or why he was brought to the place. He stood at the door, unwilling to enter a gentleman's private space, and waited with a puzzled expression upon his broad face.

Sir Geoffrey stood aside and allowed me to lift the lid to his chest. Nothing there seemed amiss. All was as I had left it. The book of hours lay upon the two folded kirtles, in the same place it had been when I last saw it. At the other end of the chest was Sir Geoffrey's fine cotehardie, also folded neatly, as it was before we took dinner. The knight saw these things also.

"All is as it was. No man has been in my chest, I think."

"We will be sure," I replied, and began lifting out garments, book, shoes, and boots. At the bottom of the chest, beneath Sir Geoffrey's riding boots, was folded his extra pair of braes. This garment seemed rather bulky. I lifted it from the chest and as it unfolded another cloth fell from it which had not been in that place in the morning. A bloodstained kirtle had been wrapped in the braes.

Sir Geoffrey looked upon the garment silently as I lifted it from the depths of his chest, then finally spoke. "'Twas Walter, then."

"Aye. This is surely his kirtle, placed here while we dined, to incriminate you. 'Tis of linen, as you might wear. I suspect it once belonged to Sir Henry, and Walter put it to his own use now that Sir Henry has no need of the garment. You return to the hall, or seek Lord Gilbert in the solar. Lady Petronilla is unwell, so he may be attending her in her apartments. I will take Arthur to confront Walter. You need have no part in the business. You may replace your goods in the chest. I will take this kirtle with me."

I folded the stained garment and placed it inside my cotehardie, under my arm, where no man could see it, then turned from the chamber and bid Arthur follow. The fellow needed to know what we were about to do, so I stopped in the corridor to quickly explain what he had just seen.

He nodded understanding, then spoke. "Cicily ain't herself, either. Heard you say Lady Petronilla's unwell. I know you ain't a physician, but mayhap you could call an' see what ails 'er?"

I promised to do so, and we then descended to the lower level and sought the cramped chamber where Sir Henry's valets and grooms had bedded for the last month. Walter expected me. He was seated on a bed, and stood quickly to his feet when I entered the room. He did not wait for me to speak, but blurted out his news.

"'Twas as you thought," he said. "There is at the bottom of Sir Geoffrey's chest a kirtle spotted with blood, wrapped in braes so as to not be found."

"'Tis no longer there," I said, and drew the garment from under my arm.

"Ah," the valet said, "you have already discovered it. Have you seized Sir Geoffrey?"

"Nay. I have come to charge you with the murder of Sir John Peverel and see to it that you are taken to the dungeon."

"What? Not so! I did but as you asked of me."

"I did not ask you to place this kirtle in Sir Geoffrey's chest."

"I found it there, while all other castle folk were in the hall, at dinner."

"Not so. I inspected Sir Geoffrey's chest before dinner. This kirtle was not amongst his possessions then, but was an hour later. Who else could have hid it there? All but you were in the hall."

I reached out a hand and pulled Walter's cap from his head. He had artfully coiled his liripipe so as to cover an ear. There was a small scabbed wound where his left earlobe should have been. I was sure that under the collar of his cotehardie I might find a scratch made by Sir John's fingernail.

Walter attempted a brave front, but he was not skilled at deception. His jaw hung slack and his eyes darted about the chamber as if seeking some heretofore undiscovered means of escape.

"I am told that your father is a smith."

Walter made no reply, but his mouth opened and closed as a trout drawn from Shill Brook and laid upon the bank.

"Was it he who made this bodkin?" I said, and drew the implement from my pouch. I would be pleased to no longer need to carry the thing about. One day the sharpened end of the tool had punched through the leather of my pouch and poked my wrist. I do not mind having upon my person blades and such with which I may help injured folk to mend, but this bodkin was used for an evil purpose and I would be glad to be rid of it.

"Did you tell him what use you had planned for it?"

"Nay," he blurted. "Me father knew nothing of it. He bears no fault in this."

"You had it in mind to slay Sir Henry before you came here, is this not so? Did you begin to plot before your cousin's death, or was it not 'til after that the notion came to you?"

Walter sat heavily upon the bed. "Wanted only to better 'imself, did Arnald," he said. "Sir Henry'd not reduce rents, him bein' so bad off, an' a Commissioner of Laborers as well, so Arnald took 'is wife an' children to take up a yardland of Sir Jocelyn Parrott. Arnald not bein' a villein, there was nothin' Sir Henry could do to stop 'im goin'. Right bitter Sir Henry was, too."

"He would not consider reduced rent to keep the man upon his lands?"

"Nay. An' he knew well enough that's why Arnald was goin' off to Sir Jocelyn. No man would pile 'is goods on a cart in January an' travel to a new place lest there was good reason."

"How did Sir Henry learn what rent Arnald paid to Sir Jocelyn?"

"Don't know. Sir Henry had spies, though. Paid folks a part of the fine if they'd tell 'im of them what was violating the Statute of Laborers."

"I am told that Sir Henry came here to Bampton to escape a plot against him."

"Aye," Walter said through thin lips. "Some of the lads had too much ale an' William overheard 'em makin' plans. Was it not for 'im, Sir Henry'd have been dealt with right proper an' I'd not have to…"

The valet fell silent for a moment, then spoke again. "Sheriff'll hang me, won't he?"

"Aye. You have confessed to me. And I have evidence now to convict you of Sir John's murder even if you had kept silent. The King's Eyre will have no sympathy for your excuse. The judges are men of property and endorse the Statute of Laborers. The court will require my witness, and I will tell what I have learned and what you have said. You must prepare yourself to meet the Lord Christ."

Walter looked to his feet. "S'pose I always knew things might turn out this way. What would you 'ave done was your kin slain for seekin' to better 'imself an' care for 'is babes? An' your father fined for chargin' a decent price for 'is work?"

I did not reply. I feared my answer.

"I have heard of a Commissioner of Laborers who was discharged when King Edward was told of his malfeasance," I said instead.

"Hah. He was probably not sendin' the King 'is proper share. So long as the King gets 'is coin he'll not much care what becomes of a tenant with but a yardland to 'is name."

It would have been impolitic for me to agree with a felon's assessment of his sovereign, so I bit my tongue and made no reply. I do not know much of the King but that he is advanced in years and not well and enjoys the company of a lady named Alice, but I suspect that Walter spoke true. This may be treasonous, but I write for my own remembrance. It is unlikely that the King or his officers will plumb the depths of my chest to seek the gatherings upon which I write of the death of Sir Henry Burley and Sir John Peverel.

I turned to Arthur. "Take Walter to the dungeon, then tell the marshalsea that I will need Bruce and two palfreys tomorrow morning. We will take Walter to Sir Roger... you will accompany me."

Arthur did not seem much pleased about this new duty. Perhaps he thought of Cicily and her indisposition. But he tugged a forelock, reached out a meaty hand for Walter's arm, and lifted the downcast fellow to his feet. I would be melancholy also if I saw in my future a dungeon, unsympathetic judges, and providing entertainment for the young scholars of Oxford as I did the sheriff's dance.

I found Lord Gilbert and Sir Geoffrey in the solar. The knight had told my employer of how matters stood, for when I entered the chamber Lord Gilbert stood and congratulated me.

"I have sent Walter to the dungeon in Arthur's care," I said. "We will take him to Oxford tomorrow. He may await the King's Eyre under Sir Roger's authority."

"Well done, Master Hugh. Well done. Sir Roger would have taken the squire to his dungeon to await the judges."

"Or Sir Geoffrey," I said. "Perhaps this business will influence the next Commissioner of Laborers appointed for Bedford to deal more wisely with the commons, and gentlemen, who run afoul of the statute. Walter will hang, but that will bring no satisfaction to Sir Henry Burley."

I said this for the benefit of Sir Geoffrey, who, I was certain, hoped to move shortly into the office, and matrimonial place, of his deceased lord.

I departed the castle feeling oddly unsatisfied. It was while I paused upon the bridge over Shill Brook that the reason for this ennui came to me. What of the portpain? Most of the portpain had been in Lady Margery's possession. Had she taken it from the pantry, or had Lady Anne? If Lady Margery stole the portpain, when and why did Walter come to have a part of it when he slew Sir Henry? And if Walter was the thief, how did most of the linen cloth come into Lady Margery's possession? Gazing into Shill Brook provided no answers.

I turned from the calming stream and returned to the castle. Wilfred seemed surprised to see me return, but men in his position are not to question the coming and going of their betters. The porter tugged a forelock and turned from me as if uninterested in what I was about. Perhaps he really had no interest in my return.

Bampton Castle dungeon lies beneath the buttery, at the base of a narrow, dark, stone stairway. Moisture gathers there in the summer, and the place is clammy with mosses. 'Tis an unpleasant place to be, as is proper. If a man has behaved in some lamentable fashion it is appropriate that he find himself in uncomfortable circumstance, the better to consider the felony which brought him there.

Two timbers, hinged on one side and dropped into a niche in the stone on the other, fastened shut the door to Walter's cell. There was, at the level of my collar, a small window in the door. I opened it and bent to peer into the cell. Walter was not visible, for the dungeon was illuminated by only a small, barred opening in the upper wall opposite the door.

Walter must have heard the small door open, for a moment later his face, apprehension in his eyes, appeared before me. This window was small, barely larger than the palm of my hand. Large enough to pass a loaf, a cup, or a small bowl of gruel through to the cell's inhabitant, but no larger.

Only a portion of my face would have been visible to the valet, and that in shadow, so he did not know who peered at him through the small hatch. Perhaps he thought some groom was bringing him a loaf. He was soon disabused of this notion, if he'd entertained it. He recognized my voice when I spoke.

"The portpain," I said. "Did you steal it from the pantry, or did Lady Margery?"

Walter stared at me for some time, looked away once, then, without speaking, disappeared from my view to a corner of his cell. I heard what sounded like a body sliding down the stones of the wall, and a sigh as his haunches reached the filthy rushes.

"You," I repeated, "or the Lady Margery, or some other? Lady Anne, perhaps?"

There was no reply.

"Why will you not answer? You can face no more severe penalty, so speak. If 'twas you took Lord Gilbert's portpain, what did you think? That you could sell the linen in Bedford when you returned there?"

Walter still made no reply.

"It must be, then, that Lady Margery stole the portpain. If 'twas you," I said, "you would have no reason to keep silent. But as you will die for your murders, you think to save Lady Margery, I think. Considerate of you, to protect the lady. Of course, the act will cost you little. But I wonder why she gave you a portion of the stolen linen. Did she know the use you intended for it? All know that Lady Margery was displeased with Sir Henry."

I heard Walter stand and move through the rushes. A moment later his face appeared through the open hatch.

"Lady Margery found I'd taken the portpain an'

demanded it of me. Said she'd find some way to return what remained of it before 'twas known to be missing."

"Why did you not say so?"

This explanation was unsatisfactory. Lady Margery had not been angry with Lady Anne for stealing Lord Gilbert's silver, but rather had been cross with her stepdaughter for being found out. Why, then, would she demand that Walter return a stolen portpain, a thing of much less value than stolen silver? Because he was but a valet, and not high-born?

"So you gave her the portpain, but only after you had used a fragment to wipe away Sir Henry's blood?"

"Aye," he sighed, "as you say."

"And did Lady Margery guess the use to which part of the portpain had been put?"

"Nay."

My mind traveled back to the day Lady Margery had seen the felonious bodkin in my hand when she left the hall, and the startled expression upon her face. Reading faces is not my greatest skill. Perhaps I got it wrong. Perhaps 'twas fear I saw there. But of what could she have been fearful? Had she been in league with Walter? If some scrap of cloth had been needed to soak away Sir Henry's blood, could they not have used some fragment brought from Bedford?

To have done so might have risked the fabric – if it was discovered, or used to incriminate some other, such as William – being identified as from Sir Henry's household. There was risk, of course, in stealing goods from Bampton Castle's pantry, but perhaps the hazard seemed less.

"They," I had said to myself. Walter had said he acted alone, but my inclination was to think otherwise. Lady Margery had accused me and the lettuce-seed potion of causing Sir Henry's death. Was this because she genuinely believed me guilty of malfeasance, or because she wished to turn suspicion from Walter, and thereby from herself? A lady cannot be accused of having a part in her husband's murder on the suspicion of a mere bailiff. If Lady Margery connived in Sir Henry's death I would need more than conjecture to accuse her.

Chapter 16

Chivalry is for gentlemen, not the commons, but although I questioned Walter sharply through the hatch in his cell door, he would say no word which might imply Lady Margery's complicity in his deed. Eventually he moved away from the door to the invisible corner of his cell and I once again heard him sit heavily in the moldy rushes. I could get no other word from him. Either the Lady Margery had nothing to do with her husband's death, or Walter would protect her from the penalty of her deed. If 'twas the last, doing so would cost him nothing. A man cannot hang twice.

I did not hesitate at the bridge over Shill Brook as I walked to my home. Perhaps I feared some new complicating revelation which contemplating the stream might bring to my thoughts.

Bessie heard the door of Galen House swing open, lifted herself to hands and feet, then gained enough balance that she could totter to me. A wide smile creased her face.

I noted how her hair, now growing in more thickly, was becoming like Kate's in color. I pray her nose will be like Kate's as well, rather than like mine.

Kate had been in the toft, but came through the rear door to see me lift Bessie, and so joined in the embrace.

My wife stood back, gazed upon me and Bessie, then spoke. "You have had good success this day, eh?"

I have never been able to conceal my thoughts and sentiments from Kate. Not that I've ever had much reason or need to do so. Perhaps the ability to construe a husband's thoughts is a gift from the Lord Christ. To men God has given muscles and strength. To women, to make up for the lack, He has given discernment. What, then, of Lady Margery and Lady Anne? Mayhap my speculation was foolishness.

Kate set before me a simple supper of porre of peas and maslin loaf, but I ate little, partly because I had dined well at the castle a few hours earlier, and partly because Kate could not resist questioning me of the day's events and the conclusion of the matter of the deaths of Sir Henry Burley and Sir John Peverel.

"The valet will hang?" Kate said when I had done.

"No doubt. Arthur and I will take him to Sir Roger on the morrow. I will be called to testify before the King's Eyre when it next meets."

"And your words will doom the man."

"Aye. 'Tis a sorry business I am called to do, but Walter could have avoided this end."

"Likely he could see no other way to find justice for his cousin," Kate said.

"Probably. We must pray that his soul be mended and some priest in Oxford will absolve him of his sins so he may see heaven's gates open to receive him."

"May it be so," Kate said softly.

Kate nursed Bessie until she fell to sleep, then took her to her cradle. While she did so I drew a bench to the toft and awaited her return. While in our sleeping chamber on the upper floor of Galen House Kate had undone her hair, so when she joined me in the toft it fell below her shoulders as it had done when first I saw her at her father's stationer's shop in Oxford.

The setting sun cast long shadows across the toft, and caused Kate's hair to glisten, the color of an oak leaf in autumn. We sat upon the bench, bathed in the warmth of the setting sun, until the shadows brought a chill to the toft and drove us to our bed.

I broke my fast next morn with a loaf and cheese. 'Tis a long way to Oxford. I found Bruce and two other horses saddled and waiting when I arrived at the castle. Arthur awaited me, and I told him to bring Walter to the marshalsea and when he was mounted upon his beast to bind his hands to the pommel. While Arthur completed this task I sought Lord Gilbert and found him entering his chapel. His face was somber.

"I am off to Oxford with Walter," I said.

"Arthur accompanies you?"

"Aye. We'll return tomorrow. What of Lady Margery?"

"She will leave this day. Her grooms are harnessing runcies to her cart as we speak. She will join me to hear prayers for Lady Petronilla, break her fast, and then set off."

"Lady Petronilla has not recovered?"

"Nay. She grows worse. Her flesh is hot, and her head aches so badly she cannot bear light, but will have her windows covered. And upon her leg is a purple bruise the size of my hand, as if she'd kicked a chair leg."

These symptoms brought me disquiet, but I did not voice my worry to Lord Gilbert, whose anxiety for his lady was great enough already.

"Have you a potion which can ease her pain?" he continued.

"Aye. I will ask John Chamberlain to accompany me when I set out for Oxford. We will pass by Galen House and I will prepare a potion. He can return with it."

Arthur and Walter were mounted and ready when John and I approached the marshalsea. The chamberlain walked behind to Galen House, where I bid him enter with me. Kate was surprised at my reappearance. I had told her that I would seek lodging with her father this night, and return on the morrow. I briefly explained my return while I went to my chest and drew from it two potent physics: the crushed seeds and root of hemp, and the ground root of monk's hood.

Monk's hood is a powerful poison, but if used in small amounts can relieve pain and reduce fever. If too much of the stuff is consumed the pain and fever will end forever. It is a dangerous plant, and must be employed only when a sufferer is in great peril. I had not seen Lady Petronilla in her distress, but the symptoms Lord Gilbert described brought me much apprehension. If her illness was what I suspected, the monk's hood would create no more danger than she already endured, and might ease the agony which would soon come to her.

I measured out the hemp and monk's hood carefully and placed the herbs into separate vials. To John I gave instructions on how much of these palliatives might be safely given to Lady Petronilla, then kissed my Kate a second farewell and mounted Bruce for the journey to Oxford.

We were not yet to Cote when Arthur mentioned again that Cicily was feeling unwell, and he was worried that whatever illness had befallen Lady Petronilla might have come nigh her. I did not wish to cause the fellow worry, so did not tell him of my suspicions regarding the Lady Petronilla, but this news made the journey even more burdensome.

Tenants and villeins were busy at their labor as we passed. Men were at work digging and cleaning ditches, children and their mothers were busy cutting weeds from pea and bean fields, and in Cote the lord's sheep were being sheared. Walter gazed intently at these scenes, as well he might, for he would not likely see such again.

Sir Roger would not hear of me seeking lodging in any other place. Arthur was sent, after dinner, to the dormitory where Oxford Castle grooms and sergeants are quartered, and I was taken to a chamber in the sheriff's private quarters. The King's Eyre, Sir Roger said, would convene on St Benedict's Day. I should think the judges will hear Walter's case then, or surely next day. The day after that he will be taken to Green Ditch, a field north of Holywell Street, and there hang for his felonies.

I made arrangements to return to give testimony at Walter's trial, then walked to Holywell Street to visit my father-in-law. Some years past I had removed a splinter of wood from his back which had penetrated under his ribs when he fell from a ladder, and for this service he offered to supply me with ink and parchment when I wished to record incidents which enliven a bailiff's otherwise tedious existence. Had he known then of the frequency with which intriguing events would enter my life, he might have reconsidered the offer.

Robert Caxton refused my coin. He said good news of another grandchild to be, and the health of the one which was, was payment enough. I returned to Bampton with a fresh pot of ink and four gatherings, upon which this account is written.

Arthur and I entered Bampton next day in a soaking rain. I was much pleased to see the spire of the Church of St Beornwald appear through the downpour. I dismounted just inside the castle gatehouse, intending to leave Arthur with the returning of our beasts to the marshalsea. My intent was to return to Galen House, a warm fire, and dry clothes. But Wilfred appeared as we passed under the portcullis, with word that Lord Gilbert was anxious for me to attend him, and I was to be told this as soon as I returned from Oxford.

I found my employer in the solar, having only then arrived from the hall and his dinner. I do not think he ate well. His face was ashen and he stumbled when he stood from his chair beside the fire when I entered the chamber.

"Ah, Hugh, I am much pleased for your return. Come, stand here close by the fire to dry yourself. Lady Petronilla is in a wretched state."

"Did the potion I sent with John Chamberlain provide no relief?"

"Don't know," he said. "She did not say... she cannot say."

"Cannot?"

"She sleeps, and will not be awakened."

"You must send to Oxford for a physician to come at once," I said.

"You are as skilled as any physician. What is to be done?"

"I am a surgeon. An illness such as has afflicted Lady Petronilla requires a physician."

"Cicily is likewise afflicted, I am told, and a scullery maid," Lord Gilbert said, "and three of the bishop's tenants in the Weald are ill with a similar malady. A surgeon will serve as well as a physician, I fear." He sighed and sank to his chair.

"Why so?"

"Since you departed for Oxford Lady Petronilla's neck has become swollen and lumpish."

"These lumps are purple?" I asked, hoping he might say "Nay."

"Aye. You feared this yesterday, did you not?"

"Aye, I did," I admitted.

"You wished to spare me, I know, so I do not hold your silence against you. But you see why I have not sent to Oxford for a physician. To what use would it be for the man to come here?"

I did not reply. We both knew the answer. Plague had returned and Lady Petronilla must, if she was in her right mind, prepare to meet the Lord Christ.

"Has she been shriven?" I asked.

"Nay. I waited for your return, to confirm my suspicion. Will you look upon Lady Petronilla and see if aught may be done for her?"

I agreed to do so, and followed Lord Gilbert as he stood from his chair and passed through a door at the end of the solar which led to a corridor. I had not before seen this private space. A door opened to the right, but Lord Gilbert passed it and entered a chamber off the end of the corridor.

Three windows, even though they were shrouded, illuminated Lady Petronilla's chamber. Fine tapestries, which she had perhaps helped to embroider, hung from the walls. Her eyes would enjoy them no more.

Two of Lady Petronilla's ladies attended her, and stood when they heard us approach. One of these women seemed unsteady, and put a hand to her forehead as she rose to her feet. Before them m'lady lay silent in her bed. Lord Gilbert turned to me, nodded to his motionless wife, and said, "What say you, Hugh? Is there no hope?"

Lady Petronilla's attendants backed away when I approached the bed. The base of her neck was dark and swollen as if over-ripe plums were there beneath the skin. I had tended William of Garstang seven years past when plague wasted his body. I knew that similar purpled lumps would be found at other, more private places upon her body.

"You must send for your chaplain," I said.

"Might she recover? I have heard that some afflicted with plague do so," Lord Gilbert said.

I shook my head. "I have heard of this also. I have never met such a one, but I trust those physicians who say it may be so. Perhaps one of a hundred may return to health, or fewer. I cannot say."

Lady Petronilla died three days hence. Hers was but the first death in Bampton when plague returned to England for the third time.

Afterword

Petronilla Gilbert did indeed die in the late spring of 1368. The cause of her death is unknown, but it is true that plague returned to England in 1368–69, so I have taken the liberty of making that the cause of her death.

Bampton Castle was, in the fourteenth century, one of the largest castles in England in terms of the area surrounded by the curtain wall. Little remains of the castle but for the gatehouse and a small part of the curtain wall which form a part of Ham Court, a farmhouse in private hands.

Many readers have asked about medieval remains and tourist facilities in the area. St Mary's Church is little changed from the fourteenth century, when it was known as the Church of St Beornwald. Visitors to Bampton will enjoy staying at Wheelgate House, a B&B in the center of the town. Village scenes in the popular series *Downton Abbey* were filmed on Church View Street, and St Mary's Church appears in several episodes.

The Abbot's Agreement

An extract from the seventh chronicle of

Hugh de Singleton, surgeon

Chapter 1

My life would have been more tranquil in the days after Martinmas had I not seen the crows. But I am an inquisitive sort of man, and the noisy host caught my attention. It is said that curiosity killed the cat. It can prove hazardous for bailiffs, as well.

I was on the road near Eynsham, on my way to Oxford. I did not travel muddy autumn roads for pleasure, although I thought some joy might follow, but to seek an addition to my library. In the autumn of 1368 I owned five books: *Surgery*, by Henri de Mondeville; *Categories*, by Aristotle; *Sentences*, by Peter Lombard; *De Actibus Animae*, by Master Wyclif; and a Gospel of St John which I had copied myself from a rented manuscript while a student at Balliol College.

I sought a Bible, if I could find a fair copy for no more than thirty shillings. Such a volume at that price would not be lavishly illuminated, but I cared more for the words upon the page than some monk's artistry. If no such Bible was to be had, I would be content with a New Testament, or even a folio of St Paul's letters.

When I told my Kate of my intentions she demanded that Arthur accompany me to Oxford. A man traveling alone with thirty shillings in his purse would invite brigands to interrupt his journey, if they knew or guessed what he carried. Or even if they did not. Arthur is a groom in the service of Lord Gilbert Talbot. A sturdy man, he weighs three stone more than me, and has proven useful in past dealings with miscreants. He does not turn away from a tussle – and who would do so, if they knew they could generally dispatch any foe? A felon who sought my coins would reconsider if he saw Arthur start for him with a cudgel in hand.

I am Hugh de Singleton, surgeon and bailiff to Lord Gilbert Talbot, on his manor at Bampton. I am the husband of Katherine, and father of Bessie, now nearly two years old, and, the Lord Christ merciful, will be father to a son, perhaps, shortly after Twelfth Night. Kate is well, so I have hope she will be delivered of our second child safely. Her father, Robert Caxton, is a stationer in Oxford, and 'twas to his shop I intended to go first. That was before I saw the crows.

The road had passed through a wood, then entered fields cultivated by tenants of Eynsham Abbey. No men were at work this day, not where they could be seen. But within barns and kitchens men and women were at bloody labor, for Arthur and I travelled on Monday, the thirteenth day of November, the time when men slaughter those animals they will be unable to feed through the winter, so that the beasts will rather feed them.

A dozen or more crows perched in the bare branches of a large oak, cawing and occasionally flapping from their places to circle down to the ground near the base of the tree. As some crows left the tree, others rose from the earth to alight in the naked branches. This oak was at the very edge of a fallow field where a flock of the abbey's sheep grazed, unconcerned about the raucous chorus above them. Sheep are not much concerned with anything, being dull creatures.

I reined my palfrey to a stop and gazed at the noisy birds some hundred and more paces distant. Arthur had been speaking of the return of plague and the loss of his wife Cicily, but now he fell silent and turned in his saddle to follow my gaze.

The man did not remain mute for long. "Carrion crows," he said. "Somethin' dead, I'd guess."

I thought the same, and said so. "Whatever it is," I added, "must be large. A dead coney would not attract so many."

"Pig, maybe?" Arthur said. "Swineherds been settin' their hogs to pannaging to fatten 'em up."

"Could be, but would a pig-man not seek a lost hog before crows could find it?"

Arthur shrugged. I dismounted and led my beast to a convenient hawthorn which grew beside the road and proclaimed its presence with many red berries. I tied the palfrey there and set off across the fallow field toward the crows. Arthur came behind me.

An old ewe raised her head, watched my approach suspiciously, then snorted and trotted away. The flock briefly hesitated, then followed.

It was a grey, chilly day, but a watery sun had broken through the clouds. Whatever it was that the crows had found lay in the dappled shadow of the bare limbs of the oak, so I was nearly upon the thing before I recognized what the crows were feasting upon. And the corpse wore black, which aided the shadowy concealment.

I was but a few paces from the body when the last of the crows, perhaps more courageous than his companions, lifted his wings and flapped to safety in the branches above.

A man lay sprawled upon the fallen leaves, dressed in the black habit of a Benedictine. Whether he was old or young I could not tell, for the crows had peeled the flesh from his face nearly to the skull, after plucking out his eyes, which they love most of all. The monk's nose and lips and cheeks were gone, and he grinned up at us while the crows protested our arrival from the branches above us.

"Holy mother of God," Arthur said, and crossed himself. "What has happened here?"

I spoke no answer, for I did not know. All that was sure was that a monk, likely of Eynsham Abbey, had died half a mile from his monastery, and his corpse had gone undiscovered by all but carrion crows.

The abbey must be informed of this, of course. I told Arthur to return to the road, take his horse and hurry to the abbey. There he must tell the porter of our discovery and ask that the abbot or prior come to the place with all haste. I would remain with the dead monk, to keep the crows away, and to learn what I could of his demise.

The man was not old. He wore no cowl, and I saw no grey hairs upon his scalp. He was not tonsured. Here, then, was no monk, but a novice.

He lay upon his back, arms flung wide, palms up. The crows had been busy there as well. I stood and looked about the place. Few leaves remained upon the trees. Indeed, most had fallen some weeks past. If the corpse had been dragged here from some other place, the leaves might mark the path, but they lay undisturbed in all directions.

How long had the novice lain here? No fallen leaves covered the youth, but the squabbling crows might have brushed leaves aside. And how long would it take the scavengers to do the injury I saw before me? Not long, I guessed.

I examined what I could see of the novice's habit, but saw there no mark or perforation or bloodstain which might betray a wound. Perhaps such a laceration was under the body. I would wait to turn the lad until folk from the abbey arrived.

My gaze fell upon the novice's feet. They were bare, and the crows had not yet discovered his toes. Would he go about in November with unshod feet? Some monks might, seeking penance for a sinful thought or deed, but it seemed unlikely that a novice would do so. If the youth died of some illness or accident, I was not the first to find him: some other man had come upon him and taken his shoes. If the novice was murdered, the man who slew him may have taken more than his life.

I thought to see if the back of the novice's skull might reveal some injury, as from a blow. It was a loathsome business to lift the faceless head. I found nothing, and as I stood over the corpse I reflected that if a man was felled by a blow from behind, he would likely fall face first into the leaves.

I heard agitated voices and turned to see Arthur leading half a dozen Benedictines toward me. At first they approached at a trot, their habits flapping about their ankles, but as they came near, and glimpsed what lay at my feet, they slowed and became silent.

Arthur had been leading the group of monks to show them the way, but as they neared the corpse he held back. One by one the monks also hesitated, until at last only one came forward to stand over the body. He gazed down upon the mutilated features and said softly, "'Tis John."

This monk crossed himself as he spoke, and his fellows did likewise. I saw them exchange glances as they did so. I am not clever at reading faces, but it seemed to me I saw neither shock nor sorrow, merely acceptance of the fact.

"Who are you?" the monk asked.

"I am Hugh de Singleton, bailiff to Lord Gilbert Talbot on his manor at Bampton."

"Ah, Abbot Thurstan has spoken of you, and the business of Michael of Longridge and the scholar's stolen books. When the abbot heard this news he would have come himself, but he is aged and frail and I dissuaded him. We all knew who it must be that you have found here."

"Who is it?" I asked. "You named him 'John.'"

"'Tis John Whytyng, a novice of our house. I am Brother Gerleys, the novice-master at Eynsham Abbey. When your man told Brother Stephen of this death, and Abbot Thurstan was told, he sent for me."

"Had the lad been missing?"

"Four days. Abbot Thurstan thought he had returned to Wantage."

"Wantage?"

"His father is a knight of that place."

"John was not enthusiastic for his vocation?" I asked.

"Nay. Oh, he was quick enough at his lessons, and seemed to enjoy study. Perhaps too much. But he found no joy in silence and prayer and contemplation, I think."

"Too much joy in his studies? What do you mean?"

"The abbey has two other novices, Osbert and Henry. Neither is as clever as John... as John was."

"Only three novices at Eynsham?" I said.

"Aye. When I was a novice, an abbot could pick and choose from lads whose fathers wished to find a place for them in a monastery. Younger sons, who'd not inherit, and would have no lands – unless they wed a widow or the daughter of some knight who had no sons.

"But now the great pestilence has come a third time, there is much land available, and a habit has less appeal than when I was a youth. John was a handsome lad. Maidens, I think, found him appealing. Although," he added, "you'd not know it now."

"And he enjoyed the company of a lass?"

"Aye. So I believe. There is no opportunity within monastic walls to observe whether or not this is so, but he was often incautious when he spoke of fair maids."

"Did you send word to his father at Wantage when he disappeared?"

The novice-master shook his head. "To what purpose? He was not happy with us, and he'd not be the first novice to reject a calling. We assumed he'd gone home, and that his father would send us word of where he was."

I studied the mutilated face at our feet and it occurred to me that, had the youth lain here under this oak for four days, the crows would have done more injury to his face than I saw.

"What has caused this death?" Brother Gerleys asked. "Your man told me that you are trained as a surgeon."

"I cannot tell."

"The pestilence, you think? Two of our house have been struck down since Lammastide... although none since

248

Michaelmas. We pray daily the sickness has passed. We are now but fourteen monks and twenty-two lay brothers."

"I awaited your arrival before turning the corpse, so you might see it as we found it. I see no sign of struggle or wound, nor is there any sign that the pestilence killed him."

"Very well, then."

I knelt beside the body to roll it so as to expose the back. No monk stepped forward to aid me, and when Arthur saw their hesitation he did so. A moment later the cause of John Whytyng's death was evident. So I thought.

In the middle of his back the novice had suffered several stab wounds. I counted three perforations in his habit. The novice-master saw these also.

"Stabbed," he said softly.

I looked down upon the fallen leaves which the corpse had covered, then knelt again to examine the decaying vegetation which had lain directly under the wounds. I stirred the leaves gently, but did not find what I sought.

"What is it?" Brother Gerleys asked.

"There is no blood here. No clots of blood upon his habit, nor upon the ground. If he died here his blood would have soaked the leaves, but there is none. There has been no rain these past four days to wash blood away, and even had there been, the lad's body would have shielded any bloodstains from the wet."

I touched the back of the dead novice's habit: it was damp. Indeed, the wool was nearly as wet as if he had a day or so earlier been drawn from a river. I lifted the edge of one of the cuts in the wool of his garment. The wound was also clean. Little bloodstained either flesh or habit.

"What does this mean?" Brother Gerleys said.

"He died elsewhere, I think, then was moved to this place."

The monk looked about him, then spoke. "Why here, I wonder. He was not well hidden, and so close to the road and abbey it was sure he would be found."

"Aye," I agreed. "Which must mean that whoso slew him did not much care if the novice was found, so long as the corpse was not discovered in the place where the murder was done."

"How long has he lain here, you think?"

"I cannot tell," I shrugged. "But there is perhaps a way to discover this."

Brother Gerleys peered at me with a puzzled expression, so I explained my thoughts.

Abbey tenants and villeins would have butchered many pigs in the past days. I had in mind that the novice-master should obtain a severed boar's head and set it upon the forest floor somewhere near this place. Then he could daily visit the skull and learn how long it would take crows to find and devour the flesh to the same extent as the injury they had done to the novice. Brother Gerleys nodded understanding as I explained the plan he should follow.

Two of the monks who accompanied the novice-master had carried with them a pallet. Brother Gerleys motioned to them and they set the frame beside the corpse and rolled the body onto it. This left John's mutilated, eyeless face upraised again to the sky. When the monks saw this, one of them turned aside and retched violently into the leaves. I sympathized. The novice's ruined countenance brought bile to my own throat.

I knelt beside the corpse again, and once more touched the black wool of the habit. The front was dry, or nearly so. Why was the back of the garment so damp? Dew would have wet the upper side of the habit, I thought.

I, Arthur, and Brother Gerleys led the way back to the road and the horses. The monks, of course, had come afoot to the place.

"Your man," Brother Gerleys said, "told me that you were bound for Oxford when you saw the crows and found John."

"Aye. This business has delayed us, but we will still be there by nightfall if we do not dally."

"Abbot Thurstan asked that you call upon him. He wishes to know what befell John."

"I cannot tell. But you may do as I suggest with a pig's head and that may tell you how long past the novice was left in the wood."

We paced in somber silence to the abbey. There I left Arthur to water the horses and followed Brother Gerleys to the abbot's chamber while the other monks took John Whytyng's corpse to rest before the church altar.

The abbot's chamber door was open when we approached, and I could see Abbot Thurstan dictating a letter to his clerk. The aged monk saw our shadows darken his door and looked toward us. As he did so I heard the sacrist begin to ring the Passing Bell.

Abbot Thurstan is an ancient fellow. He was elected to his position when the pestilence struck down Abbot Nicholas, nearly twenty years past. It was no longer necessary for the abbot to be tonsured fortnightly: he had but a wispy fringe of hoary hairs circling his skull above his ears.

The old man swayed to his feet as Brother Gerleys announced my presence. It took some effort for the abbot to do this, and I was cognizant of the honor. An abbot need not rise from his chair when a mere bailiff calls upon him.

Abbot Thurstan looked from me to the novice-master, then spoke. "It was John?" he said.

"Aye," Brother Gerleys replied.

The abbot crossed himself and sat heavily. "I thought as much. An able lad, with much to recommend him, yet he is taken, while the Lord Christ leaves me here."

I thought to myself that the Lord Christ had little to do with the novice's death, but held my tongue.

"Was it the pestilence?" the abbot continued.

Brother Gerleys looked to me.

"Nay," I said. "The lad was struck down by a dagger in the back."

Abbot Thurstan was silent for a time, then replied. "I would not wish for any man to die of plague. I have seen the agony in which the afflicted die. But I had hoped that the death was not the work of some other man's hand. When plague first visited this house nearly twenty years past, I saw Brother Oswalt try to rise from his bed and flee the infirmary, thinking he could escape his torment if he could leave the abbey. I thought perhaps John, crazed by pain, might have done likewise."

"Had the youth given sign that he was ill?" I asked.

"Nay," Brother Gerleys said.

"The pestilence can slay a man quickly," the abbot said, "but so will a blade."

"I wish you success in discovering the felon," I said.

The abbot looked from his clerk to the novice-master and then to me. "I remember," he said, "when you discovered 'twas a brother of this house who stole Master Wyclif's books. We have no man so skilled at sniffing out felons."

"Has Eynsham no bailiff or constable?"

"A bailiff. But Richard is nearly as old as me. He sees little and hears less. He is competent for the mundane duties of a bailiff, but seeking a murderer will be beyond his abilities."

I saw the direction this conversation was taking and sought to deflect its path.

"I am bound for Oxford," I said, "and hope to arrive before nightfall. The days grow short, so I need to be on my way."

"I am sorry to delay your travel. You have business in Oxford?"

"I intend to make a purchase there, and then return promptly to Bampton. My wife will give birth to our second child before Candlemas and I do not wish for her to be alone any longer than need be."

"Ah, certainly. But…"

I saw in his eyes that the elderly monk's mind was working rapidly.

"Could you not spare us a few days to sort out this calamity? Surely your purchase can wait, and there is a midwife of Eynsham who could be sent to Bampton to attend your wife till this matter is settled. I will pay the woman from abbey funds. What is it you wish to obtain in Oxford?"

"A Bible."

"Ah, Lord Gilbert must regard your service highly."

"He is liberal with wages to those whose service he values," I agreed.

"As am I. In our scriptorium there are many brothers who are accomplished with pen and ink. Brother Robert and Brother Bertran are particularly skilled. The abbey has no important commissions just now. If you will set yourself to discovering the murderer among us, I will put the scriptorium to work upon a Bible. You will have it by St John's Day, or soon thereafter."

The youngest son of a minor Lancashire knight, as I am, learns frugality at an early age. I have become modestly prosperous, but not so that I would willingly forego the saving of thirty shillings. I stood silently before the abbot, as if considering his offer, but I knew already that I would accept.

"If I am unable to discover the murderer, what then?"

"The Lord Christ," the abbot said, "commands only that we strive to do His will. He does not demand that we always succeed. So I ask only for your best effort. If you give the abbey that, it will suffice. You will receive your Bible."

"Very well. But I must return to Bampton to tell my Kate of this alteration in my plans. When will you send the woman to keep my wife company 'til this matter can be resolved? And will she accept your commission?"

"Agnes is a widow, and since the pestilence few babes are born in Eynsham to provide her a livelihood. She is unlikely to refuse my offer. I will send her tomorrow."

So it was that Arthur and I returned to Bampton that day, and I spent the evening sitting upon a bench before the hearth with my Kate, considering who might wish to slay a novice and why they would do so. I should have also considered what such a felon might do to avoid discovery.